SOLVING A COLD CASE

Daisy waited a beat and let Stephanie take control of her emotions. She could see that even now, talking about Axel brought back bittersweet memories. "What do you think happened to Axel?"

"I don't know," Stephanie said. "But I do know two things."

Tessa and Daisy both leaned in to listen.

"I know Axel didn't run away. He cared too much for his family to even consider that. He loved his mom, and he respected his dad."

"Then what's the other thing?" Tessa asked.

"Something awful had to have happened to him. I know that for sure. He never would have wanted any of us who loved him to miss him and wonder what had happened. If he could have gotten back to us, he would have."

Daisy was beginning to believe that Stephanie was right . . .

Books by Karen Rose Smith

Caprice DeLuca Mysteries
STAGED TO DEATH
DEADLY DÉCOR
GILT BY ASSOCIATION
DRAPE EXPECTATIONS
SILENCE OF THE LAMPS
SHADES OF WRATH
SLAY BELLS RING
CUT TO THE CHAISE

Daisy's Tea Garden Mysteries
MURDER WITH LEMON TEA CAKES
MURDER WITH CINAMMON SCONES
MURDER WITH CUCUMBER SANDWICHES
MURDER WITH CHERRY TARTS
MURDER WITH CLOTTED CREAM
MURDER WITH OOLONG TEA
MURDER WITH ORANGE PEKOE TEA
MURDER WITH DARJEELING TEA
MURDER WITH EARL GREY TEA
MURDER WITH CHOCOLATE TEA

Published by Kensington Publishing Corp.

Murder with Chocolate Tea

A Daisy's Tea Garden
Mystery

KAREN ROSE SMITH

Kensington Publishing Corp.
www.kensingtonbooks.com

KENSINGTON BOOKS are published by

Kensington Publishing Corp.
119 West 40th Street
New York, NY 10018

All Kensington titles, imprints, and distributed lines are available at special quantity discounts for bulk purchases for sales promotion, premiums, fund-raising, educational, or institutional use.

Special book excerpts or customized printings can also be created to fit specific needs. For details, write or phone the office of the Kensington Sales Manager: Attn.: Sales Department. Kensington Publishing Corp., 119 West 40th Street, New York, NY 10018. Phone: 1-800-221-2647.

The K and Teapot logo is a trademark of Kensington Publishing Corp.

First Printing: December 2023
ISBN: 978-1-4967-3848-6

ISBN: 978-1-4967-3849-3 (ebook)

10 9 8 7 6 5 4 3 2 1

Printed in the United States of America

This book is dedicated to my cousin Jane, who was like a sister to me in childhood and is a friend as an adult. Our shared history is a comfort, a bond, and a way of remembering those we love who have passed on . . . and those we love who make the future bright. To friendship and cousinhood!

ACKNOWLEDGMENTS

Thanks to Officer Greg Berry, my professional law enforcement consultant, who always provides the answers to my questions and as much information as I need.

CHAPTER ONE

Journalist Trevor Lundquist, his headphones mussing his brown hair, stared intently at Daisy Swanson as he asked his final interview question for his podcast, "Hidden Spaces," on a Friday evening. "How does it feel to have been instrumental in solving nine murder investigations?" His eyebrows quirked knowingly, as if he could imagine what she was going to answer.

Daisy exchanged a look with her best friend, Tessa Miller, who was the kitchen manager for Daisy's Tea Garden, housed on the first floor of a refurbished Victorian house. Tessa was now acting as assistant for her boyfriend, Trevor, in his podcast venture. Tessa's spare room in her apartment above the tea garden had become his studio.

As if Trevor wanted to nudge Daisy's hesitation, he leaned closer to the condenser microphone. "Daisy . . ."

All of Trevor's previous questions had been mostly fact-based about the last murder case she'd fallen into. "That question's not as easy to answer as it might seem," she said.

"How so?" Trevor always expected answers and cut to the heart of whatever he wanted to know.

"I care about Willow Creek and my family, friends, and neighbors who live here. When I returned to Willow Creek with my two girls"—Daisy smiled wryly at Trevor—"who are now young women, I merely planned to run the tea garden with my aunt Iris and make a new start after my husband died. But somehow, life gave me all kinds of twists and turns."

"But we're talking about *murder*, Daisy. Murders don't crash down on everyone like they've hit you."

Tessa, who was sitting beside Trevor, nudged his arm so hard that her caramel-colored braid swung over her shoulder. Daisy suspected Tessa thought Trevor was being overly dramatic for his podcast.

"Yes, we *are* talking about murders," Daisy said somberly. "I would never have chosen to be involved."

"Would you say you're overly curious?" he asked.

Now she frowned at him. She had a long fuse, and she hadn't considered that Trevor could ruffle her. But he streamed his podcast for a reason—he was trying to find a new facet to his career.

"I don't believe I'm overly curious, but I want answers when loved ones or friends need help." She knew her blue eyes were drilling into him, as if telling him not to press too much harder. After all, she could end the interview.

He seemed to get her message . . . and Tessa's. Trevor gave Daisy a mischievous smile as he asked, "Do you think the fact that your fiancé is a former detective has helped you ask the right questions when you talk to persons of interest?"

"I think the fact that Jonas is a former detective challenges me to keep the cases and our lives in perspective."

"Can I ask you a personal question? I think our listeners might appreciate a tidbit or two about you," Trevor said as if he knew exactly what his listeners wanted.

"That depends. Go ahead and ask. But remember, when you want me to bake you chocolate whoopie pies with peanut butter filling, I might forget the sugar," she joked.

Trevor laughed. "I would expect no less." After a second's pause, he suggested, "Can you tell our listeners if it's true that you and your fiancé connected over a concern with your teenage daughter?"

Daisy realized Trevor was trying to involve his audience in a part of her life that could interest them most. After considering the consequences, she decided her answer could be worthwhile to his listeners. "I know rumors run rampant in Willow Creek. I hear most of them at the tea garden. But this one is correct. My younger daughter is adopted, and Jonas helped me find her birth mother. I'm grateful for that and always will be."

Making a motion to Tessa, who was sitting at the sound console, that he was ending the interview, Trevor thanked Daisy and gave his usual closing to the broadcast. "My podcast, 'Hidden Spaces,' is about what most of us don't see, hear, or know. If you know a secret that involves our community or if you have evidence of a crime, call my tip line, and I'll follow up." He rattled off the number.

"This is Trevor Lundquist and 'Hidden Spaces' signing off."

Daisy heaved a sigh of relief that the interview was over. She leaned back from the microphone setup and removed her headphones.

As Tessa worked at the laptop at the console, Trevor studied Daisy. "You really wouldn't mess with my whoopie pies, would you?"

She smiled. "You were tough."

Trevor turned serious. "I don't want the podcast to be sensational, but it does have to engage ordinary people. My social media following is increasing. This podcast should really hike up the numbers and maybe gain me a sponsor or two."

Turning to them, Tessa said, "All posted. Comments are already coming in."

Standing, Tessa pushed back her chair and went over to the color-blocked shelf. In celebration of June and the warm evening, she'd worn a swirling tie-dyed, multicolored sundress. Her bejeweled sneakers went right along with it. The room reflected her as much as all the gizmos and equipment reflected Trevor. A trio of her paintings, which she'd created in the Victorian's attic, hung over the bookshelves. They were long and rectangular and comprised a set. The first depicted Willow Creek and the willows dipping into its banks. The second one always made Daisy stop and study it. An Amish girl, maybe in her late teens, stood at a busy intersection on her scooter bike. Her cardigan sweater was slipping over one shoulder as if the wind and the scooter had drawn it down. She stood at the light pole waiting to cross the street, her back to the viewer. The Amish wouldn't allow photos to be taken if they could help it. In the third painting, Jonas's dog, Felix, romped across their backyard. He looked joyful, ears flying, tail a golden brush against the blue sky.

Tessa picked up her cell phone and eyed Daisy. "Are you going home now?"

"No, I'm walking down to Woods. Jonas and Felix are waiting for me. He dropped me off this morning. Why?"

"Because we have no idea what kind of comments are going to come in from your interview. It might be better if you're with somebody when you read them."

"Do you have trolls already?" Daisy asked Trevor.

"Everyone has trolls on their social media feeds," Trevor answered matter-of-factly.

Trevor's phone lay on the bookshelf, too. He'd put it there before they'd started the interview. Now it was vibrating.

When Tessa handed it to him, her eyebrows were practically raised under her bangs.

As soon as Trevor glanced at his phone, he smiled. "I'll put this on speaker. It's from the hotline."

Daisy expected this might simply be a comment about the podcast . . . yet it *was* a tip line.

"Trevor Lundquist here with 'Hidden Spaces.' How can I help you?"

Since Trevor had opened the speaker on his phone, Daisy and Tessa could listen in. The male caller kept his voice low. "I know about a crime."

Trevor's face became elated and then more reserved. Daisy knew he'd had tips before about damaged property, but not anything significant.

The journalist was wary as he encouraged the caller. "I'm listening."

Silence pervaded the small room as they all seemed to be holding their breath.

"I need to remain anonymous."

"I understand," Trevor assured him.

And he did, Daisy knew. Tips weren't about the caller. According to Trevor, they were about the secret or the crime. He protected his sources.

"You have to investigate," the caller cautioned.

Daisy thought the voice sounded middle-aged or younger. It was hard to determine.

"I'll look into the crime if you give me a significant lead," Trevor informed the man.

"The lead is in an old chest. There are several chests, but one holds the secret."

Tessa looked pensive as she passed a note to Daisy. *Do you think this guy is legitimate?*

Daisy shrugged. There was simply no way to know.

"Where can I find these chests?" Trevor wanted to know. He looked as if he half-expected the man to say, "at the bottom of Willow Creek." But the caller didn't.

"They'll be auctioned off next weekend. They're included in two storage compartments at Bonner's Storage."

Trevor jumped on that information. "But auctions only happen when someone doesn't pay the rental fees for a few months."

"That *is* what has happened. One of those chests holds the secret to a twenty-year-old murder."

The line went dead.

* * *

Daisy left Tessa's apartment and made her way through the back parking lot of Daisy's Tea Garden and out onto Market Street. With each step she thought about what had just happened. The warm mid-June air with its slight breeze swirled around her yellow and white cap-sleeved top and yellow slacks. Taking a colorful note from Tessa, she'd worn neon-green clogs today.

A gray-bonneted Amish buggy drove down Market Street, its horse's hooves clomping along the asphalt. Daisy glanced at it and smiled. The buggies always reminded her to slow down and enjoy the pace of the Amish community.

Still, she heard in her head the words of the caller—*"One of those chests holds the secret to a twenty-year old murder."*

Passing shops on her trek to Woods, she saw that most of them were closed—Vinegar and Spice, Wisps and Wicks, and a few business offices. At Woods, the furniture store owned by her fiancé, Jonas Groft, she stopped in front of the main plate-glass window display, as she often did. This month, Jonas had placed a high cocktail table in the window as the main showpiece, with stools that he'd created on either side of it. In the same warm walnut of the table, a curio cabinet stood to one side. It was filled with wooden Amish toys, from a toy train to a toy pull-duck to blocks. A multi-colored rag rug had been placed under the table and chairs. A small hutch fashioned from reclaimed wood was painted in a distressed green. Daisy had loaned Jonas several teacups and saucers to add a vintage touch to the piece. The whole setup would definitely invite her inside to look around. That was the point of the display.

The coolness of the air-conditioning met Daisy when she opened the door. Out of habit, she glanced at the giant cubicle shelves along one side of the store that stretched from floor to ceiling. Ladder-back chairs stood in each of the cubicles ranging in different finishes from blue to cherry to dark walnut. Customers could order whatever finish they desired and as many chairs as they needed.

Jonas was specializing in islands now and could hardly keep up with orders. Each was unique, made from reclaimed wood with a stone, granite, quartz, or butcher-block top. Other pieces, like jelly cabinets, bookshelves, pie safes, and hope chests, were made by local craftsmen. Jonas sold the pieces on consignment.

The shop smelled like orange oil, and she liked the scent. She knew Jonas used it to shine up furniture that might have fingerprints on it at the end of the day. That was the case as she watched him rubbing over a maple dry sink. Felix, the cream golden retriever Jonas had adopted, sat on his haunches, watching Jonas's hand move back and forth and back and forth.

Jonas had large, kind hands that could convey love in the best type of way. It wasn't the fact that in his forties—trim, tall, and fit—Jonas's sexy appeal had drawn her to him. She knew she was prejudiced that he was the sexiest man she knew. But it was his loyal and compassionate heart that had coaxed her to let her walls down and let him into her life.

Jonas suddenly turned to look at her, as if he'd sensed she was there. His vibrant green eyes drew her to him almost as much as his smile. Jonas was a caring, forthright man with integrity. She had to admit, though, whenever she looked at him, an all-encompassing flicker of excitement danced through her. She could hardly believe that in six weeks he'd be her husband.

The scar down the side of Jonas's face reminded them both of his former profession as a Philadelphia police detective. But it seemed to disappear when he smiled—especially when he smiled at *her*. This evening, a wave of his thick black hair dipped over his forehead. The silver threading in the hair at his temples enhanced the laugh lines around his eyes rather than reminding her he'd once been a homicide cop who'd seen enough misery to turn *all* his hair gray.

They met at the center of the sales counter. When he wrapped his arms around her, she could feel the beat of his heart. They kissed a long while.

When he leaned away, he murmured, "I wish we were at home."

After Jonas had moved in with her last fall, the transition from dating to engaged couple had seemed seamless. They belonged together, and they knew it.

"We'll be home soon," she promised him.

Felix brushed against her leg in greeting, his fluffy tail wagging.

Stooping to the canine, she laughed. "I'm glad to see you, too." After she gave Felix the attention he wanted, she straightened.

"How did your interview go?" Jonas asked.

"I'm not sure. We'll have to check the comments on Trevor's social media stream to find out. He sent me a curveball when we were closing." She explained to Jonas about the personal question. "I answered because other families might have the same situation with adopted children."

"I'm glad Trevor didn't push too hard. I know how much he wants his podcast to propel him into more income and a better career."

"I didn't tell you about the unusual thing that happened," Daisy said, petting Felix again.

"Nothing would surprise me when you're with Trevor and Tessa."

"You know his hotline?"

"I do. I think the patrol officers caught some vandals who were smashing mailboxes because of it."

"This was a lot more interesting than that. Someone claims they know about a twenty-year-old murder."

"Whoa!" Jonas blew out a heavy breath. "That's the type of thing Trevor has been waiting for. Do you think it's legitimate?"

"I don't know. I guess it could be a hoax, but it's an involved one. Apparently some old chests are going up for sale. It's an auction that the storage company has when renters don't pay the rent."

"Old chests are going to explain a murder?"

"Supposedly one holds a 'secret'."

Jonas shook his head. "I don't know. Maybe somebody just wants the bidding to go up on the contents of those two storage compartments."

"That's possible. Trevor has a week to think about it. While he does that, I'm going to be considering wedding gowns. I'm going shopping to-morrow."

"Is anyone going with you to give you advice?"

"Mom and Aunt Iris are. Jazzi's going to cover for Iris at the tea garden, and Tamlyn is putting in extra hours. Jazzi tells me if I find something, I have to text her a picture immediately so she can okay it."

"Do you think you'll find what you want?"

"I haven't up until now, but I'm hopeful. We're going to shop at vintage stores this time instead of the ordinary ones."

"You could wear a sheet, and I wouldn't care," Jonas said with a smile.

"I don't want a ball gown, but I do want more than a sheet," she teased.

Jonas strode behind the counter to his computer. "Do you want to check out Trevor's comments before we leave, or do you want to wait until we get home? They could cause indigestion."

"Let's look now, then I can forget about it for the night." At least, she hoped she'd be able to.

Jonas sat on a stool, pressed a few keys, and then whistled. "Trevor is gaining followers. Apparently true-crime buffs tuned in. A lot of the comments are about the last murder you helped to solve."

"And the others?" She really didn't know if she wanted to look herself and read them.

"Here, sit and check them out. I think you'll find them interesting." Jonas stood and let her take up position on the stool. As Jonas had said, many of the comments were about the crime itself and the way it had been solved.

But she saw other comments, too. Some that said adopted children shouldn't try to search for their birth parents because it would hurt the adopted parents. She didn't agree with that. It hadn't been easy, but her younger daughter had needed answers.

She saw others, however, that admired Daisy for

helping Jazzi find her birth mother. Then there was the comment—*Daisy Swanson should keep her nose out of police business.*

There was another—*The Willow Creek Police Department should hire Daisy Swanson. This isn't the first murder she's helped solve.*

There were other comments like—*Daisy Swanson is too curious for her own good.*

And . . . *She could have gotten herself killed. She wasn't thinking of her family.*

"Listen to this one," Daisy said to Jonas. "Somebody thinks I have too much time on my hands."

He shook his head. "You have the gamut there, Daisy. Everybody has an opinion on everything, including you and the murder and anything else that happens in Willow Creek."

Glancing over her shoulder at Jonas, she acquiesced. "I suppose. What do you think will happen if Trevor investigates those chests?"

Jonas clasped her shoulders. "That depends on his attitude and how he goes about it. If he actually finds something, his broadcast could explode, not just in Willow Creek but with a much broader audience. Are you thinking about attending the auction with Trevor if he goes?"

"I have a wedding to prepare for, a daughter to get ready for college, and a tearoom to run."

"And a fiancé to keep company," Jonas added with a grin.

"See all that time I have on my hands?" she joked, repeating the sentiment of one of the comments.

"You haven't answered me."

"I'll think about going to the auction with Trevor,"

she said. And she would. She had to admit that buying an old chest with secrets was an intriguing idea.

"Why do you think your mom wanted to meet us *here?*" Iris asked as she and Daisy followed the walk to Daisy's childhood home on Saturday morning.

The scent of roses and lavender were noticeable as they climbed the porch steps to the covered front door.

"I don't know. I told her about the shop that sold vintage dresses, and I thought we'd visit there. But she wanted us to come here first."

After Daisy rapped on the door, she opened it. The front entrance led into the living room, where the flower-patterned sofa had a camel back and chunky legs. The side table legs were chunky, too . . . and outdated. But her dad's recliner was comfortable for him, and the pillows on the sofa suited her mom.

Rose came hurrying in from the kitchen through the dining area. She'd had her ash blond hair permed recently. It was a short, manageable cut that required the minimum of styling. She was wearing green summer slacks and a lighter green sleeveless blouse. Her lipstick was its usual bright pink.

Rose hugged Daisy and then Iris.

Iris said, "Daisy told me about the shop in Lancaster with vintage-style gowns. She has to find something soon."

"I've looked online. There are lots of beautiful dresses, but nothing feels quite right," Daisy said.

"I want to show you something," Rose explained. "I need you to come to the attic with me."

Iris's eyebrows rose. "It will be hot up there."

"Sean opened the windows, and hopefully there will be a crosscurrent. Let's do this while the morning air has some coolness to it."

Daisy followed her mother up the stairs to the second floor, Iris trailing behind. They walked down the hall to the spare room.

Rose turned around to look at Daisy before she opened the door to the attic. "Your father and I went to the town council meeting last night," she said, waiting until Iris was in the room, too.

"I heard Amelia Wiseman was in the center of it," Iris said. "A hundred-year-old celebration for the covered bridge near her bed-and-breakfast would be a good reason for her to get involved."

"She'll want to take advantage of it to promote her bed-and-breakfast," Daisy agreed.

Rose put her foot on the first step of four that led to a landing toward the attic. "Five years ago, Amelia managed to secure a grant to have that bridge restored. She spent a lot of time, effort, and some money on it, so it only makes sense she'd have a say in this celebration. I imagine the whole town will get behind it. Tourist trade should flow in for it. All the businesses will benefit."

As Rose stood on the landing, she motioned to Daisy and Iris. "It's really not so bad up here. The air is moving through. There's quite a breeze."

"Thank heavens for that," Iris mumbled.

Once they were in the attic, Daisy said, "I haven't been up here since I went to college."

The attic was spacious enough for an adult to stand up straight along the center aisle. Small windows at the centers of the points of the roof let air flow through the space. Boxes lined both sides, with chairs and small tables stashed here and there.

"Your dad and I try to come up here at least once a year." Rose pointed toward a corner. "After we return the Christmas decorations, we attempt to clean up a bit."

The old wood under the roof had a unique smell. Daisy remembered it from searching the attic for curtains to play dress-up. She also recalled that knickknacks that had once graced the rail above the kitchen cupboards were stored up here, as well as boxes of old books. Daisy's mom and dad were neat, so every box was labeled.

Iris said, "If I had an attic, it wouldn't be this organized."

"I like to know where everything is," Rose said. "Or if I don't, at least I can point Sean in the right direction. Sean keeps telling me we should empty the attic and put insulation in instead to save heating costs. But if I did that, we'd have to rent a storage unit, then we'd have *that* cost."

Iris chuckled. "It certainly is a matter of perspective. I guess you wouldn't want to empty the attic and have an auction or something?"

"I'm not ready to do that," Rose said with some vehemence. "Memories are all around me here. See that box over there?"

She pointed to one with two others that were stacked on top. "That has all of Camellia's and Daisy's elementary schoolwork inside—pictures they drew, artwork, stories they wrote, report cards, certificates of excellence . . ."

Iris said, "I get it. What's the one on top marked CARDS?"

Rose's cheeks became a little colored. She didn't

answer right away. Finally, she admitted, "There are love letters in there and cards that Sean and I sent to each other, other mementoes, too. Sometimes on our anniversary we take it out and go through everything."

"A memory box," Daisy said. "I like that idea."

"Has Jonas written you any love letters?" Iris teased.

"No, he hasn't. And the truth is, I think our generation has lost the art of writing love letters. But that gives me an idea. Maybe I should write one for him for our wedding."

"Your vows to each other will be your love letters," Rose commented with a dreamy smile on her lips. "And that leads me to why we're up here," she explained, heading over to a huge trunk that was set against one wall, protected by other boxes surrounding it.

"I always wondered what was in that trunk," Daisy said. "It was too heavy to move, and it had a lock on it. Whenever Camellia and I did come up here to snoop, we could never open it."

"I wanted to make sure that what was inside was kept safe," Rose said. "I could have explained some of it to you sooner, but I didn't think you and Camellia were interested. Besides, I think you'll understand better now." She took out a key. It dangled on a leather strap that looked old.

This trunk was huge, at least four feet long. Daisy thought about the chests the auction would be selling in about a week. Would they be holding something like what this trunk held?

The trunk was metal, big and black, with gray strapping. It appeared to have seen a lot of bumps and bruises.

As Rose put the key in the lock, she said, "This trunk came from Ireland with your great-grand-mother. It held all her earthly possessions. Her name was Heather O'Brien, and she married Timothy Fitzgerald. They wed before they came to America. I don't have anything of theirs, but Heather handed down the trunk to my mother, Lily. Lily Fitzgerald married Michael Albright."

Albright had been her mother's maiden name.

"I have this all written down for you somewhere in case you ever need it. Sean investigated our family ancestry. I don't have the patience for it."

Daisy couldn't imagine what was in the trunk. Maybe Irish linens? Something for her and Jonas to use in their home?

Once Rose lifted the lid of the trunk, a wonderful lavender scent spilled out. "Lavender and the blue tissue paper keep what I have in here fresh."

The first item she removed looked like a bedspread. She spread it out on one of the nearby tables. It was beautiful. It wasn't quilted, but it was hand-stitched. Crocheted lace edged all of it. Embroidery on the spread itself was painstakingly tiny. Flowers were embroidered in concentric circles from the center of the coverlet as far out as they could go. She could see daffodils and violets, primroses and roses, zinnias and nasturtiums. So many varieties of flowers in so many colors.

"Mom, it's gorgeous. Did you ever use it?"

"I never wanted to dress up the bed as fancy as that. Do you think you might want to use it?"

"Did my grandmother make it?" Daisy asked.

"Look down at the corner," Rose directed. "There you can see she stitched her name—Lily Fitzgerald Albright."

"I'd be afraid I'd spill something on it," Daisy said.

"You know what, honey? If you like it—and from your expression, I think you do—then I think you should use it. What good would it be to keep handing it down never used?"

"I would love to use it. I can find a dust ruffle in an accompanying color to use around the bottom of it, and it would fit perfectly, like a duvet."

Next Rose removed from the trunk linens that were pillowcases with crocheted edging. There were several sets, and she handed a few to Iris as well as Daisy.

"It's time we were surrounded by a loved one's history, don't you think?"

Daisy nodded with tears coming to her eyes, and she wasn't exactly sure why. Maybe simply because this was an emotional time.

Next Rose removed a brown box that was fairly large, about two feet long and a foot wide. When she opened it, Daisy glimpsed blue tissue paper. Rose pushed aside the tissue paper and pulled out a wedding dress that hung on a satin hanger.

Daisy took in a quick breath. "That's beautiful."

"It was your grandmother's. When she married, wedding dresses were all about lace and chiffon."

Daisy studied the dress with its capped Alencon-lace sleeves and bodice, the slightly Empire waist, and the free-flowing chiffon that flowed below that.

"I think my mother was your size when she was married," Rose said, her eyes a little misty at handling the fabric. "When you and Jonas decided to get married, I came up here to have a look at her gown. But I didn't know if you'd want to consider it for your wedding. We could have it shortened if you don't want full length. Greta at the Rainbow Flamingo could do alterations and add some sparkle if you wanted that."

"The dress doesn't need sparkle, Mom." The lace and chiffon had become creamy through the years. "That's exactly the look I wanted. This isn't my first marriage. I don't want sparkle and pearls and beads like I had on my first wedding gown. I want this one to be simply, organically me."

Rose turned to her sister. "Do you think this is Daisy?"

Iris's eyes were misty, too. "I think it's perfectly Daisy."

When Iris took the dress in her hands to examine it, Daisy hugged her mother. "It's lasted a long time, filled with memories, hurts, and regrets, but so much love. Thank you, Mom. I'm so glad you thought of Grandmother Lily and this dress. Aunt Iris, can you hold it up so I can take a photo to show Jazzi?"

Iris held the dress high as Daisy backed up to take the photo. Everything about her wedding was falling into place. She couldn't wait to tell Jonas she'd found the perfect dress. She'd just never imagined she'd find it here.

CHAPTER TWO

On Monday, Daisy stood at the sales counter studying customers who were coming and going. Slipping her hand into her yellow apron with the daisy logo, she smiled as the tips of her fingers touched the business cards she always carried. Daisy's Tea Garden had been the brainchild belonging to her and her aunt Iris.

Daisy and her aunt had purchased the Victorian with the setup for a bakery that had once existed on the first floor. In the room where she was standing—the main tearoom—they'd painted the walls a calming pale green. The glass-topped wooden tables and mismatched, antique-style chairs invited customers to linger and chat. When Daisy and her aunt offered a reserved five-course afternoon tea service, they used the yellow spillover tearoom with its diamond cut–glass windows, bay window, window seats, and crown molding. The white tables and chairs in there were complemented by the seat cushions in blue, green, and yellow pinstripes.

Tessa was carrying a tray of rhubarb muffins to

the sales counter when Daisy heard her name called. Amelia Wiseman had entered the tea garden and was waving to her. She pointed to the spillover tearoom that was partially filled. That meant the owner of the Covered Bridge Bed-and-Breakfast wanted to talk.

Daisy beckoned to April Jennings. In her early twenties, April was a fairly recent hire who was competent and seemed to guess what Daisy wanted before she had to express it. At present, April was living in the apartment over Daisy's garage and had become part of the family.

Daisy said to April, "Amelia Wiseman just came in and went into the spillover tearoom. Can you bring us two cups of chocolate tea and a plate of snickerdoodles?"

"Sure thing," April assured Daisy. Despite wearing a hairnet to keep her blond curls in place, they didn't obey. One sneaked out and curled along her cheek as she bobbed her head.

Soon Daisy was sitting across a table from Amelia. "April's going to bring us refreshments. Are you okay with that?"

"Sure. You know I love your tea and baked goods."

Amelia was in her forties. Her dark brown hair layered around her face, and she had an attractive smile. She and her husband ran the Covered Bridge Bed-and-Breakfast, but Amelia also volunteered at the thrift store, A Penny Saved, and for other community endeavors. She was a woman of boundless energy.

"How are you?" Daisy asked, genuinely wanting to know.

"I'm busy like you are, but I've come hoping to make you even busier."

Uh-oh. Amelia roped anyone she could into community projects. Daisy hoped to waylay her. "I heard the town council meeting was all about the one-hundred-year celebration for the covered bridge."

Amelia nodded with enthusiasm. "It was. Of course, I'm going to take advantage of the celebration. We'll have a stand in the field near the covered bridge along with other suppliers who will be selling wares there. I know there will be lots of mugs and buttons and shirts and caps to commemorate the bridge, but we'll have someone there to explain all the best qualities of the bed-and-breakfast, too."

In spite of herself, Daisy was thinking the celebration would be less of an historic event and more like a carnival.

"I'd like to arrange to have fireworks at the creek," Amelia went on. "But that depends on how wet the ground is and what kind of dry spell we have. We'll install solar lights for the entrance and the exit of the covered bridge as well as the long, narrow road leading to it. We're going to have an all-day celebration into the evening."

"I imagine you're going all out on publicity." If Daisy knew anything about Amelia, she knew that.

"Oh, yes, we are, and every business is going to take part. That's why I'm here."

"Uh-oh," Daisy said aloud this time. "I can see it in your eyes. You've got something planned for Daisy's Tea Garden."

"No, I don't have anything planned, but I want *you* to plan a special tea for that day."

"Oh, Amelia. I'm planning a wedding! Jazzi's getting ready to go to college. Jonas and I are figuring out plans for a workshop in the backyard. I don't know if I have time for a special tea."

Suddenly April hovered around the table. She set vintage Aynsley "Marine Rose" china teacups filled with chocolate tea in front of her and Amelia. The tea was a beautiful rich color and smelled wonderful. She also positioned a Stechcol Gracie teapot beside them with the extra tea. It was a beautiful little pot with a black background on the main portion of the pot decorated with colorful flowers in orange, red, yellow, and white. The lid had a white background with the same flowers, and the spout was a Harlequin black and white. April set the matching sugar bowl between Amelia and Daisy along with a ceramic honey pot.

"Cinnamon sugar and chocolate tea. What more could I want?" Amelia asked rhetorically.

The green Depression-glass dish of snickerdoodles had already captured Amelia's attention. She took two from the plate and set them on her dessert dish.

She was nibbling on one when April leaned down to Daisy. "I overheard what Amelia would like you to do. Maybe I could help. I can put in extra hours. Living close to you, we can consult whenever you'd like."

Daisy's first inclination was to say *no*. However, April's face was so animated, and her enthusiasm seemed genuine. Daisy knew April had experienced much tragedy in her life, and she needed excitement that was wholesome and could tire her at the end of the day so she could fall into a good night's sleep.

Amelia arched one of her tattooed brows. "I heard that. I think April has a wonderful idea.

Daisy, isn't it about time you delegated some of your duties? I know you don't want to overburden Iris or Tessa because they're helping with your wedding. But if April could plan this and execute it, maybe you should give it a try."

Suddenly April's gaze rose to the entrance of the tea garden, and she grinned.

Daisy turned her head to see Trevor and Jonas coming her way. Seated at a table for four, she motioned to the other two chairs as they greeted Amelia.

April leaned toward Daisy again. "Should I fetch two more cups of chocolate tea and maybe some rhubarb muffins?"

"Good idea," Daisy said with an answering smile. "Thank you."

Her gaze was on Jonas, and she appreciated the thrill seeing him always gave her. Today, in jeans and a pale-blue polo shirt, he looked particularly handsome. Especially when the wave in his black hair wouldn't stay in place.

"Just who I wanted to see," Amelia said to Trevor.

"Well, that's not a greeting I get often," he joked.

They all laughed. As a journalist, sometimes he was more of a bother than a friend. Jonas, who had seated himself next to Daisy, bumped his shoulder against hers playfully. She bumped him back.

Amelia went on, "How many articles is the *Willow Creek Messenger* going to do about the covered bridge's anniversary?"

"That's a good question," Trevor said. "I'm just preparing an in-depth one for the day before the anniversary. Do you have something else in mind?"

"Of course, I do. I'd like an article on the history of the covered bridge, but I'd also like a piece on the plans leading up to the anniversary and how we're going to celebrate. We need to get the information out to the public so they know what to expect. If we make enough noise, maybe we can encourage some bloggers to pick it up for social media."

Trevor snitched a snickerdoodle from the plate. "I can pitch it, but I don't know if it will fly."

"What other news is there in Willow Creek right now?" Amelia asked, raising her hands in frustration.

"Do you listen to my podcast?" Trevor asked her. "I posted a short one this morning about a tip that came in to my hotline."

"I haven't listened to your most recent one. What was the tip about?"

"I might be investigating a twenty-year-old murder. That could be big news. The paper could follow along with articles summing up what I find out."

Jonas interjected, "I don't think your editor will go for that. He usually follows directives coming out of the Willow Creek Police Department."

With a scowl that Trevor directed at Jonas, he muttered, "Don't be a spoilsport."

"You know I'm right. Do you really think Morris Rappaport and Zeke Willet are going to go along with what you want to do?" Jonas questioned him.

The detectives were Jonas's friends and had become Daisy's friends, too. She tried not to get in their way and to respect their methods, but she wasn't sure Trevor would do the same.

April came across the threshold into the spill-over tearoom with a tray of goodies for Jonas and

Trevor. She set them down and exited without interrupting their conversation.

"Tell me all about this," Amelia said. "What's going on? Is this gossip or rumor?"

"Not gossip or rumor." Trevor stirred a bit of sugar into his tea. "After my podcast, a call came in to the hotline. Daisy and Tessa were both there. They heard it." He motioned to Daisy. "Tell Amelia so she knows I'm not pulling her leg."

"A call did come in to the hotline," Daisy affirmed.

Amelia didn't look impressed. "In the past, those tips weren't consequential."

"This time could be different," Daisy said. "A man called in and told us there was a chest being auctioned off by a storage unit company, and it would have a secret to a twenty-year-old murder."

Amelia's eyes grew wider and then narrowed again. "And you believed this?"

"I checked into the auction," Trevor said. "Two storage compartments are being auctioned off. One has three chests, and the other has two. One out of five chances we'll find something. That's if we buy the contents of both storage units."

Amelia was quiet long enough for Daisy to ask, "What are you thinking?"

Amelia picked up one of the rhubarb muffins and examined it, but Daisy didn't think she was really seeing it. "Horace and I will be redecorating a few of the rooms at the B and B. I could use a chest or two and any antiques. I imagine those storage units might hold other items, too."

"Assorted furniture and I don't know what else," Trevor said.

"What if I go along?" Amelia offered. "I might

be interested in bidding. I'd be bidding on the whole unit, right?"

"That's right," Jonas agreed.

"I'm prepared to bid on one of the units, too," Daisy added. "I could find a chest for Jazzi to take to college. I think she'd like that. If we win the bids, we could examine the chests to our hearts' content."

"We'll examine those chests until we find the secret," Trevor resolved.

Jonas picked up his rhubarb muffin and held it like a crystal ball. "We'll find the secret, as long as this isn't a hoax."

Trevor scowled at him, but the expression didn't faze Jonas. As a former detective, he was used to scowls, mumbles against him, and even more.

Amelia raised her cup of tea. "I say, be hopeful. We could find a treasure as well as a secret."

More than anything, Daisy hoped they'd find the treasure and not evidence of a murder.

The June evening, bringing scents of honeysuckle and roses to the patio, was absolutely balmy as Daisy, Jonas, and Jazzi finished supper. Jonas had grilled steaks. Daisy had brought home cabbage apple salad from the tea garden to accompany them.

As Jazzi cleared the picnic table and carried remnants of their dinner inside, Jonas covered Daisy's hand with his. "So we're actually going to bid on the contents of the storage compartment next Saturday?"

"We'll see. If the auction price flies too high, I'll forget about it."

"Do you think Trevor will?"

"Not a chance," Daisy said, already worried about Trevor's involvement in the cold case.

The sliding-glass doors to the patio reopened. Jazzi hurried outside followed by Vi, Daisy's older daughter, and her son, Sammy. Sammy was a year and a half and one of the joys in Daisy's life. Vi and Foster had unexpectedly become pregnant when they were in college. Vi had quit school, had Sammy, and suffered with postpartum depression. Now they were getting their lives back on track. They'd moved out from the garage apartment and into a rental house near friends of Daisy's.

As Sammy toddled over to her, Daisy extricated herself from the picnic bench and scooped him up. "How are you, big boy?" She tickled his tummy as she asked.

He placed his little hands on either side of her face and giggled, babbling as he did. He was voicing several words now, but most were only recognizable to him . . . and sometimes Vi. His mom had dressed him in red shorts with a red-and-white-striped shirt. A dog face grinned at them from the shirt.

As soon as Felix had seen Vi and Sammy crossing the patio, he'd left his spot by Jonas's leg to greet the little boy who often played "roll the ball" with him.

"It's good to see you," Jonas said to Vi. "We were about to have dessert. Do you think Sammy would like a lemon tea cake?"

"I think he'd love one," Vi said. "And so would I, but I'm watching my calories, especially carbs."

As far as Daisy was concerned, her daughter was

a perfect weight. But as she did in many instances, she held her tongue.

Vi sat on the bench beside Daisy, who had lowered herself with Sammy. Sammy was trying to pet Felix, and she let him down so the dog and little boy could have an adventure.

Jonas said, "I'll watch them," as Sammy ran after Felix to the tomato garden near the patio.

Jazzi offered, "I'll get the tea cakes and a cup of milk for Sammy."

Vi had clipped her honey-blond hair back at the temples. It was getting longer again and waving on her shoulders. She brushed it away from the bateau neckline of her pink blouse. She was wearing mauve-colored shorts tonight, and she crossed her legs, one of her flip-flops bobbing up and down. "Jazzi tells me she's enjoying her job at the Rainbow Flamingo."

"She wanted a job somewhere other than with me, and I can understand that. She's earning money for college expenses."

"I wish our jobs didn't have to take up our whole lives," Vi said with a frustrated sigh.

"Does yours?" Daisy asked, surprised. Vi worked part-time at Pirated Treasures, an antiques shop on Sage Street.

"No, of course it doesn't. The problem is, there are complications. Foster's working so many hours. Sammy is more mobile and getting into more things. I can't take him along to Pirated Treasures like I used to. I'm afraid he'll damage something or get hurt. I can't constantly burden my family with daycare. Brielle's been babysitting him a few hours at a time, but she's getting ready for college just like

Jazzi is. She's doing administrative work for her mom at home."

Brielle Horn's mom was a lawyer, and Daisy could see how Brielle could help with some of the filing and paperwork. Brielle, who was Jazzi's age, had needed a port in a storm, and Daisy's home had been that for a while. But now she was happily living with her grandmother and her mom again. Her grandmother's former home was the one Vi and Foster were renting.

"Is Foster enjoying his new job?" Foster had graduated from college in May and secured a job with a software company. With his degree in business management and his tech skills, he could go far.

"I think he likes his new job, but he's under pressure to perform. He wants to succeed, and I understand that. But he's also taken on other projects. You know that."

Daisy did. Foster, once her employee, still managed her website and social media accounts. "I can find someone else to take over my website," she pointed out.

"Your website is the least of his responsibilities. He's doing the PR campaign for the homeless shelter and spending many evenings on that. Once it gets up and running, he wants to help *them* succeed, too. He's even helping to sort through applications for counselors and volunteers."

The homeless shelter had been a controversial project the town had undertaken. But plans for it were progressing nicely. "How many websites is he handling now?" Daisy asked.

"About fifteen. It doesn't seem like a lot, but he updates them once a month and that type of thing. And he takes on new ones. He's spending a lot of time right now on Amelia Wiseman's because of the bridge and the celebration for it."

"Have you spoken to Foster about all this?" Daisy asked.

"I have, but it doesn't do any good. I don't want to nag him. I don't want to be that kind of wife. But I also want to enjoy our new place and do the landscaping for it. I want him to spend more time with Sammy. At night he's so tired that Sammy's in bed and asleep before Foster even gets to him."

"Are you having meals together?" Daisy asked like the mom that she was.

"Many nights, but you know what a meal is. Sammy has it all over his face and on his high-chair tray, and supper lasts about ten minutes. I love Sammy. I love Foster. I love our new home. I'd like to enjoy all of it."

Just then, Jazzi returned outside with a dish of lemon tea cakes and a pitcher of iced tea. Vi took a plastic cup from the stack on the table and poured herself tea while Jazzi went back inside for Sammy's sippy cup.

Daisy studied her older daughter, circling her mind with anything she should say, could say, or wanted to say. Finally she decided on, "Foster's only been at his job a few weeks. Give him a chance to figure out his routine. In the meantime, maybe your gram, Aunt Iris, and I can help you with childcare in the evenings. Then you can spend time at Pirated Treasures if you want. With daylight and Otis's security system and the tourists walking by, you should be safe there."

"I don't only want to work in the evenings when family is free," Vi complained. "And it seems waste-

ful to pay for daycare so I can work during the day
and make less money than daycare costs." Vi took
a few swallows of tea. "I didn't mean to dump all
this on you. I just came for a visit, and to watch
Sammy play with Felix and have fun."

Daisy motioned Jonas to come back over to the
table. "Then let's turn on the hose, wash those little hands, and have some lemon tea cakes."

Vi gave Daisy a smile, and Daisy knew at least for
now her daughter's concerns were pushed into
the background.

Surprised at the setup at the storage compartment center on Saturday, Daisy found the man in
charge while Jonas, Felix, Amelia, and Trevor looked
around.

The storage facility in a rural area of Willow
Creek consisted of a two-floored building mostly
composed of concrete blocks. To her amazement,
the auction wasn't going to be held at individual
units inside the edifice. Rather, all the former
renter's belongings had been separated into two
areas in the gravel parking lot.

And . . . the name of the storage unit's welcome
sign had been changed. Instead of BONNER'S STOR-
AGE CENTER, it now read SMALL TOWN STORAGE.

At a corner office in the building, she found a
rotund man in a yellow baseball cap, the bill
pulled down over his eyes. His orange T-shirt had
sweat stains under his arms and on his back. He'd
obviously been engaged in physical labor. Moving
the contents of the units to the parking lot?

"Hello," she said through the Plexiglas window with its reception-style opening. "Can I ask you a few questions?"

The man looked up at her. "Sure. About the auction today? We want to get this completed as soon as possible."

"I noticed the name on the storage unit sign has changed. What's going on?"

"I'm Bill Horton. I was the manager of Bonner's Storage Center, and Small Town Storage kept me on."

"The ownership has changed?" she asked.

"Sure has. We're part of a chain now."

"Is that why the auction happened so quickly? Usually aren't auctions advertised online to pull in a bunch of people to bid on the merchandise?"

"The new owner didn't want any backlog. He wants all the old business taken care of. Understand?"

"Is that why the auction is in the parking lot?" she probed.

"It is. I have new renters coming on board, and I wanted them to fill up the storage units. If you're interested in renting, I can sign you up."

"Not right now. I'm here for the auction."

"I didn't even hire an auctioneer for this. Not enough merchandise to warrant his commission. All I want to do is empty the parking lot. I'll be out shortly, and we'll get started."

Taking the hint that the man had business to conduct, Daisy returned outside and met Jonas and Felix, who were looking over the merchandise in the two piles.

"The storage facility has been taken over by a new owner," Daisy explained.

Amelia and Trevor came over to join them.

"What do you think?" Jonas motioned to the contents of the storage unit to his left.

Felix was nosing around the furniture, sniffing old scents and new.

Jonas said, "I'm particularly interested in that pile. Two chests are there and old tables and chairs. I think I can refurbish them and sell them at Woods."

"That's fine with me," Daisy confirmed. "That green chest could work for Jazzi."

Amelia nodded as if she was pleased with that decision. "Good. I like the contents of the other unit. There are three chests and a few stained-glass panels. Those panels would be gorgeous in the windows of the bed-and-breakfast."

From what Daisy could see, the stained glass was designed in a flower motif, one with an iris and one with a rose. "My mom would probably love them," Daisy said.

"But I have a place to put them." Amelia's smile was sly. "I can name one of the rooms the Iris Room and the other the Rose Room. What do you think?"

There was an older woman wandering around, as well as a man in khakis and a polo shirt.

"That will be great if you can win the bid," Trevor reminded her. "These are being sold as lots, not as individual pieces. That doesn't make sense to me because they'd get a lot more the other way. But if the center was sold and the manager wants to just rid himself of the old contents, that's why he's doing it this way."

"The man who called you knew about this auction before it was even posted in the *Willow Creek Messenger*," Jonas said.

Trevor nodded. "Someone had an inside track."

Bill Horton was crossing the parking lot. Daisy glimpsed someone else near the corner of the storage unit building. Although it was early morning, the temperature was already in the low seventies. The fellow at the storage unit corner caught Daisy's attention because he was wearing gray. She'd almost missed him because his hoodie was the same color as the concrete building. She couldn't see his face because as soon as she glanced toward him, he turned away and ducked behind the building.

Could that have been Trevor's caller? Could he have been watching to see if Trevor had taken the bait?

Before she could alert Trevor, the office manager began with the first section of merchandise that Jonas was interested in. Jonas and the man in the khakis bid on the lot, and Jonas won the bid. Trevor was elated.

In an aside, Amelia said to Daisy, "You bid, too, if we have to knock someone out. I'll pay you if you win it."

As soon as the manager started the bidding on the second collection of merchandise, the woman who had been milling about bid also. So, Daisy got into the action. Since Daisy and Amelia were determined to win the bid from the older woman, she dropped out. Daisy ended up winning the bid.

Jonas elbowed her. "You might have bid more than what all of it is worth."

"I know Amelia is pleased with the panels. She nudged me to keep bidding."

Jonas gave her a knowing look. "The bottom line is, you can't resist a twenty-year-old mystery, can you?"

She didn't have to answer him because *no*, she couldn't resist.

CHAPTER THREE

In case Amelia or Jonas won their auction bids, Trevor had driven Amelia's SUV, pulling a trailer behind. Jonas hoped anything else would fit in his SUV.

With a grunt, Trevor handed a console table to Jonas, who positioned it in the trailer.

Studying the table, Amelia said, "I might want that for the bed-and-breakfast."

The table had a mahogany veneer with a checkerboard and diamond inlay. Daisy agreed it would add interest to one of the bedrooms.

Trevor next handed over a schoolhouse chair that had seen lots of wear, as had the case pieces and storage cabinet. But Daisy knew that Jonas could work any furniture into something beautiful. He'd let Amelia have the pieces she preferred, and he'd refurbish the rest.

"None of this is worth much in its present condition," Amelia noted. She'd brought two old quilts, which she used to wrap the stained-glass panels.

After Amelia had taken the panels to the back

seat of her SUV and secured them, she returned to Daisy and Felix, who was sitting by her foot. They all looked thoughtfully at the five chests, which appeared to be variations of a small steamer trunk. The first one was wood seamed with metal strips that created square-like designs across all sides of the chest. Two metal buckles aligned along the middle strip on the front surface. Another sturdier latch had been secured at the center.

"I particularly like that one," Amelia said, pointing to the second chest waiting to be loaded. "I can use it as a coffee table in a sitting area. It's probably too heavy and bulky for Jazzi to take along."

Daisy suspected Amelia was right. The trunk, which appeared solid and heavy, had a flat top, probably pine, in a reddish-brown color.

"That hardware is cast-iron," Amelia pointed out. "The guys will probably need our help lifting it."

The lid of the chest was fastened with four buckles and a latch that had three strong back hinges. Amelia undid the buckles and flipped open the lid. There was a pine tray inside that could be lifted out. Worn leather handles were attached to both ends of the trunk.

The day was heating up already, the sun bright on the brass fixings on the next trunk. Daisy imagined this one could interest her daughter. The green wood chest was half the size of the others. Leather fittings secured and fastened the brass mounts.

"That's certainly scuffed with some stains," Amelia said, as if she couldn't possibly be interested in it.

"It's vintage and looks well-used. I think Jazzi

would appreciate the authenticity. It's a good size that could slip under her bed."

"Are you sure she wouldn't like this better?" Amelia had moved to stand beside a leather-handled wicker chest that was wider at the top than the bottom. She flipped the lid open. The insides were bare.

"I'll take photos and give her a chance to look it over," Daisy said, already doing that with her phone. "The latch isn't very secure."

"If Jazzi doesn't want it, I can probably paint it a trendy color and use it in a bedroom to store duvets and quilts."

The final chest was a dome-topped steamer trunk. Knowing more about antiques and vintage items than Daisy, Amelia explained, "That's steel-clad wood. Another heavy one. It's seen its share of use from the looks of it."

Daisy raised the lid on this one and knew it was a chest she would want to explore. It housed several boxes and compartments.

An hour later, Felix seemed excited trotting back and forth with Jonas and Trevor as they carried furniture from the trailer into Jonas's workshop at the rear of Woods. Jonas had decided to unload everything there that Amelia didn't want. Her husband, Horace, had come to pick her up at Woods. Trevor would drive the trailer with the rest of the furniture and sundry items back to the B&B.

As Daisy drove Jonas's SUV home with two of the chests inside, she realized the morning was already gone. Jonas was staying at Woods to take another good look at the furniture he planned to restore or revamp. His store manager would drop him off at home later. Daisy wanted to examine the two chests in the back of the SUV, but she had gardening to do . . . and cleaning, too. If she didn't plan her time wisely, dust bunnies as well as weeds could get ahead of her. She'd take a cursory look at the chests but wait until Jonas brought them inside after he returned home to examine them more carefully.

To that purpose, she parked the SUV in front of the garage at the path to their barn home.

The chests produced no secrets at first glance. Saving her curiosity for later, Daisy went inside the house and gave attention to Marjoram and Pepper, her two felines. A tortoiseshell, Marjoram had striking markings. One side of her face was mottled with tortie colors of tan, brown, and black. The other side of her face was dark brown. Various colors from orange to cream spotted her back and flanks while her chest was cream and rust. Pepper, on the other hand, was a tuxedo, black with white fluffy patches on her chest.

After Daisy grabbed a cup of lime yogurt for a quick lunch, she vacuumed the downstairs, taking throw rugs outside to shake on the patio. Jazzi would run the sweeper upstairs later. After she finished, she plucked her straw hat from the closet and went outside to the garage for her gardening implements. Soon she was ankle-deep in weeds as she pulled them from the surrounding plants in the vegetable garden. She only paused to smooth on additional sunscreen before turning back to her task.

Jazzi came home before Jonas. After she washed up, she helped Daisy cut up tomatoes and lettuce and grate cheese for tacos. "Was the auction exciting?" she asked as she set the dishes in a row on the island.

"Not a bit," Daisy answered. "I got a little *zing* when I won the bid. Amelia pretty much got first dibs on everything we won, but Jonas didn't seem to mind."

"I peeked in the SUV. I think I will like that green chest if we can clean it up. The other chests in the photos you texted me were too big."

As Jazzi went outside with paper plates, cups, and napkins, Jonas came inside. He kissed Daisy, and they almost got carried away. With a chuckle, he leaned back and held her by the shoulders. "I think you got some sun. You look cute with a red nose."

"I do *not* have a red nose. My hat protected me." He'd tapped the tip of her nose, and she could see in his eyes he was thinking about kissing her again when Jazzi returned inside.

Within fifteen minutes, they were eating tacos on the patio and drinking iced tea. "Your tomato plants look good," Jonas remarked.

"I spent most of the afternoon weeding the garden. The zucchini vines look hardy."

Jazzi asked, "Are you going to bring those chests into the house? I looked at them but didn't see anything noteworthy. The one I'd like for college does have a liner inside, but I didn't feel anything under it." After a pause, she said, "FYI, Mark is coming over later. Okay?"

"Of course, it's okay," Daisy assured her. Jazzi was dating Mark Constantine but they'd decided to attend different colleges. They'd only have the rest of the summer to spend time together.

"I could have Mark help me bring the chests into the house, especially the heavy one," Jonas said.

Jazzi nodded. "I'm sure he'll help. He listens to Trevor's podcast. He'll be curious about them, too."

After supper, they played fetch with Felix, talked about the wedding, and went over the site in the backyard where Jonas's workshop would be built. Shadows took over the yard as the sun went down.

"Do you feel like a game of Cat-Opoly?" Jonas asked Jazzi. "You said Mark won't be here for another hour."

"Sure," she agreed. "I'll set it up."

Felix helped.

Once a barn, the building had been turned into a cozy home by Daisy's renovations. She'd bought the property with her deceased husband's insurance money, which had made possible her new life in Willow Creek. The second floor had been divided into two bedrooms with a bath in between them that suited her daughters perfectly. An architect had helped Daisy design the downstairs for coziness and practicality. An open stairway at the rear of the living room led to the upstairs. Marjoram and Pepper often sat there looking over their domain.

Daisy had switched on the wagon-wheel chandelier, and it glowed in the living room. That opened into the dining area and kitchen. A stone fireplace, used often in the winter, stretched from the hearth to the ceiling in the dining-room space on the east wall. Daisy and Jonas's bedroom was behind the living room with a short hall that led into the kitchen. The powder room located under the stairs, and with it a tiny laundry room, suited their needs.

For now Marjoram and Pepper perched on the blue, cream, and green upholstered sofa. Marjoram meowed at Daisy loudly. When she and Jonas settled in for the day, it was time for the felines' snack.

Daisy brought the treat bag from the kitchen and shook it. "If you want treats, you have to come into the kitchen. You know that."

Marjoram gave her another meow and carefully walked down the back of the sofa to the seat cushion and then jumped to the floor. Pepper yawned and then came down the arm of the sofa to the coffee table to the floor, avoiding Felix. However, Felix wouldn't be ignored. He scampered to the kitchen with the felines, expecting his peanut butter biscuit.

Daisy had just put the cats' treats in their dishes and given Felix his biscuit, when her phone on the counter buzzed, playing its tuba sound. The caller was Trevor.

"You got my message?" he asked.

She studied her phone's screen and saw she did, indeed, have a voicemail. "I'm sorry, Trevor. We were outside, and I left my phone in here to charge. What's going on?"

"Nothing. That's just it. I looked at the chests that Amelia brought home. I couldn't find anything. Have you examined yours yet?"

"We didn't bring them into the house. Mark is coming over later and will help Jonas unload them."

"I'm disappointed. I hope your chests turn up something. It must have been a prank," Trevor moaned morosely.

"You don't know that. I'll let you know if I have any news."

After that, Daisy ended the call. She looked out the window to see if the lights were on in the apartment over the garage. They were. That probably meant April was settled in for the night. Daisy felt protective of her because she didn't have any family. That had to be a lonely feeling.

Daisy took a plate from the knotty-pine cupboard and set it on the island. She'd brought home chocolate-chip cookies from the tea garden, and she arranged them on a plate.

The game of Cat-Opoly was stretching long when Daisy's phone played again. She'd brought it into the living room because sometimes Vi called this time of night after she'd settled Sammy in bed. However, the caller was April.

"I'm just calling to check out something," April said. "I heard a noise behind the garage, some kind of motor. It wasn't in the driveway. Are you guys doing something back there?"

Daisy glanced at Jonas. "No, we're not." She reported to Jonas what April had told her.

"I'll check it out," Jonas said. "Tell April to stay inside."

Daisy did that and watched Jonas head out the sliding-glass door from the kitchen to the patio with Felix. Jazzi gave her a look.

"You stay here," Daisy ordered. "I'm going to back him up."

"With what?" Jazzi called after her as Daisy followed Jonas and Felix out the sliding-glass doors.

Jonas could move faster and stealthier than she could even with Felix by his side.

Suddenly she heard Jonas shout, "Hey, you!"

Daisy hesitated, then raised her phone, ready to call 9-1-1 if necessary.

Felix and Jonas had taken off through the field behind the garage when Daisy heard the rumble of an engine. It revved up loudly, a pulsing sound into the night, then faded away.

Only slightly out of breath, Jonas returned to the driveway and spotted Daisy. "What are you doing out here?"

She lifted her phone. "Backup."

He shook his head, took a deep breath, then studied his SUV. "I couldn't see much. Somebody dressed in black. He was carrying what looked like a crowbar. Whoever it was took off on a four-wheeler. That was the noise April must have heard when he arrived."

Closing in on the car, looking for signs of damage, she was glad she didn't see any. "We don't have to wait for Mark. I can help you carry the chests inside." She lifted her arm in a Popeye gesture to show Jonas her biceps. "I do have muscles from lifting trays at the tea garden."

Jonas laughed. "You've proved that more than once. I think we know now that Trevor's tip was legitimate. But I don't think the intruder will be back. Mark will be here soon."

"I want to tell April what's going on. I think I'll invite her to come over to the house for the night."

"While you do that, I'll call Trevor and tell him what happened."

"Are you going to call Zeke?" This could be a

matter for the detectives. Except what had really happened? Some stranger had been in their backyard.

Jonas must have had the same thoughts. "Nothing was damaged, and we don't really know anything for sure right now. I think I'll wait to contact Zeke or Morris."

Walking toward the garage door, Daisy texted April to tell her she was coming up. Once at the side door, she punched in the code. When the door opened, she flipped the light on inside and then headed for the stairs. April was waiting for her in the small apartment.

After Vi and Foster had moved out their belongings, Jonas had moved a sofa from his furniture store into the living-room area, along with a table and two chairs for the small kitchen. Daisy's aunt Iris had made April an afghan when she'd moved in, and April had spread it over the back of the sofa. The apartment was still sparse, but April was making it her own. She'd brought in a braided rug for under a wicker coffee table that she'd found at a flea market. Daisy could see April's laptop sat on the coffee table. She'd been probably streaming something.

April asked, "What's going on?"

"We don't know exactly, but I can make a pretty good guess. Trevor Lundquist started a podcast."

"I know, I listen to it," April said. "You did an interview with him. That went well."

"I thought it did. But after the podcast, Trevor received a call on his hotline."

"About a crime?" April was as interested as other podcast listeners in Willow Creek's happenings.

"Possibly. We were told there would be an auction of merchandise from a storage compartment. So Amelia Wiseman and Jonas, Trevor, and I bid on the items. There were chests up for bid. One of those chests was supposed to hold a secret to a twenty-year-old murder."

"Wow." April's eyes were wide. "Did you get the chests?"

"We did. I have two of them. That's where things get a little complicated. Amelia has the other three. Trevor said he didn't find anything in those. I haven't really examined these two completely because they were in Jonas's SUV. We got busy, and Mark was going to help him bring them in as soon as he arrived."

"But . . ." April drawled.

"But then you called that you heard something out back, so Jonas came out to look. Apparently someone came across the field in a four-wheeler. We suspect he was going to try to break into Jonas's SUV to find out what was in the chests."

"Is Jonas okay?"

"He's fine. The guy ran off, jumped on his vehicle, and went back the way he'd come."

April glanced around her apartment and back at the kitchen, where a window looked out to the back. "Do you think he'll be back?"

April had been through trauma in her young life, and Daisy didn't want her to be afraid any more than she'd want her daughters to be frightened.

"I doubt it. As soon as Mark arrives, we'll take the two chests inside. In the meantime, I have a feeling Jonas is going to keep watch over his SUV. But I don't want you to be afraid of staying here. Do you want to come over to the house for the night? You can sleep in Vi's old room. I'm sure Jazzi would be glad to have company up there."

"Oh, I don't know. I'm a grown-up and all. You're giving me a break on the rent, which I'm grateful for. For so long, my life wasn't in my own hands, and now I feel like I want to be independent."

There was a "but" underlying April's tone.

"April, are you afraid here? I don't want you to be, and there's no reason you have to be. You can come over to the house for the night. Then we'll see where things go from there. Besides, wouldn't you like to look at those chests with me?"

A slow smile spread across April's pretty face. Dimples even formed on either side of her mouth. "That would be kind of fun, wouldn't it?"

"I'll wait for you to pack a bag, and we'll go over together. I'm not sure I want to be outside alone in the dark."

April had headed for her bedroom, but she stopped and turned to look at Daisy. "I don't believe that for a minute. You're the bravest person I know. Are you *ever* afraid?"

"Of course, I'm afraid. But I'd rather not be put into circumstances where I have to be brave or courageous. Courage is just something that happens when you want to get out of a predicament you didn't intend to be in, and you don't have another way out."

April laughed. "It won't take me long to pack up pj's. I'll be ready in a few minutes."

And she was.

April was no sooner settled upstairs in Vi's old room when Mark arrived and helped Jonas bring in the two chests, setting them in the living room.

That was the best place for them all to see exactly what was inside of them.

Felix was already sniffing around them while Marjoram and Pepper looked on. Marjoram had jumped up onto the deacon's bench at the front window while Pepper moseyed around out of Felix's way. The cats and Felix were companions of sorts now, but they still didn't cuddle or sleep together. Daisy didn't know if that would ever happen.

Daisy brewed chocolate rooibos tea. It was a robust tea infused with cocoa husks and sweet vanilla. Since it was an organic decaffeinated tea, it was good to drink in the evenings. Along with the tea, Daisy produced cheese biscuits to munch while they sipped.

Everyone seemed to relax, and Daisy explained about the other pieces they'd bought at the auction along with the chests. "Jonas took anything he could fix or renew into the shop."

"I'd like to see your shop sometime," Mark said. "I have no idea how furniture is made, but I use it all the time."

Everyone laughed.

"It's an art," Jazzi said. "I've seen Jonas work the planer, the sander, and the lathe."

"Listen to you," Mark said with a smile. "You know all about it."

"I've been to Jonas's workshop a few times." She asked, "Are you going to still work in town even when you have your workshop out here?"

"I'm not sure yet," Jonas said. "I might store all the reclaimed wood here and build my pieces from that. Or . . . I might just do special-order pieces here. Clients could pick them up when they're finished. I have to talk to my manager about it. It would be nice to have a design office here away from sawdust and noise."

Jazzi finished a biscuit, then she wiped her hands on a napkin and stood, going over to the two chests. "Can I open the green one?" she asked Daisy.

"Sure. Maybe we can paint the outside and shine up the brass?"

April joined Jazzi as she lifted the lid, and they stared inside.

Mark couldn't help but be interested, too. "Is this what's called a steamer trunk? You know, like people used to travel on ships?"

"Could be," Daisy said. "It's not as large as the other ones."

The inside of the chest was empty except for the tan satin lining that was pulling away from the sides and the bottom. Could some kind of secret be held behind that lining or underneath it?

Jazzi's nose wrinkled, then she frowned. "Can we take the lining out and redo it?"

"I'd like to take the lining out to see if anything is underneath, and if you want to redo it, that will give us a chance to look at the whole trunk bare."

Taking hold of a corner of the lining in the lid, Jazzi pulled. The material was old, almost thread-bare, and it came away easily. Except for the glue marks around the edges of the lid, there wasn't anything else there. Jazzi ran her hand over the inside of the lid, feeling carefully in case anything might be hidden that she couldn't see with the naked eye. Nothing was.

She told Mark the story of the chest, and his

brows wrinkled. "We couldn't be looking for a computer chip or anything that small, could we?"

After thinking about it, Jonas shook his head. "I don't think so. If we're looking at a twenty-year-old crime, my guess is the secret is contained in a less tech-oriented way."

After Jazzi had taken the lining from the top of the trunk and laid it on the floor, Felix began exploring it—nosing it, pushing it, lifting it with his paw.

"What do you think, buddy?" Jonas asked him.

The dog took the lining in his mouth and shook it back and forth, and then dropped it.

"That about says it all," April joked.

Her gaze on the bottom of the trunk, Jazzi took a corner from the side and pulled gently. The lining came away from the glue, loose between the corners. The bottom was all one piece of material and again tore when Jazzi tugged on it.

"You can line it with anything you want," April said. "Even fur."

"We'll have to go to Quilts and Notions," Jazzi suggested. "I'm sure Rachel would have something there that I'd like to line it with. Don't you think, Mom?"

"Oh, I'm sure she would. If you don't see anything you like, you can probably order it."

Rachel Fisher was a good friend of Daisy's from childhood. She was New Order Amish. She and her husband owned Quilts and Notions, a fabric and quilt store not far from Daisy's Tea Garden.

"An animal print might be nice." Apparently, Jazzi's imagination was already working.

Jonas was examining the leather straps that

lifted the lid. "I can replace these so they're stronger, then it won't matter how many times you lift it up and down."

"I think it will be perfect," Jazzi decided.

Rising to his feet, Jonas picked up the fabric. "I'll stash this in the trash. I'm going to go outside and have a look around. Why don't you examine the other chest?"

Daisy gave him a worried look. They had a security system, and there were motion-detector lights all around the house and the garage. Maybe those had spooked their would-be burglar, too.

Jonas simply lifted his phone. The underlying message was clear. He would call Zeke if anything untoward happened.

When they moved to the second chest, April wrinkled her nose. "This one smells musty."

"There's no telling where it was stored," Daisy mused.

The top of the trunk was slightly domed. Daisy unhooked the buckles for the lid and then the center lock. If there had ever been a key, there wasn't now, and the lock was broken. When she lifted the lid, she saw the inside of the trunk had many compartments. A cardboard-type folder was attached to the lid. She undid a small ribbon and opened the envelope top. She didn't realize she was holding her breath until she saw the envelope was empty. When she turned to the little latches, the wood with the envelope fell down and she could see into the domed top of the trunk. Nothing was there. On the right side of the dome, however, a playing card–sized photo of a woman in old-fashioned gear was pasted.

"How old do you think that is?" Jazzi asked.

"Impossible to know."

There was a small compartment under the picture with a little leather latch. It was about half the size of an old-time cigar box. Daisy lifted the narrow lid. Again there was nothing inside. The interior of the trunk itself smelled mustier than the outside. She didn't see anything there except dust and some crumpled old leaves.

April and Jazzi were still studying the picture in the lid when Daisy's phone vibrated and played its tuba sound. She lifted it, half-expecting it to be Jonas saying he'd found something else outside. But it wasn't. It was Amelia.

"Hi, Amelia. We were just examining our chests. We didn't find anything, though."

"Something is definitely amiss," Amelia said. "I have a storage shed out back, and Trevor helped me move everything into there. But someone just broke into my shed. These chests must hold a secret that someone doesn't want us to find."

CHAPTER FOUR

With the musty scent of the old chest still in the air, Daisy tapped the speaker icon on her phone. That way all of them gathered there would hear what Amelia had to say. When Daisy heard the sound of the sliding-glass door, she knew Jonas had returned inside.

"Go over it all for us, Amelia. Tell us what happened. I have you on speakerphone."

When Jonas came into her purview, she motioned to her phone. With an inquiring expression, he stood by the sofa, and Felix settled on the floor beside him.

"Who all is there?" Amelia asked.

"Me, and Jonas, Mark, Jazzi, and April. They were examining the chests with me."

Daisy heard shuffling and a scraping sound. Amelia must have made herself more comfortable on a chair. She began with, "Trevor and I went over those chests with a fine-tooth comb this afternoon. He was so disappointed we didn't find anything."

"I'll bet," Jonas muttered, lowering his hand to Felix and stroking his flank.

"I think Trevor wanted to head over to your place right then," Amelia went on. "But I told him not to barge in. He should give you a chance to do your own examination."

"Thank you for that. Jonas and Mark just brought them in a little while ago, and . . ." She hesitated, not sure if she should tell Amelia the rest. But then she did because it sounded as if Amelia had had a break-in.

"Jonas chased away someone who was going to try to break into his SUV."

There was a surprised "oh" from Amelia, then she offered vaguely, "We've definitely stumbled onto something. It looks as though you have the chest with the secret."

"Why do you say that?" Daisy asked.

"Besides the fact that Trevor and I examined the chests, the person who broke into the shed didn't find anything either."

"Or maybe he did," Daisy countered. "Tell me what happened at your place and when."

"I'm not sure *when*. Trevor and Horace helped me move the chests into the shed. After we combed over them, Trevor left, probably before noon. After that, I was inside until I went out to the shed to look through the lamps and wall hangings again. That's when I saw the padlock had been wrenched off."

"Like, with a crowbar?" Jonas asked.

"That could have broken it, I suppose," Amelia said. "The things in the shed were shuffled around, but I don't believe anything was missing.

The clasp on one of the chests was broken, too. I can't remember if it was that loose when we moved the chest inside."

Jonas entered the conversation again. "Did you call the police?"

"No, nothing was stolen. I couldn't see the point. Did you call?"

"No, no damage was done." Jonas was frowning. "But maybe we *should* call."

"If Trevor reports all of this on his podcast, the detectives will know what happened," Daisy reminded them.

Daisy heard Amelia click her tongue before she said, "Do you really think he'll do that?"

"If he wants to create interest, he will," Daisy maintained. "Keep in touch and I'll do the same."

After good-byes, Daisy ended the call. Mark studied Jazzi and then Daisy. "You certainly do have an interesting life."

Mark's grin relayed the sentiment that an interesting life was a good thing.

Daisy wasn't so sure.

On Monday, Daisy carried rhubarb muffins and a glass of chocolate iced tea to one of her favorite customers on the patio, Fiona Wilson. As she walked past a pot of lemongrass, her leg brushed against it, and the scent followed her as she continued to Fiona's table. Herb pots were interspersed with pots of petunias in pink, purple, and yellow along the patio's edge. Between those containers sat whimsical statues—a bronze cat seated on a stone reading a book, glasses perched on its nose, and a dog with a ball in its mouth. Yellow-and-white-striped umbrellas provided shade over the white patio tables.

As Daisy unloaded the items on the serving tray, she said to Fiona, "Are you still eating soup in the warmer weather?" Usually Fiona bought a quart or two of soup to take home and have for the week.

"I think I'm going to load up on salads this week, and just take home one quart of soup. It's lovely out here this time of year. I love sitting on your patio. I wish I had one."

Around seventy, small and slender, Fiona wore her curly hair chin-length with a gold clip over her right temple. Daisy knew she lived in a first-floor apartment without a backyard.

"You can come and sit on my patio anytime you want," Daisy offered. Daisy had been busy all morning and hadn't taken much account of her surroundings.

At that moment, she noticed the blue sky beyond the umbrella, the fluffy clouds, and the boughs of the maples practically intertwining near the creek that flowed to the rear of the tea garden's property. She also recognized Iris and Marshall Thompson only a table away at the edge of the patio. Herbs and flowers framed them as they were settled in chairs close to each other at the table.

A lawyer, who had come to Daisy's aid in more than one murder investigation, Marshall was six-foot-two with thick snow-white hair. He always looked impressive. Even today, he looked professional with a blue oxford shirt and navy slacks. No tie, but that was his idea of casual. He had been dating her aunt since fall. In fact, her aunt Iris had been dating two men—Morris Rappaport, the detective whom Daisy was friends with, as well as Marshall. They were two very different men.

After a few more words to Fiona, Daisy approached Iris and Marshall's table to say hello. However, she was only two feet away when she saw the expressions on their faces. They seemed to be having an intense conversation. She was about to turn around and walk away when she overheard Marshall telling Iris, "I've been patient up until now. It's time for you to decide whether you're going to date me or Morris full-time."

After that ultimatum, he pushed back his chair, stood, and without even acknowledging Daisy, headed to the driveway that led to the front of the tea garden and Market Street.

Usually, her aunt wore a positive expression. She was a happy person, optimistic, trying to see the best in everyone and everything. Her ash-brown curls were natural and framed her face, hanging almost to her chin. The curls fluffed when she walked. When she wore a hairnet at the tea garden, a few slipped out. Apparently, she'd taken off her hairnet to meet Marshall. Today she was wearing a cranberry T-shirt, cream slacks, and her white sneakers. In her sixties, Iris usually didn't look her age. But now Daisy could see the lines around her aunt's eyes and around her mouth quite clearly.

Daisy pulled out the chair Marshall had vacated and sat facing her aunt. "Are you okay?"

Iris's eyes looked misty, and her lower lip quivered. "I thought dating was supposed to be fun."

Daisy patted her aunt's hand. "I guess that depends on whom you're dating."

With obvious effort, Iris forced a weak smile.

"Yes, I suppose that's true. You and Jonas didn't always have fun, did you?"

That was an understatement. "As you know, Jonas and I had a complicated road."

"It looks like my road is complicated, too," Iris acknowledged with some exasperation. "I didn't want it to be."

"Did you know Marshall was coming here today?"

With a swift glance at her phone, Iris answered, "Yes, he texted me. I told him we could have tea on the patio." She motioned to the iced tea glasses. "But he was very cut-and-dried about what he wanted."

Close to her aunt since she was a child, Daisy suspected Iris wanted her to keep prompting her. "And what does he want?"

Iris wrung her hands together. "He wants to date me full-time . . . or to cut off our friendship entirely, I suppose."

As softly and gently as she could, Daisy reminded her, "You've known for a while you would have to make a decision."

"Yes, you and Tessa have pointed that out more than once. I just didn't know if I was ready."

"Drink some tea and take a breath," Daisy advised. After her aunt did, Daisy pointed out, "They're both upright and caring men. They just have different outlooks on life and different personalities. Aunt Iris, you know this is all about feelings."

Iris nodded. "It is. Maybe I don't think I know either of them well enough to make this type of decision."

Daisy remembered when she'd made the decision to date Jonas exclusively. "You're talking about a serious decision."

"At my age, it *has* to be serious." Iris's chin came up, and her shoulders squared. "But it also has to be the right one for me."

A man's character often revealed itself, not just in his words, but in his actions, too. "How do you feel about Marshall giving you an ultimatum?" Daisy asked.

"I didn't expect it, and it shook me up. I'm going to have to figure out why."

Daisy patted her aunt's hand. "You'll figure it out. You have to do what's best for *you*."

"I think I'd like to take a vacation to Bora Bora," her aunt said with a smile back in place now.

"But I would miss you."

Iris shook her head. "I know. And I can't escape from my problems. They'd just follow me."

Daisy couldn't help but point out the obvious. "Some women would think dating two men, with both of them wanting a relationship, would *not* be a problem."

"I guess I'm not meant for one of those dating shows," Iris said acerbically. "Let's get back to work so I can think about something else."

"Upcoming July specials?"

"Anything other than men." Iris picked up her glass of iced tea along with the one Marshall hadn't taken a sip from. On the way to the door, Iris stopped to say hello to Fiona, and then she followed Daisy back into the tea garden, where luncheon customers were arriving.

"I'll get my hairnet and apron. I'll be in the kitchen shortly," Iris said.

After Daisy washed up, she joined April at the

sales counter, where she was loading more rhubarb muffins into the tray.

"How do you come up with your recipes?" April asked her.

April looked pretty this morning in her short-sleeved dress covered with a pineapple pattern.

"I'm not sure about that," Daisy admitted. "I guess I just take the ingredients that are available to me in the season, mix them up, and come up with something, either baked goods or usually salads."

"Your grated carrot salad is delicious with the sour cream, lime, and honey dressing. I wish I could be as creative."

"When you find something you like to do, the creativity will come," Daisy promised.

"I like working here," April said. "I like mingling with people. Your customers are very different than the ones at the Farm Barn were." April had once worked at a farm-to-table family restaurant that had now been sold to a new owner.

"Is that good or bad?" Daisy asked with a laugh.

"I'm not sure. Your customers here come in expecting to be companionable with each other. They recognize each other from who's come and gone other days at the same time. I've noticed that about your customers. Then there are the tourists, of course. You even know some of them."

"Some of my customers have been coming since the tea garden opened."

"I think I'll move back to the apartment over the garage tonight." April finished loading the muffins onto the tray and closed the case.

"You feel safe going back there?"

"I do. My guess is that the intruder was after

those chests. Do *you* feel safe knowing that some-body might want them?"

"I have a good security system. Felix is a wonder-ful guard dog. And I'm sure Jonas will be alert to any strange noises."

April had picked up the baking sheet that had held the muffins to take it back to the kitchen when Daisy recognized two men walking into the tea garden. Trevor came in first and then glanced back over his shoulder to check if Jonas was follow-ing. He was.

Trevor's hair looked as if he'd run his hand through it about a hundred times. He often did that if he was agitated or nervous. Even Daisy rec-ognized that habit of his. Jonas, on the other hand, looked composed and much too stoic. Daisy recognized *that* expression, too. He was going to tell her something she didn't want to hear. She tried to concentrate on the fact that he looked un-believably attractive today in a yellow Henley and khaki slacks. But he didn't have his usual smile for her, and his green eyes looked worried.

Tamlyn Pittenger was nearby. She was a full-time employee and always kept a scrupulous eye on their customers and their tea services. She was about the same age as April and wore her long brown hair in a knot at the back of her head. Her cheeks were full, her wide lips were lightly glossed, and her bangs dipped to her brows.

Daisy motioned to her. "Can you handle the sales counter for a little while?"

Tamlyn glanced over the room of customers. "Sure."

Trevor targeted his course straight for Daisy as

she came around the counter. He jammed his pointer finger at her office, and she knew what that meant. This was a consultation. When she looked toward Jonas, he nodded that that's what they should do.

Once the three of them were in her office and Jonas had closed the door, she asked, "Tea and a muffin?"

Trevor shook his head. "I don't think so. Of course, after we talk, we might need tea with plenty of caffeine."

Daisy sank down into her desk chair, and Trevor and Jonas took the other two chairs in the small space.

"Is everyone all right?" she asked, suddenly concerned for her family.

"All your loved ones and friends are fine," Jonas said to ease her mind.

That left a multitude of possibilities.

Trevor leaned forward in his chair and propped his elbows on her desk. He studied her, watching her closely. "A man around thirty-five years old was found dead in Willow Creek near an overturned canoe."

Daisy was saddened at that thought but didn't understand why Trevor and Jonas looked so worried.

Jonas took over now. "The man didn't drown, Daisy. He was murdered."

It was as if Trevor couldn't wait to jump in. "He might have died of asphyxiation and was most likely dumped there. A burner phone was found in the high grass along the creek."

Studying the two men, one whom she dearly

loved and one whom she respected, Daisy still didn't realize what all this had to do with *her*. "Did you know this man?" she asked Trevor.

"No, I didn't. But my instincts are telling me something you're not going to like."

"What's that?" she asked warily.

"I believe the call I received and this murder could be connected. There is only one way to find out."

CHAPTER FIVE

"What do you think Trevor is going to do?" Daisy asked Jonas that night as they sat on her sofa, acoustic guitar music playing in the background. Felix lay spread out on the hardwood floor by the outskirts of the rug.

"We don't know what Trevor will do next, but whatever he does, I hope he does it with the blessing of Chief Shultz and the detectives."

Daisy had opened her laptop to the file containing all their wedding arrangements. But her mind danced around their conversation with Trevor. "Have you checked with Zeke to see what's going on with the body they found?"

"I put feelers out, but so far they haven't identified the person. He *was* in his mid-thirties, though."

"So, it could have been our male caller."

"It's possible, but don't borrow trouble, Daisy."

Turning her gaze on Jonas, she could see his worry. "You don't want any complications before our wedding."

"'Complications' is a nice way of putting it,"

Jonas said with a grimace. "I'd like us to just keep our minds on the day we're planning and our future."

It was tempting to kiss Jonas—oh, so tempting. They had a couple hours alone to go over wedding plans since Jazzi was babysitting Sammy while Vi was working.

With willpower she'd rather ignore, Daisy turned her attention back to her computer file with a sigh. "This is the to-do list for the things that still have to be accomplished," she said, waving to the screen. "My mom, Iris, Tessa, and Vi found bridesmaid dresses, but Jazzi is still wavering. I don't know what's holding her up. Goodness knows, she likes to shop. Finding a pretty dress for a summer wedding shouldn't be that hard."

"Jazzi might want to look perfect for our wedding."

Daisy flopped her head onto Jonas's shoulder. Then she peered up at him with a slanted glance. "As long as Jazzi is present when we say our vows, what she wears doesn't matter."

He brushed Daisy's blond hair over her forehead, amusement in his eyes. "Would you care if Jazzi wears a clown suit?"

Daisy sat up again, her eyes back on the laptop. "I merely want everyone to be comfortable. After all, we might have a very hot day to contend with."

"Just so I'm clear on what you're saying, that means me, Foster, and your dad don't have to wear suits?"

"Again, I merely want everyone to be comfortable. I don't care about photo ops for an album. I want guests to take photos on their phones and send them to us, so we have a lovely record of our day. What we're wearing is the least important part of it."

"Does that include you?" he asked with a wink.

"I think you'll be surprised at what I'm wearing. I'm very pleased with it." She hadn't told him anything about her trip to the attic with her mother and Aunt Iris. Her wedding gown was going to be a surprise.

"All right. As far as what the guys wear, I have an idea. I'll talk to the others about it."

"Uh-oh. Is this a surprise?"

"Just like the gazebo."

Jonas was building the gazebo at an Amish friend's farm. They would take their vows in it. But Jonas wouldn't let her see it until it was brought to the yard before the wedding. That gazebo would be positioned in their backyard for years to come. Every time they looked at it, they'd remember their commitment to each other. Tomorrow morning Gavin Cranshaw, Foster's father, who was a contractor, and a partial crew were coming over to lay the foundation for the structure.

"Are you considering Bermuda shorts and Hawaiian shirts?" she joked.

He didn't answer her, but he did kiss her.

Somehow wedding arrangements got set aside for at least an hour.

Jonas was brewing chocolate tea, and Daisy had mixed up a blueberry coffee cake for the following morning and had popped it into the oven when the doorbell chimed. She checked the monitor in the kitchen. "It's Tessa and Trevor."

"I'm always glad to see them," Jonas mumbled. "But I have a feeling Trevor has done something and wants to consult with us about it."

"'Consult' is a very, very broad term for what Trevor does when he meets with us." Trevor often wanted their ideas, but he also had several of his own.

When Daisy opened the door to her friends, Tessa floated in, her sundress a swirl of purple and yellow. She'd tied her hair in a high ponytail in deference to the heat. Her hair was long enough to flow to her midback. Her outfit was bright, but her expression was anything but relaxed.

Trevor, on the other hand, in a gray T-shirt and red shorts, looked excited. "I have news," he said, his expression sly.

Marjoram and Pepper had settled on the deacon's bench to wait for Jazzi to come home. Felix, however, was excited to see their guests. He wound around their legs, and Tessa stooped to pet him. When she looked up at Daisy, she just shook her head as if Trevor was exasperating her. Daisy couldn't wait to find out why.

"I'm just brewing chocolate tea," Jonas said. "Care for a cup?"

Trevor took a deep breath and headed toward the sofa. "It's cool enough in here. Sure, I'll take a cup of hot tea."

"Me, too," Tessa agreed, going to sit beside him. Felix followed them and sat beside Tessa, hoping to encourage more strokes along his flank.

Ten minutes later, they'd settled around the coffee table. For their chocolate tea, Daisy had used four vintage Churchill Blue Willow teacups and saucers that had been made in England. The cups were sturdy. She'd also included on the tray a lead-crystal sugar bowl with a lid and small sugar spoon.

She knew Trevor liked sugar in his tea. The tray had high wooden handles and hydrangeas painted on the wood under the glass.

Jonas took the tray and set it on the side table. After he sat on the arm of Daisy's chair, he gazed at Trevor. "Spill it."

Trevor took a sip of his tea, set the cup and saucer on the coffee table, and leaned forward on the sofa. His eyes glittered with excitement. "I kept the caller ID number for the anonymous caller who gave the tip about the chests."

"Of course, you did." Jonas let loose a resigned sigh.

"Don't give me that look," Trevor said. "You know I'm on top of this."

"That's what I'm afraid of," Jonas said.

"Me, too," Tessa seconded in a low voice.

Daisy just wanted to hear what Trevor had to say. She gave him a go-ahead signal with her hand.

He grinned at her encouragement. "You'll be pleased to know that on a hunch, I gave the number to the police. A half hour ago, I just learned that the caller ID number was identical to the burner phone's number."

"Are you telling me one of the detectives told you that?" Jonas asked, obviously befuddled by that thought.

"Of course, they didn't. But I have my contacts. You know that."

"Possibly the dispatcher?" Daisy wanted to know. She'd long been suspicious that that was the case.

"I don't reveal my sources."

"Unless it suits your purposes," Jonas murmured.

"That's not true, Jonas, and you know it. I'm a reputable journalist, and that's why I'm going to do what I'm going to do next."

Tessa laid her hand on Trevor's arm. "You're really deciding to do this?"

"You know I am, baby. It's just what I need to jump-start my career, and I'll be doing a public service at the same time."

"And just what are you going to do?" Daisy asked, anxiety sneaking up her spine.

"'Hidden Spaces' is going to take the public along through this investigation every step of the way. I've already started. In the next podcast, I'll inform listeners about the phone number from the tip line and the burner phone." He rubbed his hands together. "This is going to be so exciting." He glanced around. "Why aren't you all smiling?"

Tessa was the first to express her concern. "Because I think it's dangerous. You won't be dabbling with vandalism anymore. You could be dabbling with a murderer."

Jonas waved his hand at Tessa. "She said it all."

Trevor's mouth set in a straight line, his determination evident. "Great careers aren't formed without risks. I'm going to take a risk."

"And pull the rest of us in it, too." Jonas concluded.

Daisy dearly hoped that wouldn't be so.

Daisy was drawn to her kitchen's sliding-glass doors to see the activity outside. Early this morning, Gavin Cranshaw had arrived with two members of his crew to start the work for the concrete slab that would be the base of the gazebo. This was

Gavin's wedding present to her and Jonas. Gavin had quickly become family after Vi had learned she was pregnant and the couple decided to marry. Since then, they'd gone through Vi's pregnancy, the birth of Sammy, Vi's postpartum depression, and the couple trying to stand on their own feet. Gavin had even been integral in solving a murder with Daisy.

The first thing the men had done this morning was build a wooden frame using two-by-fours to mark the desired area, which was about fourteen feet square. They'd driven landscaping stakes into the ground at the corners. After they removed the frame, leaving the landscape markers in place and tying string around the area to delineate the square, a backhoe had started its work. It dug about four inches down in the entire area. Afterward a truck had brought in scoops of gravel and dumped them into the area. Jonas and Gavin compacted it with hand tampers. Then they dumped in more gravel and did the same again.

As Daisy stared through the glass doors, she realized Jonas and Gavin were two sides of the same coin. While Jonas was around six feet tall with black hair, strong, lean, and always projected a former detective's vigilance, Gavin was around six-two with a square jaw and sandy-brown hair that always became more blond in the summer. Three children—Foster, Ben, and Emily—looked up to him.

Felix was nosing around the landscape stakes, every once in a while darting off to chase a squirrel or maybe a rabbit. As Daisy went outside and crossed the patio, she overheard the men. Jonas was telling Gavin, "The gazebo will always remind us how much our wedding day meant. I hope it will be a constant reminder of what it took us to get here, and how we should work hard at staying this connected always."

Gavin caught sight of Daisy and smiled. He motioned to what they were doing. "What do you think?"

"I'm glad I have an active imagination."

Both of them laughed.

Gavin revealed, "The concrete will be poured tomorrow. We'll put the two-by-fours back in when we're done here. Tomorrow, we have to wet the frame and gravel, pour in the concrete, and screed it."

"What's that?" Daisy asked.

"We take a two-by-four-inch board across the entire surface. It brings the concrete to the proper grade. After it loses its sheen, we smooth it over with a concrete float."

Jonas said, "They'll probably run a stiff broom over it so the surface isn't slippery."

"Then we spray it, cure it, and seal it," Gavin said easily, "before we remove the frame."

"This is a lot of work, Gavin. Thank you. We appreciate this so much," Daisy said.

"I appreciate everything you've done for Vi and Foster. I don't know how they would have managed being married if you hadn't stepped in."

"Family does for each other," she said simply.

"I like the idea that this gazebo is going to remind you of what you mean to each other." Gavin looked over at Felix, who had run into the field. "Couples need reminders."

The breeze ruffled Gavin's hair as he turned back to them. "I worked too many hours when I was building my business, and my marriage suffered for it."

"Did your wife understand what you were building?" Jonas asked.

"I think she did, but I still have regrets. Once the kids came along, we hardly saw each other. When she died, I practically fell apart. Foster, Ben, and Emily all made me see I couldn't lose them, too."

Daisy and Gavin had spoken of this before, and she definitely understood.

"I don't think anybody can look back over their lives and not have regrets," she observed. Gavin deserved to move on and be happy, like anyone else.

"I'm worried about Foster," Gavin revealed.

Daisy took a few steps closer to him. "Vi stopped in, and she said the same thing. Why are you worried?"

"I think Foster's falling into the same trap I did, and I'm not sure he knows how to stop it."

After listening to all of it, Jonas asked Gavin, "Do you think Foster needs an intervention?"

"I'm not sure. At least not yet. I want to give him a chance to come to some realizations on his own. But I know what damage can happen in the meantime."

As if that topic caused too much worry, Gavin changed the subject. "Tell me about these chests you found."

"I wish we had just found them," Daisy said. "Did Foster tell you?"

"Not much. Something about an auction?"

Daisy explained about the auction and then said, "Trevor's podcast got a tip on his hotline that one of the chests could hold a secret to a twenty-year-old murder."

Gavin leaned on the long-stemmed tamper and whistled. "Wow. Not again, Daisy."

"We didn't find anything in the chests," she told him, holding her hands up as if she were completely innocent.

"But . . ." Jonas drawled, "someone was going to attempt to break into my SUV to get at them, and that same person probably broke into Amelia Wiseman's shed to look at the chests *she* bought. We don't know if they got what they wanted."

"So, what now?" Gavin asked.

Daisy exchanged a look with Jonas. "Well . . . Trevor is still involved. We found out that the number that came in on his tip line is connected to a burner phone that was discovered near the man who was found in Willow Creek."

"The man who drowned?"

"Possibly murdered. The police don't know his identity yet. They're working on it."

Gavin stood up straight again. "So now there's a possible *double* murder?"

Jonas shook his head. "There's no way to know. All this could be supposition on Trevor's part. On the other hand, with the phone number that came in to his hotline being the same one attached to that burner phone, it's hard to know."

"Are you going after this?" Gavin asked Daisy.

"I have no reason to," she said calmly.

Gavin just made a grunting noise. "And what about Trevor? He has a nose for news that sometimes involves you."

"His nose is possibly going to lead him into big trouble," Daisy said. "Tessa is worried about him, too. It's sort of a situation like Foster's, I guess. Trevor can't see that he's treading into water that's too deep for him."

"What's he planning?" Gavin asked.

"He's planning on making his 'Hidden Spaces' podcast a true crime podcast. He's going to go after this in real time, explain about the hotline tip and the burner phone."

"So, he's going to bring the hounds of hell down on himself?" Gavin asked.

"He's hoping for more tips," Jonas explained. "He's hoping callers will tell him what they've seen and heard. Somehow, he'll figure out how this goes back twenty years and what it has to do with the present murder."

"You do know, don't you, that that's crazy," Gavin said, studying Daisy.

"Yes, I do know that's crazy. That could bring the killer right out of the woodwork . . . or out of the chest, so to speak."

Gavin's expression was practically sour. "But you're hoping it goes nowhere."

"I am. I want the police to handle this, not Trevor."

"Do you think Tessa will back him?" Gavin wanted to know.

"I'm not sure," Daisy admitted. "She's loyal, I know that. She's helped me in the past with investigations. That was more to protect me when I interviewed suspects and make sure I wasn't doing it alone."

"It's possible she wants to protect Trevor," Jonas said seriously. He finished tamping his quarter of the square, then came over to stand with Daisy. He laid the tamper on the ground and circled her waist with his arm. "We always do want to protect those we love . . . but sometimes we can't."

Gavin finished the area he'd been tamping, put down the tamper, and came over to stand with them.

"That brings up another subject I've been meaning to talk to you about."

"Something else to do with our kids?" she asked with a smile.

"No. This has to do with me, and yes . . . my kids," he added.

"Trouble with Ben or Emily?" His son Ben was fourteen and Emily sixteen.

"I asked them what they thought about me dating."

Daisy's smile widened. "Do you think you need their permission?"

Gavin shrugged his broad shoulders. "Maybe not 'permission'. But I wanted to know where they stood on the subject, and I don't *like* where they stand."

Jonas laughed out loud. "What does *that* mean?"

"Emily said she'd think about it, but Ben . . ."

Daisy could tell from the expression on Gavin's face and his silence that he didn't even want to consider what his younger son thought.

"I know they loved their mother, and I did, too. They're getting older. They'll find their own lives. You and I talked about this a few months ago, Daisy. Now I think I have a different outlook than I did then."

"Have you met someone?" Daisy asked, hoping that was so.

Gavin sighed and looked totally uncertain. "One of the volunteers at the homeless shelter and

I have been talking. I like her. I thought it would be nice if we went for coffee."

"You and I have tea together," Daisy pointed out mischievously.

"Yeah, she might like tea, too. I haven't asked. The thing is, if the kids are going to be negative about it, do I even want to have her around anything like that? Before you ask, she's divorced but doesn't have kids."

"What are you going to do?" Daisy asked.

"I was hoping you might talk to Emily and Ben." Gavin's expression was streaked with embarrassment.

"Do you really want me to interfere? That could be trouble," Daisy warned him.

"Trouble for me, not trouble for you. I know you'd be tactful. What do you think?"

After considering his request, she decided, "I think talking to Emily will be easier than talking to Ben. But he and I made a connection when Foster was acting so weird before we knew Vi was pregnant. Maybe that would still hold. I'd talk to them separately, not together."

"That makes sense," Jonas said with a nod. "You don't want to embarrass them any more than necessary."

"I think Emily is going to be babysitting Sammy on Friday evening. Maybe you could stop in at Vi's then?" Gavin asked.

"Sure, and what about Ben?"

"Ben's doing his service hours for school by working at that new grocery store east of town. Maybe you could talk to him on his break."

"I'll see what I can do," Daisy assured him. "But don't expect miracles."

"I expect, at least, you might make them see my side of things."

"I'll try. Now, while you guys finish this up, I'm going to drive to the tea garden. We're having a reserved tea this afternoon."

Jonas brought Daisy closer for a kiss before she left.

Since it lasted awhile, Gavin asked, "Are you practicing for your wedding day?"

"Practice makes perfect," Jonas jibed.

Daisy headed for the garage and her workday.

CHAPTER SIX

Arranging flower containers on the front porch of the pale-green Victorian with its white and yellow trim, Daisy placed a bucket of fuchsia petunias on one plant stand and a white and purple mix on another. She'd already placed a ceramic pot of rosemary and thyme on the white metal table beside a white wooden cane-seat rocker. Last night Jonas had helped her heft a three-foot-deep colorful ceramic container with arrangements of pink and white geraniums over to the corner. She believed the front porch should send a message of welcome, inviting customers inside.

She was about to deadhead a few of the purple petunias when her phone played. Outside with cars and buggies passing by, the scent of the hot summer sun on the pavement and freshly mowed grass riding the air, her phone's tuba ring tone didn't sound as loud. She was perplexed when she saw the ID of the person who was calling—Detective Morris Rappaport.

"Good morning, Detective. Did you call to make a reservation for our next five-course tea?"

It was a standing joke between them. First of all, Morris claimed he didn't like hot tea. And second, he insisted those little sandwiches would hardly whet his taste buds, though he *had* been on a diet for the past six months.

At her question, he grunted dismissively. Without any preamble, he said gruffly, "I think I need your help."

Did this call have something to do with Aunt Iris? Did he want her to put in a good word? "You know I'll help however I can. What do you need?"

"First of all, I want you to keep everything I tell you to yourself."

That, in itself, was ominous. This conversation might not be about her aunt.

His voice was deeply sober. "You know about the young man found in the creek?"

"I heard something about it."

"He was thirty-six," Morris informed her. "Thirty-six, and his life cut short. We had a missing person's report, and his wife identified the body this morning."

"I'm so sorry," Daisy said empathetically. But she still didn't see what this had to do with her.

"His wife's name is Beth Ann Kohler."

Daisy recognized the Kohler name. It was common in the area. "Is the name supposed to be familiar to me? Has she come into the tea garden?"

"That I don't know. But I do know this, Daisy."

Daisy could hear the detective's deep sigh through the phone line.

"The woman is hysterical. I can't question her as I need to."

Little prickles rose on Daisy's neck even though it was eighty degrees outside already. She had a feeling she knew where this was going, and she hoped she was wrong.

Morris's next question proved she wasn't.

"Can you come down to the station and help?" He sounded exasperated and frustrated.

"Morris, you can't be serious. Maybe you should give her a day to process the death of her husband."

Now his voice held the power of his position, no friendliness at all in his tone. "This is my job, and this is a murder." His voice softened just a tad when he continued, "The chief is all over me and Zeke because the last investigation took too long to solve, according to the mayor. No credit for solving it, of course. Will you help? I don't want to traumatize the woman any more than she's already been traumatized. Imagine your husband doesn't come home one night, Daisy. And then you find out he was strangled and dumped in the creek."

Daisy sank down onto the rocking chair next to the table with the herbs. Morris knew exactly what buttons to push to target her emotions.

"When do you want me there?" she asked.

"As soon as possible."

Five minutes later, with Iris assuring Daisy that her staff could handle whatever came up, Daisy drove her blue Dodge Journey down Market Street. After she turned into the parking lot of the Willow Creek Police Department, she took a deep breath and glanced at the Daisy's Tea Garden bag she'd brought with her. Then she stared at the building that housed the police department.

Smack-dab in the middle of downtown, the police department building was almost as old as the town itself, which had been settled back in the late eighteen hundreds. The building had been refurbished often, but its brick exterior needed sand-blasting. Maybe that could be added to the agenda at the next town council meeting. After all, a few years ago, the council had allotted funds for automated front doors and reinforcement of its only jail cell, according to the report in the *Willow Creek Messenger*. Daisy had been inside the building more times than she wanted to count.

She picked up the bag on the passenger seat, disembarked from her car, and trudged toward the electronic front doors. Inside, Daisy caught sight of the dispatcher, whom she didn't know. She did know two of the others who were part-time. The woman appeared to be in her mid-twenties, brown hair highlighted with violet and fuchsia. Huge pink glasses sat on her nose. Right now, she was wearing earphones and typing on the computer.

The reception area was cut off from farther back in the room by a wooden fence. The swinging door in the middle always reminded Daisy of a gate from an old-time movie. Six desks with computers sat beyond the gate, officers at three of the desks. The murder was probably keeping them all occupied. One of the officers was Bart Cosner.

He motioned Daisy inside the gate. "Follow me," he said.

Daisy had heard those words before, too. In fact, Bart was the one who had spoken them when she had been in the police station during her very first investigation. These days she knew exactly where she was going. She followed Bart to the right and down a short hall. Detective Morris Rappaport appeared from his office.

The detective was near sixty. The grooves along his mouth cut seriously deep, and he had plenty of other lines on his face. His thick blond-gray hair never saw any styling gel. On this summer day, he was wearing brown slacks and a cream oxford shirt with the sleeves rolled up to his elbows and the neck open. His shirt was wrinkled, and Daisy supposed he might have been there all night. It was his MO when a police investigation was going on. Nothing was more important to him than solving the murder. When she'd first met him, they'd been at cross purposes. But over the past few years, they'd learned to respect each other. Hence this call today.

Morris's shoulders slumped as he said, "She's still crying. I can't get anywhere with her. Zeke couldn't either, and he's usually good at interrogating, especially when he has to be gentle about it."

"And what makes you think *I* can help with this?"

"Because you have two daughters. People talk to you. I'm sure you can do this, Daisy."

"And what exactly is *this*? If I help, I need to do it my way," Daisy countered.

Morris knew how to scowl better than anyone she knew. "And what exactly is *your* way?"

She lifted the bag she'd brought along. "There are some chocolate tea teabags in here and a few snickerdoodles. I'd like you to make a mug of hot water. I'll drop in a teabag. Maybe you can bring me a paper plate?"

Morris continued scowling at her and ran his hand up the back of his neck as if it was stiff. "This isn't a tea party, Daisy.

"You asked for my help, so let me help. You can record what she and I say, but I want to be alone with her, at least at first."

"This is against protocol," he muttered.

"Bringing me in to help is against protocol," she reminded him. "Does Chief Schultz know you're doing this?"

"No, and I want to keep it that way. He's not here right now."

Daisy merely shook her head. Morris was all about the rules, and for once he was going against them.

"All right. I'll bring a mug of hot water. No paper plates, but we have napkins. Just go in," Morris said, motioning to the door. "I kept her in my office instead of an interrogation room. Just say you want to help her talk to me. She doesn't have to know anything more."

Daisy wasn't so sure about that. "Aren't you going to introduce me?"

"As soon as I start talking, she cries more. You can introduce yourself. When I bring in the hot water, I'll start recording."

As Morris hurried off to the break room, Daisy opened the office door. Morris's office was as cluttered as usual, the old wooden desk covered with file folders. His computer and printer to the side of the desk were plastered with Post-it Notes. Three filing cabinets lined one wall. The tall, narrow bookshelf beside them was stuffed with manuals and research books. There were no wall hangings or photographs, just gray walls that she supposed were intended to promote an official ambiance.

A young woman whom Daisy suspected was a few years younger than herself was seated on the interviewee side of the desk, holding a mound of tissues in her hands. She was wearing an orange-and-white-patterned T-shirt, orange shorts, and leather sandals. Her strawberry-blond hair was tied in a straggly topknot. Her bangs were a short fringe, her brows a lighter strawberry-blond than her hair. Her face, Daisy suspected, was usually very pretty with wide-set brown eyes, a narrow nose, full mouth and a petite chin. Today, however, her cheeks were streaked with tears. They were redder than her pale complexion said they should be. The freckles spattered across her cheeks were almost blotted out by her high color. She was terribly upset, and her tears were flowing.

Scanning more than Beth Ann Kohler, Daisy spotted the gray metal folding chair against the wall. Before saying anything, she placed the bag with cookies and teabags on the desk. She went over to the chair, unfolded it, and placed it face-forward toward Beth Ann. Beth Ann hardly looked at her. Maybe she thought Daisy was another detective.

Daisy said gently, "Mrs. Kohler. I'm Daisy Swanson."

Beth Ann looked up at her, her eyes still swimming with tears. She wiped a tissue across her nose and nodded.

Daisy wasn't exactly sure how to start, but she explained the situation as best she could. "The detective told me you're having trouble with his interview. I'm sort of a consultant. I'm here to help you talk to them about what happened with your husband."

Beth Ann blew her nose and mumbled, "I'm sorry. I just can't get it together."

"That's completely understandable," Daisy assured her. "That's why I'm here to help. I've been through some traumatic situations myself."

"You lost your husband?" Beth Ann demanded.

"I did, but not in the way you have. My husband died of cancer. But I do know that lost, world-tilting feeling that nothing's ever going to be the same again."

Beth Ann blew her nose again, eyeing Daisy. "Are you a psychologist?"

"Absolutely not," Daisy said with a very small smile. "I've helped the detectives with a few of their investigations."

"Did you say your name was Daisy Swanson?"

"Yes, I did."

"I've read articles about you. You have a tea shop or something."

"Daisy's Tea Garden. I run it with my aunt."

"So, the detective brought you in to talk to me?" Through her tears and sniffles, Beth Ann looked perplexed.

"He thought it might be easier than talking to him. Detective Rappaport can be a little gruff."

"That other one was nicer," Beth Ann said. "But I was just too upset to talk. They couldn't seem to understand that."

At that moment, Detective Rappaport opened his office door and stepped inside, looking sheepish. He held out the mug to Daisy.

Quickly, Daisy procured a teabag from the bag and dropped it into the mug.

"Daisy thought you might like a cup of tea," Morris awkwardly explained. In his other hand, he held out a napkin. "She brought cookies, too."

Daisy removed cookies from the bag and set the napkin on the desk.

The young woman looked at the mug of tea and smelled it. "Nice," she said.

"It's chocolate strawberry," Daisy told her. "I believe tea has a calming effect."

A recording system sat on Morris's desk in between the file folders. He set it on top of one of the stacks. "Mrs. Kohler, I'd like to record your interview with Daisy. Would that be all right?"

"I . . . I guess so. I don't think I have anything important to tell her . . . or you."

"I'll decide that," Morris said, back in his police persona.

Beth Ann's face seemed to crumple again.

Morris said to Daisy, "I'll give you fifteen or twenty minutes, then I'll be back."

After he pressed the button on the console, he gave the date and the time and Beth Ann's name. Then he left the office. Daisy was hoping that Beth Ann would forget about the recorder once they began talking.

After Morris left the office, Daisy let Beth Ann take a few sips of her tea. Afterward she set the mug on the desk near the cookies. She eyed them but didn't take one.

"Mrs. Kohler, I'd like to start by . . ."

With a hiccup, the young woman said, "Please call me Beth Ann."

"Sure, and you can call me Daisy. What was your husband's name?"

"His name was Henry." Her tears started rolling again.

"Why don't you tell me about Henry? Tell me what he liked to do."

"It's hard to say," Beth Ann answered.

Talking about a deceased person's life was difficult to summarize. "What was his job?" Daisy asked, starting with an easy question.

"He was a physical therapist. He worked in that building at the edge of town where doctors are moving in. He really loved his job—working with people, seeing them get back on their feet."

"Did he have any hobbies?"

After considering the question, Beth Ann nodded. "Mostly he spent his spare time outside in the yard. He went fishing now and then. He just finished planting cone flowers for me." Beth Ann broke down in tears again, holding the tissues to her face.

Daisy gave her a few minutes and then let her blow her nose. Morris had been right. Beth Ann was very upset, though not hysterical. She was probably trying to remember everything about her husband that she didn't want to forget.

"I know this is hard, Beth Ann, but anything you can tell the detectives might help them, even the smallest things."

Beth Ann ran her hand across her cheek, wiping away more tears.

Daisy took a stab in the dark. "Do you know what happened the day Henry went missing?"

"I don't know," she answered with a hiccup. "All I know is that Henry went out to run errands and didn't come home Saturday night. We always check in with each other a lot. We liked to know how each other's days were going. Do you know what I mean?"

"Yes, I do. I'm engaged, and my fiancé and I often do that, too."

Thinking about the other investigations she'd been a part of, Daisy considered what to ask next. "Can you tell if anything unusual happened in the last month or so?"

"'Unusual'? I'm not sure I know what you mean."

Daisy didn't want to lead Beth Ann in the wrong direction . . . or in any direction, really.

"Did Henry talk about anything unusual that happened, at work or with friends? Had he changed in any way?"

At first Beth Ann was shaking her head, and then she stopped. "Now that you mention it—" She trailed off and looked over Daisy's shoulder as if she were thinking about the time frame Daisy had mentioned. "He's been acting odd for the past few weeks."

"Odd how?"

"I'm not sure exactly. His laptop had been stolen from his car, and I thought he was upset about that. He would often go to the window in the living room and look out at the driveway. I thought he was imagining who could have taken it. Whoever it was, they broke the car window, and we had to get that fixed. It was an expense we hadn't counted on."

"Did he act as if whoever broke in might return?"

Beth Ann thought about that. "He told me to make sure when I was alone in the house that I locked the doors. I always did. He knew that."

"Do you think he was afraid someone would break into the house?"

"It seemed that way. Maybe something was going on that I didn't know about. Obviously there was, or he wouldn't be *dead*."

She put her hands and the tissues to her mouth to stifle a sob. Daisy wasn't going to keep pressing, not until this woman had a little time to grieve, and the detectives shouldn't either. But there was one more question she could ask. "Did you know your husband had a burner phone?"

"No! The detective showed it to me, and I'd never seen it before. But he might have kept it in his work messenger bag or in his desk. I never went through his things. We didn't have that kind of marriage."

"I understand," Daisy said. And she did. Apparently Henry and Beth Ann had trusted each other.

"I suppose the detective asked you for Henry's everyday phone?"

"That was an odd thing, too," Beth Ann informed Daisy. "Detective Rappaport told me he found it in Henry's car, parked at the physical therapy facility. That was strange because it was a Saturday."

That was something Daisy hadn't known about . . . that Henry Kohler's car had been found at the place where he'd worked.

"They're not telling me what was on either phone."

Whom had Henry texted or called? Had he bought the burner just for his call to Trevor?

"Have you ever heard of Trevor Lundquist's podcast, 'Hidden Spaces'?" Daisy asked.

"No, I haven't. But Henry listened to podcasts all the time, all different kinds. He would have his earbuds in while he was doing yard work outside, when he took a walk, or even on the way to work, even though it wasn't a very long drive." Beth Ann inhaled a giant breath and picked up the mug of her tea. She took another few sips, set it down, and picked up one of the cookies.

Daisy said, "I'm going to talk to the detective. He'll probably come back in and try to ask you a few questions. Do you think you're up to it?"

"I'm feeling more in control. I can try."

That was all any of them could ask of this very recent widow.

Suddenly Daisy made a decision. She took out a business card and set it next to Beth Ann's mug of tea. "My number is on the card if you need to talk . . . about anything. Losing a loved one is hard."

Beth Ann looked at the business card and picked it up. "Thanks."

Daisy stepped outside of the office and left the door open a few inches. Morris was waiting, and he motioned to her to come down the hall a couple of feet so Beth Ann wouldn't hear them. She quickly summed up her interview with Beth Ann, telling him about the stolen laptop.

Morris put his hand to his forehead as if he had a headache. "At least that's a clue we can pursue. We don't have much else. Forensics is still processing the evidence and the scene."

Daisy hesitated, then expanded on the stolen laptop, telling him that Beth Ann had said Henry had been acting differently in the few weeks after it was stolen.

"He was probably paranoid," Morris said.

"Maybe or . . ."

Morris circled his finger in the air as if to tell her to hurry up because he had a lot to do. As if she didn't realize that.

"I want you to listen to me for two minutes."

He slanted her a sideways glance, then looked back at the door to the office where Beth Ann was enclosed inside.

"You know about Trevor's podcast, right?"

"Your interview?" he asked in a clipped tone. "You did a decent job, and he put you on the hot seat at the end."

"That's not what I'm talking about. You know he received a call on his tip line."

"Something about an auction and old chests. I didn't bother with that one."

"Maybe you should listen to it."

"Daisy—"

"Someone was going to break in to Jonas's SUV. The chests were inside, but Jonas went out and chased him off. Someone also broke into Amelia's shed. We both had won bids on the chests. Ours were in Jonas's SUV. Amelia's were in her shed."

"Amelia Wiseman?"

"Yes. She had stored three chests in there. Nothing was stolen, so she didn't call you either. Trevor believes the old murder is connected to *this* murder."

Before Morris could open his mouth again, she went on. "I'm worried about Trevor. He has sources I know nothing about, and now with the podcast and hotline, he has even more. He's going to pursue this, you know. We don't know if anything is connected for sure, but it seems awfully coincidental that the same phone that was used for the tip line also turned up near the murder victim. Don't you think?"

"I'm not an idiot." Morris scowled. "Of course, I see the connection. But we have to deal with what we have. Right now I have a body, a canoe, and a burner phone. Forensics is all over it. But I'm going to tell you something that you already know, and I would like you to reiterate it to Trevor Lundquist. He is going to put all of us in danger."

CHAPTER SEVEN

Daisy preferred to shop locally in Willow Creek whenever she could to support community businesses. But this evening she and Jazzi were outfitting her younger daughter for college. For that, Daisy preferred going to a big-box store in Lancaster.

As they traversed the aisles choosing a set of towels, a travel cosmetic bag, hair products, and hand wash, Jazzi checked the list she'd made on her phone. She was wearing a denim shorts overall outfit tonight with a white crop-top tee. Her long black hair, sleek and glossy, fell down her back. Daisy thought she looked too young to be setting off for college.

Diverting the conversation from what they were doing, suddenly Jazzi asked, "Why did you go down to the police station this morning?"

"How did you hear about that?"

Jazzi's expression was mischievous. "Word gets around. One of the customers at the Rainbow Flamingo saw your car parked in the police lot. That cat decal on your back window is a giveaway."

Daisy really shouldn't have been surprised. Willow Creek was a small town with many gossips . . . or, as they would defend themselves—concerned citizens. "Willow Creek doesn't need cameras on the streets."

Jazzi laughed. Then she sobered. "Was it about someone trying to break into Jonas's SUV?"

"No. Detective Rappaport needed my help with something."

"Something like . . ." Jazzi's voice trailed off.

"I'm not supposed to talk about it." Daisy hoped her daughter would accept that because she wanted to respect Morris's wishes.

Picking up a pack of sticky notes at the end of the aisle, Jazzi dropped them into the basket. "Does this concern the investigation about the victim found in the creek?"

Daisy should have guessed Jazzi would probe until she found the answer she wanted. "It could."

"Mom, come on. Spill it."

Her mind circling the information it held, Daisy considered what she should say and what she shouldn't. She had to give Jazzi something, or her daughter would keep poking at her or find answers somewhere she shouldn't.

"Jazzi, I'm really not supposed to talk about what went on at the police station this morning."

"I understand if you can't give me definite details. But you know as well I do that people and officers were milling around the station while you were there. Word will get out about what was happening there."

Jazzi's reasoning was mostly correct. The word was probably already out that Beth Ann Kohler had been at the police station this morning. Still . . .

Choosing her words with care, Daisy continued

pushing the cart, her voice low. "A witness was at the police station with the detectives. She was so upset she couldn't tell them anything they needed to know."

"Was this a relative of the person who was killed?"

Unfortunately, Jazzi had deductive reasoning skills.

Daisy didn't answer.

"So, Detective Rappaport brought you in to calm her down?" Jazzi probed.

"That's about it. By the time I left, she was able to answer their questions. I took along tea and cookies."

"Of course, you did," Jazzi said with a wry smile. "So, Detective Rappaport is going to call you a consultant now?"

"I don't know what he's going to call me," Daisy admitted.

After Daisy pushed their basket into the next aisle, Jazzi slipped her phone into her crossover bag. However, the subject they'd been conversing about wasn't closed for Jazzi because she asked, "Did you tell Jonas the details?"

"I told him who the victim was and why I went to the police station."

"But you didn't say what you talked about."

"No. Jonas knows Detective Rappaport counts on me so he didn't poke like you are."

"Jonas has a lot of trust in you just to let it go like that."

"He knows I'll tell him when the time is right."

"In spite of Detective Rappaport?"

"Yes, in spite of Detective Rappaport."

"He trusts you, and you trust him," Jazzi decided, looking pensive.

This was an important teaching moment, and Daisy didn't take it lightly. "I do. I couldn't marry Jonas if I didn't trust him as well as love him."

As if Jazzi accepted that and didn't need more, her daughter checked over their basket. "I think we're done here. Let's go shop for my bridesmaid dress. There are a few shops at the outlet down the road that might have something we both like."

"Do you have a particular color in mind?" Daisy wondered what her daughter was thinking and what had prompted the desire to shop tonight.

"I'm not sure. Aunt Iris's dress is yellow, Gram's dress is sort of mauve, Vi's is lilac colored. Tessa's dress is a swirl of pastel roses. Do you know what Aunt Cammie is wearing?"

Daisy's sister had informed her with a text and a photo the style and color of her dress. "Aunt Cammie's dress is pale green."

"That doesn't leave me much choice, does it? I'm sorry I waited so long."

Daisy stepped away from the cart and crossed to her daughter, laying her hands on Jazzi's shoulders. "There's no color code or theme or whatever. All we have to do is find something you like. I don't even know what the guys are wearing. Jonas said it will surprise me."

"No tuxedos?" Jazzi seemed perplexed.

"Nope. The July evening is too hot for jackets. I want everyone to be comfortable and enjoy themselves . . . including *you*."

With her lips quirking in a smile, Jazzi nodded.

Five minutes later, as Daisy and Jazzi were checking out, Daisy's phone rang. Thank goodness the tuba noise didn't sound too loud from her pocket. Still, customers around her turned and stared.

Jazzi motioned her outside. "I'll wheel out the cart. Take your call."

As Daisy checked her phone and spotted Beth Ann Kohler's name on the ID, she hurriedly stepped on the pad to open the electronic doors and walked outside. Moving to the right, away from foot traffic, she answered the call. "Hello, Beth Ann."

"Hi, Daisy. I want to thank you for talking to me at the police station. It was easier talking to *you* than to *them*."

Daisy guessed Beth Ann meant the detectives. "I understand how upset you were. You were in shock. What can I do for you?"

"Can you meet with me to talk again?"

Daisy's mind played possible scenarios for the request. "Sure, I can. My daughter and I are shopping for . . ." Daisy stopped. She was fairly certain Beth Ann wouldn't want to hear about her wedding plans.

Beth Ann was waiting. Maybe she didn't want to push Daisy to meet.

Daisy said, "Why don't you come to the tea garden tomorrow when it's convenient for you. I'm sure we can find a quiet spot to talk and have tea."

Beth Ann was quick to jump on the suggestion. "That will work for me." Her voice became thick with sadness. "I have arrangements to make. And I'm not exactly sure how long all of it will take."

Understanding the gamut of tasks that had to be accomplished when a loved one died, Daisy gripped her phone tighter. "Simply come in and ask any of the servers where I am. They'll guide you to me."

Daisy just hoped she'd know what direction to take with Beth Ann and their conversation.

* * *

The following morning at 10 a.m. Cora Sue Bauer poked her head into Daisy's office. Around fifty years old, Cora Sue was a dependable full-time server at the tea garden. Her shade of red hair was helped by chemicals, and their customers liked her bubbly personality. Her royal-blue T-shirt and indigo slacks under the yellow apron with the daisy logo made her look like a colorful bird. Daisy wasn't sure why that description had occurred to her today.

"Beth Ann Kohler is here to see you," Cora Sue said.

Daisy hadn't given her staff any details about Beth Ann, simply told them a woman named Beth Ann Kohler would be coming in to talk with her.

Daisy asked Cora Sue, "Are there many customers on the patio?" It was a warm, sunny morning, and the atmosphere would be perfect there for a quiet talk.

"No one is there now. The morning breakfast crowd all left," Cora Sue said.

"I'll take Beth Ann out there. Can you bring us hot chocolate tea and rhubarb muffins?" Daisy was already on her feet. She didn't want Beth Ann to get jittery and change her mind about talking.

"Sure thing," Cora Sue assured Daisy and went to prepare the servings.

A few minutes later, Daisy and Beth Ann were seated out on the patio at one of the round tables. The light wind lifted the canvas edge on the yellow-and-white-striped umbrella, rustling it. Some of the herbs along the patio were still wet with morning dew. With a pale-blue sky and cottony white clouds above the umbrella, Daisy hoped

Beth Ann could relax as they talked. She was dressed today in a navy-and-white-patterned flared skirt and a white blouse. The outfit was casual but suitable for the serious errands she had to run.

To help the woman feel comfortable, Daisy asked, "How did the rest of your interview go?"

"It was okay. I tried to answer Detective Rappaport's questions the best I could."

"That's all he could ask for."

Her encouragement seemed to prod Beth Ann to go on. "I basically told the detective what I told you. He was interested in the laptop . . . if it was work-related or personal. That kind of thing. But I couldn't sleep at all last night."

The side door of the tea garden opened, and Cora Sue brought out a tray with tea in a pink-and-gold-trimmed teapot, sparkling sugar in a cut-glass bowl, and the muffins. She set two Royal Copenhagen blue-flowered braided cups and saucers to the side of their glass plates. Then she quickly left, knowing Daisy wanted privacy.

Beth Ann looked nervous as she poured a cup of tea and sprinkled a little sugar in her cup, stirring it around. She picked up her teacup. It shook in her hand, and she set it back down again. The cup clinked against the saucer.

She folded her hands in her lap. "I don't want to break down again, and that's why I came to you. I don't know if what I remembered will be of any good to the detectives or not, and I didn't want to go to them and start something I couldn't finish."

Daisy made eye contact with Beth Ann, blue eyes on brown ones. "You can tell me anything."

Beth Ann nodded, tried again to take a sip of her tea, and this time succeeded. "The detective said something about a possible connection to something that happened twenty years ago?" she asked.

Daisy wasn't surprised Morris had talked to Beth Ann about that. "It's possible. Henry's burner phone number is the same number that was on Trevor Lundquist's ID when his tip came in about a twenty-year-old murder."

"One of the reasons I couldn't sleep last night," Beth Ann explained, "was my mind was going in circles, yet in all directions, too. Do you know what I mean?"

"I certainly do."

"As *I* was having trouble sleeping," Beth Ann mused, "I remembered Henry always had trouble sleeping. Even from when I first met him."

That was interesting, but Daisy wasn't sure why Beth Ann might consider that fact important. "Do you mean he woke up often?"

Beth Ann pushed her hair away from her cheek. "Not exactly. The problem was nightmares. He wouldn't wake up screaming or anything like that. He'd simply awaken suddenly. I could feel his body go rigid and jerk, and that would wake me up, too."

"Did you ask him about the nightmares?"

"I did. But he always brushed them off. He just said he woke from anxiety because of work. He was thinking about his patients and that type of thing. But you know, the more I thought about it, I began to believe that waking up like that was more like a panic attack than a nightmare. He'd go all pale. He would take in deep breaths. He never talked about what he dreamed."

Trying to be tactful, yet find out information

that would help the investigation, Daisy asked a personal question. "Would you say you and Henry had a close marriage?"

Without hesitation, Beth Ann nodded. "We did. We shared most things. But he wouldn't talk about this. And you know what else?"

"What?"

"He would never talk about his teenage years. Doesn't that seem odd to you?"

Henry Kohler's teenage years would have been twenty years ago. This wasn't anything that detectives could do anything about, but it *was* another link. Trevor would think it was important.

"Besides the detective, Trevor Lundquist, the reporter, is looking into what happened to Henry," Daisy mentioned.

"I listened to his podcast last night. I don't know if it's a good thing or a bad thing. Yet, if he gets answers, I suppose it could be good."

"Do you mind if I tell him about what you just told me?"

Beth Ann shrugged. "I don't care."

"Do you know anything about storage units that contained old chests that were up for auction?" Daisy asked.

Looking puzzled, Beth Ann shook her head. "No, I don't."

Since that seemed to be a dead end, Daisy turned in another direction. Detective Rappaport had asked Beth Ann about the laptop, and she was going to ask, too. "Do you know what Henry kept on his laptop that was stolen?"

"It was his personal one. Mostly he had saved old photos on it that he'd scanned. I thought he was keeping a history of his family. He was evasive about that, too. He'd just say they were photos of his friends."

"His friends now, or his friends back then?"

"Maybe some of both. I'm not sure."

The rhubarb muffins were warm from the oven. Beth Ann picked up hers and broke it in half. There were soft chunks of rhubarb and walnuts in a fluffy dough. Daisy mirrored Beth Ann's actions, knowing that often helped connect with a person. She'd studied and read some body language books. It was a fascinating field. She didn't know nearly enough about it, but she had picked up some tips. They ate their muffins in silence until Beth Ann looked nervous again.

Daisy didn't jump on her reaction. She just waited and took another sip of her tea.

There were crumbs on Beth Ann's plate, and she pushed them around with her fork. Daisy waited until she made a circular pattern with them, and then she asked, "Is something else bothering you?"

Looking up, Beth Ann nodded. "Yes, it is. Again, I didn't go to the police because I didn't want to get anybody in trouble. I didn't want to say something that wasn't true."

"Run it by me, and we'll go over it together."

Fingering the handle on her teacup, Beth Ann looked lost in thought. "The detective asked me a lot of questions, and most of them I didn't have an answer to. But I did remember something, and I can answer one of his questions."

"What was the question?"

"He asked me if anyone wanted to hurt Henry."

Daisy's heart rate picked up, and she considered that Beth Ann could be giving her a real clue. "You said you don't want to get anyone in trouble?"

"No, I don't. But one of Henry's patients at the physical therapy center was particularly upset with him."

"Was this recently?"

"He'd been a patient for a long while. His name is Callum Abernathy."

"And he was a patient of Henry's?"

"Yes. He was in a roofing accident, and he broke his leg. It was a bad break. Because of confidentiality, Henry couldn't tell me much. But because of what happened at the center, he did."

Daisy leaned forward a little. "What happened?"

"Like I said, Callum Abernathy had to have surgery, and I think he broke his leg in two places. He expected to be as good as new after his physical therapy sessions."

"I know about physical therapy," Daisy empathized. "My fiancé was injured, and he had to go through it more than once. It can be difficult and painful."

"Yes, it was for this Mr. Abernathy. He wanted to be pain-free and do everything he did before. But, of course, that wasn't possible. Although he could walk without a cane, he was still in pain. Two months after he started physical therapy, he had a really loud fight with Henry at the PT facility."

"When was this?"

"It was the week before Henry died . . ." Beth Ann's voice seemed to stick in her throat. "Before Henry was murdered."

"What can you tell me about Callum Abernathy?"

"Not much. I saw him once while I waited for Henry after work and his car had to be worked on. Callum was a big, hefty man, and he looked dangerous."

Daisy knew *looking* dangerous wasn't the same thing as *being* dangerous. And a loud fight, a verbal fight, didn't necessarily mean the man had murder on his mind. Of course, it was hard to tell anybody's motives, or their mental state for that matter.

She understood Beth Ann didn't want to go through the whole interview process with the detectives all over again. But this was something she should tell them.

"Did you sign a statement yet about what you told the police?" That was a requirement.

"No, I'm supposed to stop in and do that. I was just going to wait awhile."

In the most reassuring voice Daisy could muster, she said, "I think you need to ask to talk to Zeke Willet or Morris Rappaport when you go in to sign your statement. You can tell them about Henry's nightmares or not. I don't know if they'd be interested. But they *will* be interested in Callum Abernathy."

After that bit of advice, Beth Ann seemed to relax. Daisy had the feeling that this meeting with Beth Ann was a practice run for Beth Ann for when she did talk to the detectives again. Daisy knew they would be going back to her whether she went in, signed her statement, and had another interview, or if she merely signed her statement and left. Beth Ann was a source and a suspect, whether she realized it or not. The detectives were determined to glean anything from her that would help them solve this case. Daisy realized how involved she herself was now.

She and Beth Ann talked about Willow Creek. Daisy explained how she'd gone to college, fallen in love, and then lived in Florida before she'd moved back a few years ago. Sharing easily now, Beth Ann told Daisy about her online associates degree in medical coding. She was happy working at the dental practice, where she'd been hired a few years ago.

"Henry and I lived in a little two-room apartment and managed to save most of our earnings so we could buy our house. Neither of us has family anymore. A few months ago, Henry and I started thinking about having kids." Her eyes misted, and she turned away from Daisy. "Now that's never going to happen."

Two customers exited the side door of the tea garden, to-go cups of tea and baked goodies in hand. They sat at one of the tables beside Beth Ann and Daisy, looking toward them and smiling.

Beth Ann checked her watch. "I have to go. I have an appointment with Reverend Kemp to talk about a service for Henry, even though we don't know when we're going to have it yet."

Daisy stood when Beth Ann did, feeling as if she wanted to give the woman a hug. But she didn't know her well enough yet. She walked Beth Ann around the side of the tea garden to Market Street, and then she went back inside.

After glancing across the tearoom and noting that everything seemed under control, Daisy stopped in the kitchen.

Tessa gave her a knowing look. "Fruitful conversation?"

The aroma of cinnamon sugar in the snicker-doodles that were baking filled the kitchen and wafted out into the tearoom. Tessa was pouring batter with blueberries and pecans laced through it into bread tins.

"I think it was," Daisy responded to Tessa. "I'm going to give Trevor a call if you don't need me in here."

"We're good," Tessa said. "I'll catch up with you later."

After a nod, Daisy went into her office and closed the door. Taking her phone from her pocket, she pressed her icon for favorites and dialed Trevor.

He picked up on the first ring. "Found something?"

"Not exactly. I just spoke with Beth Ann Kohler. She ran a couple things by me. I think she's going to talk to the police again."

Trevor had already known about Daisy's "help" to calm down Beth Ann, though she didn't know his source. He'd phoned her about it last night. "Tell me," Trevor said.

Daisy didn't think Beth Ann would appreciate Callum Abernathy's name going out on the airwaves with Trevor. He was a suspect the police were going to have to explore with interviews and lots and lots of questions. But she did want to run something else by Trevor. "I think I found a link that connects the two murders. I think, as you said, Henry was involved somehow."

"Something good I can broadcast?"

"No, I don't think this is anything you can broadcast. But it might be something to look into somehow. Beth Ann told me that Henry often had nightmares. Nothing specific about them, but he would wake up with panic attacks. He didn't sleep well, not as long as she had known him. And when she talked to him about their teenage years, he didn't want to discuss his."

"And you're thinking that when he was a teen-ager, he was involved in a murder."

"If not involved, maybe he saw something or heard something. Something that kept him awake at night."

"Hmm," Trevor said. "I need to think about this. With the first episode about this murder, I gained followers and subscribers. I even have a sponsor in-terested. I'm going to keep going any way I can."

It was that "any way I can" philosophy that Daisy didn't like. Maybe she could help keep Trevor on an even keel, maybe not.

"I think I'm going to head over to Amelia Wiseman's after work to take another look at the chests," she said.

"Do you really think you'll be able to find some-thing she and I couldn't?"

"I don't know, but it's worth a try, don't you think?"

"Sure. I can't meet you there, though. I have an appointment in Harrisburg. I'm looking into the forensics of the case."

"No problem. When I do get home, I'm going to spend some more time examining the two chests at my place, too. I think Henry was your caller. His tip to you was specific. We're missing something. I'm going to see if I can find it."

CHAPTER EIGHT

As an inn should, the Covered Bridge Bed-and-Breakfast welcomed anyone who came to its doors. The first thing that took Daisy's attention today was the quilt that hung over the open banister on the second floor. A huge turquoise-and-navy starburst on a background of white graced the middle of the quilt. Daisy could make out partial sunbursts surrounding that. A wide navy border surrounded the white background. It was stunning.

The dining room for the B&B was to her right. When Daisy peered inside, she spotted quilted place mats at the center of each table positioned under a vase with two daffodils.

"Daisy?"

Amelia had called to her from the doorway that led to a parlor down the hall near the stairway.

"Hi there," Daisy called back. "Your dining room is so welcoming."

"Our guests are all out touring. Several were driving to Gettysburg today. When you called, I wel-

comed the chance to stop cleaning a bedroom for
tomorrow's guests."

"Do you still have quilts for all the beds?"

"I do. All handmade in Willow Creek." Her expression turned sly. "That starburst quilt is for sale.
Are you interested?"

Daisy laughed. "Not today. I'm only interested
in finding a secret in those chests."

"Do you really believe there is one?" Amelia motioned Daisy to follow her.

"Trevor and I both think there's a link between
the present-day murder and something that happened twenty years ago."

"Then let's get to it," Amelia said.

After all, Amelia was a no-nonsense type of
woman. Daisy appreciated that.

Daisy caught the scent of lavender as soon as
she and Amelia exited the back door of the bed-
and-breakfast. Daisy knew Amelia's husband oversaw the landscaping along with a handyman. A few
ceramic pots overflowed with red geraniums, white
vinca, and light-purple impatiens. Fuchsia-colored
impatiens had also been planted along the path-
way to a set of faux-wicker lawn furniture on the
patio that surrounded the firepit.

Amelia gestured to a second path of octagonal
stepping-stones that led to a large blue and white
garden shed, which looked a little like a small
house.

The afternoon sun beat down on Daisy's hair,
which she'd let loose over her shoulders. The heat
of the sun felt good after being in air-conditioning
most of the day.

A ramp leading to a double door opened to a

twenty-by-ten-foot space. Amelia said, "When we first erected this, we thought we'd use it for the riding mower and other gardening equipment. But it soon developed into my storage space. I like to change up the looks of the bedrooms . . . and the common area of the inn, for that matter."

Daisy didn't visit the inn often, but when she did, it always looked refreshed. Inside the shed, she could see why. "You have enough pieces in here to furnish another inn!"

"That's what Horace says."

Amelia's husband kiddingly complained about his wife's penchant for collecting things. But he admired her decorating know-how.

Recognizing a few pieces from the auction, Daisy headed to that corner of the shed. The beautiful glass panels of the iris and rose had been propped against the wall. There was a four-light metal chandelier base, a brass and hand-painted floral globe light, what resembled an adjustable desk lamp, and a white milk-glass bedside table lamp. All were possibilities to use at the inn. But what really drew Daisy's attention wasn't a piece of furniture or lights from the auction. It was a four-poster headboard and foot frame. The headboard had the outline of a cloud. The posters were carved, and it all had a mahogany finish.

She pointed to it. "That is beautiful."

Amelia gave Daisy a sly smile. "I had to struggle with Horace to agree to buy that. But it will look amazing in the pansy bedroom."

Each of Amelia's bedrooms was titled with a descriptive name. Daisy suspected the pansy bedroom sported pansy wallpaper on at least one wall.

Amelia went on, "We attended a public sale. The bidding went high because those four posters are actual mahogany. Horace declares we should use it in *our* bedroom. Maybe we should."

Daisy knew Amelia and Horace's suite spread across the third floor of the inn. They were on-site practically twenty-four hours a day.

"Amelia, have you ever experienced a break-in before?"

The skin on Amelia's forehead wrinkled with her frown. "Absolutely not. In fact, we only attached the padlock after the last Willow Creek murder. Our security cameras only protect the inn. Now, however, we'll be putting a few out here, too."

Spotting the chests from the auction, Daisy said, "You didn't take these inside?"

"Not yet. I want to clean them up or shine them up first. I'm not exactly sure. I might even paint the one."

"You're not afraid the intruder will return?"

"Apparently, he or she didn't find what he or she wanted. And the chests are still here. We put another padlock on the door, and it hasn't been broken into. What did you do with your chests?"

"They're in the house right now. I'm going to go through them again after I go home. Do you mind if I look at these?"

"Not at all. That's what we're here for, right?"

As Daisy opened the first chest with its cast-iron buckles and hinges, it creaked. A musty smell rose up from inside.

"I'm going to have to open them and set them in the sun for a while. That should help the dampness. If the smell doesn't go away, I don't know what I'm going to do. I might spray them with disinfectant, too. That should kill any mold or mildew."

Daisy considered the problem of the musty odor. "I think Otis at Pirated Treasures wads up old newspapers and puts them in anything that smells musty. He takes them out after a day and then puts in more."

"That's a good idea. I could try that in one of the chests. I also read about another method. You're going to laugh."

Daisy straightened to study Amelia. "Why am I going to laugh?"

"Because you have cats. The article I read said to take old nylons, cut them off below the knees, and then fill them with charcoal-based cat litter. You leave that in whatever smells musty for about a day. If that doesn't do it, then you put a small bowl with white vinegar in the chest or trunk, and you let that set overnight. Does that chest you got for Jazzi have a musty smell?"

"You know, it doesn't, now that I think about it," Daisy said.

"To keep that fresh, just put dryer sheets inside until she uses it. That ought to do it."

The first chest that Daisy had opened was the one that held a wooden tray inside. After she lifted it out, Amelia took it from her and set it on a nearby table.

First Daisy went over to Amelia and checked the tray. It formed a square and a rectangle with a divider between the shapes.

"Be careful or you'll get a splinter," Amelia warned. "That happened to Trevor."

Daisy could see the wood on the inside of the

tray was rough. She skidded her hands along the interior, taking special care where the divider separated the two sections. But everything seemed to be solid wood. There was nothing there.

"You know, a trunk like this could cost up to five hundred dollars," Amelia said. "Do you know how lucky we were to get these chests?"

"The office manager didn't seem particularly concerned with anything that had been inside the storage compartment," Daisy revealed. "He just wanted to get rid of the lot. It didn't make much sense to me, but I guess that's business as it is now."

Hunkering down, Daisy studied the outside of the chest and ran her hand over each of the cast-iron buckles and clasps.

"They are solid," Amelia pointed out. "Trevor wanted to get a screwdriver and pry loose a couple of them. I told him no deal."

"He might still do it yet if we don't find anything. He might even buy the chest from you to do it."

Amelia gave a wry chuckle. "You sure have Trevor's number."

"I've worked with him for a while."

"Worked with him?"

"He shared clues with me when we were looking at a case as long as I promised to give him an interview after we solved it."

"I see," Amelia murmured. "And now that the *Willow Creek Messenger* isn't publishing as much, Trevor puts that kind of thing on his blog."

"His blog and now his podcast."

Still hunkered down, Daisy scooted around the corner of the chest to look at the leather straps on the sides. "Do you think these were the original handles?"

"Hard to tell. They seem somewhat worn, so they might have been."

"They're made of two pieces of leather stitched together. Did Trevor want to take these apart?"

"I told him that if somebody put a secret in these chests that they wanted us to find, that wasn't a likely place."

Amelia's acerbic reply made Daisy smile. Coming to her feet, she then stooped over to examine the inside of the chest. Again, she could easily get a splinter if she wasn't careful.

After another good look, Daisy went to the wicker chest next. That one didn't smell as musty as the wooden one.

"What do you think if I paint it bright purple?" Amelia asked.

"For the pansy room?" Daisy asked.

"Exactly. I think that would be unique, and it will hide the couple shreds of wicker that have torn off. It will probably cover that black stain, too. Trevor saw that this one was empty, and nothing much could be hidden inside wicker."

Daisy continued brushing her hand over it. "I wonder if the storage unit manager would give out the name of the person who rented the shed."

Amelia looked thoughtful. "How would that help?"

"I'm not sure. But Henry had some reason to think proof of a crime was hidden in the chests. If I got that name, maybe the police would follow up."

"Let me remind you," Amelia said, "the detectives won't go on a chase for something they're not sure about."

"I guess that's true," Daisy agreed. "But it wouldn't hurt to ask."

* * *

When Daisy returned from Amelia's, she found Jazzi with Marjoram and Pepper upstairs in Jazzi's bedroom. Her whitewashed furniture, her bedspread, and curtains that were blue trimmed in white usually emphasized the neatness of her room. Jazzi was Daisy's neat freak. She liked everything to be in its place.

Nevertheless, this evening that wasn't the case. Clothes straggled across Jazzi's bed and even hung over the corner of the headboard. Marjoram, in bread-loaf position, sat atop a few sweaters stacked on Jazzi's desk, her golden eyes targeting Daisy as she stepped into the room. Pepper, on the other hand, lay on her side on the floor of Jazzi's closet and meowed.

"She's as confused as I am." Jazzi's gaze slid around the disorder.

"You can't be packing already," Daisy claimed with mock alarm.

Wrinkling her pert nose at her mom, Jazzi moved two purses from her desk chair to the edge of the bed. "I'm sorting, eliminating, and deciding on donations to A Penny Saved."

Willow Creek's thrift store was a popular venue for budget concerns of teens as well as adults. "Are you trying to figure out what you'll take to college at the outset?"

"I am. I can't decide if I want to include a few fall outfits. Mostly I'll just need jeans and tees."

"Unless you want to dress up for something."

"I have good jeans and old jeans. It's not like I'll be dating."

"Won't you?" Not wanting to press too hard, Daisy hadn't asked where Mark and Jazzi were leaving their relationship when each left for different colleges.

"No dating. Mark and I will reassess where we stand at Thanksgiving. Don't worry, Mom. I *will* be making new friends."

From experience, Daisy knew life could make unexpected turns and detours. Not everything could be planned out. Jazzi would see that more clearly away from home. Still . . . she was going to miss her younger daughter like crazy.

"Shippensburg isn't that far. I can always bring you an outfit you forget or need."

Jazzi teasingly shook her finger at her mom. "From everything I've read, I should spend at least six weeks away without a visit. But you can text as much as you want," she added, her voice catching.

It was obvious Jazzi would miss *her*, too.

Turning to her desk and running her hand down Marjoram's dark-brown, golden, and cream fur, Jazzi asked, "What have you been up to? You're home late from the tea garden."

Daisy gave in to the change of subject. "I was at Amelia's inn examining the chests again. We didn't find anything. Do you want to help me look at the two we brought home?"

"Before or after I clean up this mess?" Jazzi's brown eyes twinkled.

"Before. This mess could take you the rest of the night."

Pepper meowed as if she agreed and followed Daisy as she left for downstairs.

Jazzi ran down the steps after Daisy, the two cats following along. The cats could obviously see they were headed to the corner of the room where the chests sat. Marjoram surged ahead and jumped up on top of the larger one.

"Okay," Daisy said. "We'll look at Jazzi's first since you like your perch."

"Does Jonas think your conversations with the cats are odd?" Jazzi asked with humor in her eyes.

"He talks to Felix."

Shaking her head, Jazzi flipped open the buckles on the green chest. With it open, Daisy could easily see all the inside without the lining. "You'll have to go to Quilts and Notions and pick out the fabric you want for this."

"I can stop in tomorrow before my shift at the Rainbow Flamingo. How much do you think I need?"

"If you're getting forty-five-inch width, probably three yards. You'll have to take the measurements of the chest and give those to Rachel. She'll be able to tell you better."

"Are we going to use glue?"

"Ask her about that, too. I think there's fabric glue."

"Should we use the hand vac?" Jazzi asked.

"That would be good." They often used the small vacuum cleaner to sweep up cat litter and dust bunnies.

After Jazzi went to the laundry room for the handheld sweeper, she ran it over the inside of the chest. As she did, Daisy slid her hands over every edge of the inside. She found nothing. "Did you decide on the color you'd like me to paint the outside of the chest?"

"I can paint it," Jazzi said. "I think I'd like to make it a robin's-egg blue, not too flashy, not too bright. But it will make a statement. Do you think I'll have to remove the buckles and hinges?"

"Probably, unless there's a way you can tape them so you won't spread the paint on them. Ask Jonas about that. He'll have a better concept of what you have to do."

When they moved on to the second chest, Daisy knew she'd have to be more careful examining it because there were more parts. The boxes inside were made of a stiff composite material. One by one, she and Jazzi removed them and ran their hands over them. Daisy had no idea how old they were, but only one corner was peeling on one. The blue border of the picture was faded and worn. One of the buckles was broken. Maybe Jonas would know how to replace it. The outside of the chest with its pattern of wood squares in between the cast-iron strappings was solid. She ran her fore-finger along the edge inside. She could easily see there would be nothing else hiding there.

Then she studied the bottom. It looked like teak, which was unusual. The rest of the wood seemed to be pine. She'd become familiar with woods since knowing Jonas.

She pointed to it. "That teak panel seems un-usual, don't you think?"

"Unless the bottom of the chest was stained. Who knows what people stored in here," Jazzi said.

Pepper came up beside Daisy and ran her nose along the bottom of the chest. Daisy stood away from it, then looked inside again. "The bottom seems thicker than the sides."

"Wouldn't that make sense?" Jazzi asked. "The bottom has to be the sturdiest."

"Yes, but why not use the same wood? The teak looks newer."

Now Jazzi was interested in the inside of the chest, too. "Do you need tools?"

"I don't want to damage the chest. I don't know what we're going to use it for yet, but still . . ."

Jonas's main toolbox was huge and heavy and was located in the back of the garage, where he kept his weight bench and weights. "Jonas has a small toolbox in the laundry room for minor repairs. I'll get that. Maybe there will be something in there we can use."

Soon Daisy was back with a metal toolbox that held a hammer and other implements. Pushing a tape measure aside, she found a chisel and what looked like a paint scraper. It was metal and thin. She grabbed that, knowing she might be able to use it as a lever.

Kneeling on the floor, she slid the slim piece of metal down the side of the chest. She was able to insert it between the wall of the chest and the teak edge, and that's what gave her hope. That teak panel wasn't original to the chest. The teak slid incrementally, maybe an eighth of an inch, to the side.

"I don't think it's glued down," she said with excitement.

"You could find something icky underneath," Jazzi warned. She was kneeling beside Daisy, her shoulder touching her mom's. She was intent on looking, too.

On the other side of the chest, Pepper had put her paws on the edge and was standing up, peeking in.

Jazzi waved her hand at the cat, and Pepper jumped down with a *meow*. "I don't want you to get hurt."

With the chisel in the corner and using the paint scraper as a lever, Daisy lifted, and the piece of teak wood popped up.

Daisy stared down, not sure what she was seeing.

"Do you want to call Trevor?" Jazzi asked.

"No. I want to look at this stuff first."

There was a layer of yellowed papers. "If they're twenty years old, I need to be careful with them."

"Maybe they're older than that," Jazzi warned.

Daisy slid her fingers under a few loose-leaf pages, then carefully lifted them out and spread them on the floor.

"Those are math computations," Jazzi said. "They look like calculus."

There were three pages, and Daisy separated them. None had any words on them, just math. Working out a formula? Working out a problem?

In between the loose-leaf pages, she found two newspaper clippings. Handling them carefully, Daisy slipped them out. She read the first one with Jazzi looking over her shoulder. The clipping was a story about an upcoming Mars exploration *Rover* launch into space that summer. There was no date on the clipping, but they could easily look it up.

The second clipping concerned the Willow Creek track team and a bake sale to raise funds for the team's travel expenses. Daisy read it, then reached down into the chest and found two more loose-leaf pages with more math equations. When she lifted them out, a photo fell from between them.

Daisy heard the sliding-glass doors open in the kitchen.

Jonas called, "Anybody here?"

Felix came scampering into the living room. Daisy held up her hands before he walked on the papers that rested on the rug. Felix knew hand signals as well as voice commands, and he stopped short and sat.

"What's this?" Jonas asked.

"A clue." In her hand she held a wallet-sized photo of a teenager with a man and a woman. "Jonas," Daisy said. "We're going to find out who these people are and what happened twenty years ago."

CHAPTER NINE

A s Daisy walked into Willow Creek's police station early the following morning to keep an
appointment with Zeke Willet, she thought about
her conversation with Trevor the night before. He'd
been as excited as she'd been about the photo, not
so much about the rest of what she'd found. He'd
said, "The clippings are only important insofar as
they give us a date around whatever happened."

He'd been correct about that. But Daisy still
considered that the pages of math equations could
be significant in some way.

"Anything we found could be connected to
whatever the crime was," she surmised.

"It all could belong to whoever was involved *in*
the crime," he'd said. "We should try to secure the
name of the person who rented the storage units."

That conclusion was one of the reasons Daisy
had made an appointment with Zeke.

She didn't have to wait in the reception area
long. Zeke came out to the space behind the fence
and beckoned to her. He opened the swinging gate
for her, and she followed him to his office. Today

Zeke was dressed in black jeans and a white T-shirt. When they reached his office, she noticed a gray linen sports jacket folded over a side table. She also noticed he'd recently had his blond hair trimmed. His jaw seemed even more square than usual. That happened when he wore a determined expression.

"I know you're busy," she said as she sat before his desk, a manila folder in her hand.

"I am. I also know you well enough to realize you wouldn't be here unless you had something important to tell me. Morris said you were a big help with Beth Ann Kohler."

When Zeke had first moved to Willow Creek to take a position with the police department, he and Jonas had been former friends in the Philly PD. They'd been on the outs because of the death of Jonas's partner. At first, Daisy and Zeke had had a relationship as contentious as his and Jonas's. But Daisy and Zeke had learned to respect each other, and Zeke and Jonas . . . they were almost back to a friendship they'd once shared in Philadelphia.

"You don't suspect Beth Ann of anything, do you?" Daisy asked.

Zeke gave her a hard stare. "You know at this point everyone is a suspect."

She sighed and leaned back in her chair. This was the script the PD followed at the start of an investigation. She decided to set aside the subject of Beth Ann for now. "Have you listened to Trevor's latest podcast?"

"I listened to your interview on 'Hidden Spaces' before this case dropped on us. Morris told me about Lundquist's latest podcast and the tip he got . . . something about chests. It sounds like nonsense."

"It isn't. Trevor and I both believe there's a connection."

"Do you have any proof?" Zeke was always about the facts . . . only the facts and the evidence.

"I don't have proof, but I have this." She slipped the manila folder across the desk to him.

With a frown, Zeke opened the folder. After he looked inside, separating the loose-leaf papers, the articles, and the photo, his frown deepened. "What am I supposed to make of this?"

"Take a look at the photo."

After he did, he looked back at Daisy. "And?" he asked, leading her into whatever she wanted to tell him.

"And I want to find out who those people are."

"Daisy . . ." He let her name trail off, and she knew what that meant.

"I know you don't have time to go on wild-goose chases. I get that. But Trevor's tip paid off. All these items were hidden in one of the chests."

"What do you mean *hidden?*" Zeke's eyes bored into hers.

"They were hidden under a panel in one chest. Most likely Henry knew they were there if he was the tipster."

"Even if he was the tipster, I have to follow leads and work on *his* case. I'm not going to pursue nebulous information about an old photograph when Henry isn't even in it."

"Zeke, I want to find out who *is* in the photo and who rented those storage units. I don't know if the manager will give up the name of the person who rented them. Will you make a call to him to smooth the process?"

"I think you should see what *you* can do first.

You know I can't go looking at irrelevant clues." He lifted a stack of papers. "These are interview request sheets the chief has to approve. Beth Ann Kohler came in this morning to sign her statement, and she gave us another lead."

Zeke glared at Daisy when she didn't seem surprised. "You knew, didn't you?"

"Beth Ann came to me and told me about Callum Abernathy. I advised her to tell *you*."

He plopped the papers on his desk. "I'm calling him in as soon as I can."

Preparing herself for Zeke's reaction, she informed him, "Trevor is going to do another podcast, and he's going to talk about what I found in that chest. He thinks he can coax people to come forward that way."

Instead of erupting like Morris would have, Zeke scowled. "You know, don't you, that Trevor's podcast is a lousy idea?"

"That depends on who's looking at the idea," she pointed out. "He thinks he'll find out more about the photo, about the clippings, even about the math scribblings."

Zeke studied the math scribblings again. "None of it makes sense to me. And it even makes less sense that you want to go after this, Daisy. You have so much on your plate right now."

"Everybody keeps telling me that," she said with a wan smile. "But I found the photograph, and now I want to satisfy my curiosity. Maybe all I'll ever get out of this is knowing who those people are in that old photo. But that will be something."

Zeke shook his head. "You are constantly going to be a challenge to Jonas, aren't you?"

"Apparently he likes the challenge."

Zeke laughed out loud. "I guess that's so. If you find a real connection to this case, Daisy, then let me know. But for now, I have to follow evidence that leads to whoever killed Henry Kohler."

Returning to the tea garden after her appointment with Zeke, Daisy was met almost immediately as she came in the back entrance to the kitchen by Cora Sue. The room was buzzing with activity, as it always was in the morning. Eva was baking cookies, and Tessa was readying salads. Daisy would put the ham and cabbage soup on as soon as she washed up.

However, Cora Sue crossed to her and prohibited her progress. "I think you ought to talk to Iris."

"Where is she?" Daisy asked, looking around but not seeing her aunt, who was usually in the kitchen as well as Tessa and Eva in the morning.

"She's at the sales counter. Something about making sure all the baked goods were arranged properly. But I don't think that was really it. I think she just needed something to do to keep her hands moving."

That was a warning to Daisy. If Iris needed her hands moving, her mind was moving, too. Something was up.

Daisy washed up and then went to the sales counter, sidling in beside her aunt. Tamlyn and April were serving customers.

"How are you this morning?" Daisy asked brightly.

Iris gave her a look.

"Did you have a date last night?" Daisy couldn't imagine what else would have her aunt in a tizzy this morning. And she *was* in a tizzy. She was rearranging chocolate-chip cookies as if it were the biggest puzzle on earth.

"Yes, I had a date last night," Iris said in a clipped tone.

"Do you want to talk about it, or do you want me to leave you alone?"

Iris sighed, straightened, and put her latex-gloved hands on top of the sales counter. "I had a date with Morris. We went bowling."

"You like bowling, right?"

Iris nodded, then looked at Daisy askance. "Yes, I like bowling. I've gotten a lot better at it since Morris and I have been trying our hands at the lanes. I do throw fewer gutter balls."

"All right, so if you enjoy bowling, and you enjoy being with Morris, and you throw fewer gutter balls, what's the problem?"

"Two men are the problem." Her voice was so emphatic that Daisy took a step back.

Daisy and her aunt had always confided in each other. For decades, they had been closer than Daisy and her mom, though that was changing now. "Are the men the problem? Or is your process of deciding whom you want to seriously date the problem?"

"Two men are the problem, as well as the whittling process. But Morris and I had a troubling discussion last night."

Iris dipped her hand into the sales counter tray and brought out two chocolate-chip cookies. Taking a napkin from under the counter, she put them on it and slid it over to Daisy. "Want a cookie?"

Daisy almost laughed, but she didn't. She hadn't had breakfast, and a cookie and a cup of tea would serve her well.

She accepted the cookie to mollify Iris. After she took a bite, she asked, "So, tell me, what did you and Morris talk about?"

Iris suddenly closed the sales case. "Can we go to your office?"

Daisy checked the tearoom and noticed everyone seemed quite content. April was serving a table of four, and all appeared happy there. They were chatting with April as if they were old friends. April did have a talent for making customers feel comfortable. Tamlyn was pouring tea at another table.

"Sure, let's go to the office for a few minutes."

Iris picked up the napkin and the other cookie and followed Daisy into her office. After she placed the cookie on the desk, she took off the latex gloves and dropped them into the waste can.

Daisy asked, "A cup of chocolate tea?"

"Sure. Chocolate and problems always go well together," Iris muttered as she sat.

Daisy boiled water in the electric tea maker, then poured it into two mugs. She dropped in chocolate teabags and handed a mug to Iris. "Let it steep for a few minutes. It will give you more of what you need today."

"What I need is a problem solver," Iris almost moaned.

Daisy couldn't imagine what was troubling her aunt so. But something serious was. "So, tell me what you and Morris talked about."

"Maybe I shouldn't have, but I told Morris about Marshall's ultimatum—that I have to make a decision . . . that I can't continue to date both Morris and Marshall, according to Marshall."

"What did Morris say?"

Iris studied the tea in her mug. "He got very quiet."

Getting to know Morris over the past few years, Daisy realized he was an up-front guy. He didn't hold back. He didn't pull punches. Nevertheless, this situation with Iris might persuade him to act differently.

"How long did he stay quiet?"

Her aunt raised her gaze to Daisy's. "At least five minutes while we ate our pizza. Then he finally said that I have to remember he's a cop."

Not sure what Morris had been suggesting, Daisy muttered, "As if you could forget that." Daisy remembered the first murder investigation she'd been involved in. Iris had been a suspect, and Morris Rappaport had gone after her hard. "What did you say to that?"

Iris's shoulders squared. "I told him I certainly know he's a cop. I reminded him that he interrogated me most thoroughly once upon a time. When I said that, he gave me one of those crooked smiles of his."

"And what did *that* mean?"

"It meant that we have a history, and that investigation is one of the things that ties us together."

"I know Morris is a man of few words. Did he explain anything?"

After biting her lower lip, a habit her aunt displayed when she was confused, she continued, "What he said was very puzzling. Morris told me he's not only a cop, but that he's a cop with a checkered past. He didn't explain *that.*"

It was obvious her aunt was troubled by what Morris had told her. "You know Jonas was in a complicated situation with his partner and then with Zeke. I guess things can get even stickier when you're an officer of the law than when you're an ordinary person."

"Possibly," Iris agreed. "But to me, a 'checkered past' means something happened to him as a cop. I can't imagine Morris doing anything wrong. Not ever."

"Sometimes situations aren't always black and white," Daisy reminded her aunt. "Through Jonas I've learned cops have to put themselves in danger, and that the job always comes first."

"Morris as much as told me that. And then he asked if I could become serious with a man who sees crime up close for a living."

That was Morris, trying to clearly lay out what was important to him. "*Can* you see yourself with a man like that?" Daisy asked.

Iris sighed. "I'm not sure."

That evening, Daisy drove down the lane to the house that Vi and Foster were now renting from Glorie Beck. It had been renovated before Vi and Foster moved in. The white clapboard on the outside had become cream siding. A small roof over the porch as well as the floorboards were gray. The window trim had been freshly painted, too, the same gray. Daisy knew the heating system had been updated to include air-conditioning. In the large pantry in the back off the kitchen, a window had been installed, and it had become a nursery for Sammy.

Although she hadn't wanted to accept the limitations of her arthritis, Glorie now lived with her daughter, Nola, and her granddaughter Brielle about an acre away from her old house. Gavin had overseen construction on the new house, which included living quarters for Glorie that made her feel as if she were still independent to a certain extent.

Since Emily Cranshaw was babysitting Sammy tonight, Daisy had texted her that she would be arriving for a visit and what time. Emily opened the door with Sammy grabbing onto her leg.

Daisy laughed and scooped up Sammy into her arms. "How are you two getting along?"

Emily grinned and pointed to the toy mess in the living room.

Vi and Foster had imprinted their personalities into Glorie's house. The gold, green, and blue rug under the coffee table that Vi and Foster had used at the apartment was cluttered with blocks, a busy box, and a few stuffed toys.

"I can see that you two have been busy."

Emily was a pretty girl who was going to be a beautiful young woman. Her shoulder-length hair was sandy blond and turned under just a bit at the shoulders. Her bangs fluttered over her blond brows. She was wearing fuchsia shorts and a fuchsia-and-white crop top. Her feet were bare, as were Sammy's. His navy shorts and white shirt with a sailboat imprinted on the front looked a bit disheveled, with cookie crumbs dancing across the sail on the boat.

Daisy pointed to his shirt. "Those look like oatmeal-raisin cookie crumbs."

Emily laughed. "Only *you'd* be able to tell. Vi says at least they have some nutritional value."

Emily was plainspoken like her dad and had enough confidence to express her own opinion. Gavin had always claimed she kept him on his toes.

Motioning to the kitchen, Emily said, "Vi left iced tea in the fridge. Do you want some?"

"That sounds good. Do you want to sit at the table?"

"Sure, we can pull Sammy's high chair over. He only had one cookie, so he can have another one, Vi said."

"Are there enough for us?" Daisy asked with a grin.

"Yes, there are."

Daisy pulled Sammy's high chair over to the table while Emily took the pitcher from the refrigerator and set it on the gray-speckled Formica counter. The round-top refrigerator and stove were vintage, but they worked, and that was all Vi cared about. Emily took Sammy's sippy cup from the counter and set it on the table. Daisy took off the lid, and Emily poured in milk from the quart in the refrigerator.

When they were all settled, Emily looked Daisy straight in the eye. "Did you come to see Sammy, or did you come to see *me*?"

Daisy broke her cookie in half. "I didn't come to check up on you, if that's what you mean. Vi will only be gone a couple of hours, and I'm sure you can handle that."

"I can. She texts me every hour, and I text her back, usually with a photo or a video. I know that gives her confidence that I can take care of Sammy."

Sammy broke his cookie into lots of crumbs. Then he picked up a piece and stuffed it into his mouth.

"I think you have this babysitting thing down pat."

Emily set Sammy's sippy cup on the high-chair tray. "It's nice to save money for college so I know I can help Dad pay for it. And when I babysit for someone else, I know Vi will recommend me if I do a good job."

"Yes, she will. And I would, too."

"Because you're friends with my dad?"

"No, because I think you're a capable young woman."

"That's nice to hear, but you still didn't answer my question."

Daisy took a few swigs of her iced tea, knowing that she might as well come clean with Emily. "I do want to talk to you about something."

"Did my dad ask you to?"

This teenager was sharp. "Your dad always wants the best for you."

Brushing her bangs to the side, Emily responded, "I know. What did I do now?"

"You didn't do anything. Neither did your brothers."

Emily's brown eyes narrowed as her lashes swept down to her cheek. "This is about what Dad asked me, isn't it? About him dating."

Daisy had thought about what she could say to Emily, but she mostly wanted to draw out the teenager's thoughts and feelings. "He said you seemed to be on the fence."

"Are you supposed to give me words of wisdom . . . or tell me what he thinks?"

Daisy laughed.

As Sammy picked up another bite of his cookie, ate it, and then brought his fists up and down on the tray, crushing the cookie into tiny crumbs,

Daisy admitted, "I don't have any words of wisdom. But I do think your dad wants to know how you really feel, and he's afraid you won't tell him."

"What do *you* think about my dad dating?" Emily's question was sincerely curious.

"Honestly?"

"Always," Emily said, meaning it.

"I think you and Ben and Foster are growing up. Your dad looks at you, and he knows the three of you might not be around forever. You're going to want to have your own lives, just like when Vi and Foster moved out of my garage apartment and moved in here."

"But they're not that far away."

"No, but it's not like having them next door either. I met Jonas, and we're going to get married and start our own lives. If I hadn't met him, and Vi and Foster moved out and Jazzi would be going to college, I think I'd be pretty lonely."

After taking a few bites of her cookie and finishing it, Emily took a swig of the iced tea. "I'll always love Mom."

"Of course, you will, and so will your dad."

Emily looked down at the table and moved her napkin to the right and then to the left. "I don't remember her as much as I used to. I pull out our photo albums and look at them again, so I do remember." There was a subtext in Emily's words . . . and sadness.

"That's a good thing, right? I do that, too. I want to remember Vi and Jazzi growing up with their dad in Florida."

Finally, Emily's feelings flowed more freely. "I get sad sometimes when I look at the pictures."

"I do, too," Daisy confessed. "But the memories

are sweet, too, aren't they? Don't they bring smiles as well as tears?"

Emily thought about that for a second, then nodded. "Ben doesn't like the idea of Dad dating at all."

"He's younger than you. None of us likes things to change too much."

"It would be a change, wouldn't it? Dad going out on dates? It seems so odd."

"My guess is, he wouldn't want to bring anybody home to meet you and Ben and even Foster unless he's really serious."

"That could take a long time, right?" Emily asked brightly.

"Yes, it could. On the other hand, he could meet somebody he really likes right away."

With a frown, Emily shook her head. "I don't know if I'm ready for that."

"How did you feel when Vi came into the family?"

"I felt okay. She was fun. Ben liked her, and I liked her, too."

"How would you feel if your dad met someone, and you actually liked her? If you could go shopping with her? If you could go to concerts?"

"Or she could cook meals for us," Emily said practically.

Daisy had to chuckle. "Yes, she could. On the other hand, she might just want your dad to bring home takeout."

"Then nothing would change," Emily said with a straight face.

Sammy pointed to the living room. "Toys, toys, toys."

"Vi said that was his first word," Emily revealed.

"Then let's go play with him. But, Emily, if you talk to your dad about this, tell him how you feel. Then you'll both know where you stand."

"I want to go to that paintball park in Lancaster. Maybe if he takes me there, we can talk."

"I'll give him a heads-up," Daisy offered.

Emily grinned at her and gave her a thumbs-up sign.

Daisy decided not to waste any time on her search to find the identity of the faces in the photo she'd discovered. The next morning, she visited the storage unit facility, where she found the manager pushing a dolly stacked with taped cartons across the parking lot. Daisy waited for him at his office.

He adjusted the bill of his cap and smiled at her as he rounded the corner and pushed the dolly to a standstill by the office door. After he stepped inside, he pulled up the waistband of his jeans and faced her through the Plexiglas partition.

"You're back. I don't have any auctions today, might not for a long while."

"The new management takeover seems smooth," she observed. It was always better to make friendly conversation when you wanted information in return.

"Yeah, pretty smooth. Are you thinking about renting space?"

"Not right now, but I'd like to pick your brain if you'd let me."

"About fees and the size of the compartments?"

"No." Maybe using a little of Trevor's celebrity

might help. "By any chance, have you listened to Trevor Lundquist's podcast, 'Hidden Spaces'?"

The manager's interested gaze and quirk of his lips said he had, or at least he'd heard of it.

Her last supposition was confirmed when he said, "Not yet. But I'm going to listen to it soon. He's trying to solve a murder—that guy who was found in Willow Creek. A couple people who came to get stuff from their units were chattering about it in the past couple of days."

Daisy ran her hand down the thigh of her yellow-and-white-striped Capris, not sure if what she was about to do was wise or not. "I'll let you in on a secret. Maybe you can keep this confidential."

She had his attention now. With an almost-flirty wink, the manager agreed. "I guess I can do that, especially if the secret is a good one."

"You know Trevor was here on Saturday with the person who bought the contents of one of the storage units."

The manager pointed his finger at her. "And you bought the other one."

She continued, "Trevor is talking on his podcasts about what we bought at the auction and how it plays into the murder." She wasn't going to give too many details, just enough to trade for this man's cooperation.

"Is he going to mention this place?"

"I'm sure he will. He wants to be transparent with all his information."

"Wow! Do the police know what he's going to say?"

Wasn't that an interesting question? "Not specifically, but they do know what information he has."

"But they're not happy he's spilling it, probably."

No comment on that either. "I came today to ask you a very important question. Maybe your name could come up in one of Trevor's podcasts."

The manager puffed out his chest under his red T-shirt. "That would be great. It might impress my new bosses. What's the question?"

"Can you give me the name of the person who rented the storage units and then couldn't or didn't pay?"

The manager considered her request and glanced at the laptop on his desk. "Do you think he's tied into the murder?"

Inhaling a deep breath, Daisy told the truth. "Listen to Trevor's podcast for details, but he thinks the murder that happened in Willow Creek recently is connected to a crime from twenty years ago. I think so, too. The detectives won't invest time into that until we prove there's a connection."

The manager looked over at his laptop again. "If I tell you, maybe you should keep my name out of it."

"Trevor can do that, or he could just mention your name and say that you've been helpful with the auction and all."

The manager pushed up the bill of his cap. "That's okay, I guess. I remember the man's last name but not his first. Give me a minute."

He went over to his laptop, tapped a few keys, and then a few more. Finally he looked up at her. "His name was Ernie Strow."

"Do you know anything about him? Were you here when he rented the units?"

"I was here. I'd say he was around sixty, and he didn't have much to say. He moved everything in himself from an old, rusted pickup. After the first month's rent was in arrears, I sent a notice and then for five months more after that."

"Do you know where the notices went? The address?"

"The notices went to a PO box. But even if I give you the PO box number, I bet the police would have to get more information."

And that's exactly what Daisy told Jonas when they'd both returned home that evening. Jonas had listened as she told him about her visit to the manager.

"So, he was willing to give you information," Jonas recapped.

"He was, but he only had so much. We have a name. Do you think Zeke will help with the PO box?"

"There's only one way to know," Jonas said picking up his phone and hitting a favorites number.

Five minutes later, he gave Daisy a look that she recognized. "He won't help us, will he?" she asked.

"He said he's too busy, but I don't think that's the bottom of it. I don't think he likes this whole idea. You know he doesn't like Trevor's podcast."

"Yes, he's made that very clear. But there is a next step."

Jonas put his arm around Daisy and pulled her over to the sofa. "And what's that? We should make supper?"

"No. We might not be able to get info on the PO box, but maybe we can find out more information on the Strow family."

CHAPTER TEN

Sunlight streamed in the diamond-cut glass on Monday in the spillover tearoom as Daisy helped finish serving the five-course reservation-only tea. This type of tea kept all her servers on their toes as they carried out each course, cleaned crumbs off the tables, and poured more tea. Their customers had the option of two different brewed teas, and Iris kept those going in the kitchen. Usually most of her customers finished around the same time, and that was true today.

As Daisy helped April clear the last of the dishes from the tables, April asked, "Can we consult in your office? I have some ideas I want to show you for the covered bridge tea."

Daisy and Iris had decided to let April supervise that tea and see what she could do. Maybe they'd have someone else in a supervisory position to take over their duties now and then. That would give them much-needed breaks they really hadn't had since they'd started their tea business.

About fifteen minutes later, with the spillover tearoom back in order, Daisy met with April in her office. April looked fresh and summery today in a flowered blouse and white slacks. She was still wearing her DAISY'S TEA GARDEN apron. She had, however, removed her hairnet, and her blond curls swung around her face. She sat in the chair across from Daisy's desk with an iPad in her hand.

She'd also laid a folder on the desk. "I'd like to start with how we'd decorate the tea garden."

Daisy and Iris often decorated for their special teas. She was pleased April had considered how they could bring the tea to life in the tearoom itself.

April opened the folder and pushed it toward Daisy. "These photos are all pictures of the covered bridge at different levels of its construction and history . . . its reconstruction, too. I can have a few of the photos made into little poster boards that stand and set one on each table. Others we could have blown up larger . . . maybe use one in front of the sales counter, one behind the sales counter, and one over by the entrance."

"I like that idea," Daisy said. "These would sort of be picturesque emblems of what we're doing that day, similar to what we used when we had the Alice in Wonderland Tea with the lifelike cutouts."

"Exactly," April agreed.

That tea had been April's first day serving at one of the special teas.

"We have to stay within our budget constraints," Daisy reminded her.

"I'm aware," April said. "I found a business in Lancaster that will give us a good deal on them."

"And they'll guarantee to print them in less than two weeks?" Daisy asked.

"Yep. I already checked. And if they don't, we

get an even bigger discount. So, of course, I've narrowed down when we'll need them."

Daisy smiled. April *was* good at this.

Next April pressed the photo gallery icon on her tablet and turned it around to face Daisy. "Look at these last two photos. I baked cookies last night, and I thought we could use these for the tea. They're sugar cookies decorated like miniature covered bridges. I understand there's a horse and buggy parade that day to the covered bridge."

"There is. Planners are hoping Amish and English will appreciate the town's history together. From what I understand, there will be farmers with their wagons, a few men on horseback, and even a hayride wagon for kids. Of course, the horse-drawn tour wagon with about twenty seats will join the parade, too. He drives tours all around the county."

"Scroll to the next cookie," April suggested.

When Daisy did, she saw the horse and buggy–shaped cookies. "I showed the cookies to Iris this morning, and she liked them, too. They're in the kitchen if you want to take a bite and see if you like the taste. I can always add more vanilla or even make some lemon."

"Both the flavors will be popular," Daisy agreed. "In fact, for the horse cookies we could even make chocolate sugar cookies. I have a good recipe for those."

"Since adults will mostly be our core group for this tea, instead of children like with the Alice in Wonderland Tea, I don't think our servers will have to dress in anything other than our Daisy aprons. So, if we have Ned Pachenko play his guitar again, maybe he could dress in something old-fashioned," April posed.

"That idea works. Maybe he could find some

old-fashioned folk songs to strum on his guitar. Or he might have some other ideas. He's well-versed in all types of music," Daisy explained.

"I also understand," April said, "that Amelia Wiseman is going to be selling commemorative plates for the one-hundredth anniversary at her stand at the covered bridge itself. What if we bought five of those plates wholesale from her and then give those away by drawing ticket stubs?"

Daisy grinned. "I'm glad I put you in charge of doing this."

Daisy was still praising April for her organizational skills when there was a rap on her door. When she looked up, she was surprised to see Jonas.

After she motioned to him to come in, he asked, "Are you busy?"

After greeting Jonas, April said, "I'm finished with all my points for now . . . if you're happy with all of it."

"I am," Daisy assured her as April rose from her chair.

Before April exited the office, she asked, "Would you like some tea and a couple of cookies?"

Jonas shook his head for both of them and pointed to the teabags on Daisy's credenza. "We'll just have some strong chocolate black tea instead. We're good."

After April left, she closed the door. When Daisy looked at Jonas, she asked, "What's going on?"

"How about we make that tea, then we sit down for a discussion."

"About what?"

"About my research." Jonas had an affinity for the Internet and getting around on it even more than she did. Maybe it was because of all his years

as a homicide detective . . . maybe it was just because he enjoyed the tech world.

Because she was anxious to learn about what
he'd discovered, she didn't question him at first.
She just went to the credenza, poured hot water
from the teapot sitting there, and then added
chocolate black teabags to both of their mugs. He
had pulled two chairs together in front of her
desk, so they sat knee to knee. They didn't like bar-
riers between them when they talked.

Dressed in jeans and a navy Henley short-sleeved
shirt today, Jonas leaned forward, his green eyes
intense. "I told Trevor about the name Ernie Strow
for his podcast. He's going to talk about the chests
again and the fact that Ernie Strow rented those
storage compartments. He's hoping to shake out
some information from that. In the meantime, I
researched the name."

Daisy took a sip from the mug of her hot tea and
savored it. "I'm ready. What did you find?"

"From public records, I found out there was an
Ernie Strow who was married when he was twenty-
eight to a woman ten years younger than he was
named Susan."

"Do you have any indication this is the Ernie
Strow we're looking for?" She doubted Jonas
would have mentioned it without more facts.

Jonas picked up his mug from the desk and
took a few bracing sips before he set it back down.
"The time frame fits—and wait until you hear what
I learned next. From birth records, I learned they
had one son named Axel."

"I can tell from your expression that there's more,
isn't there? Maybe we should have had April bring
in packs of sugar to make this more palatable."

Jonas leaned forward, then took her hands in his. "I used a common search engine and found a news story about the Strows. I also searched their names on other databases I have access to."

"Law-enforcement databases?"

"Yes. Axel went missing when he was sixteen."

"Oh, no," Daisy said, slipping her hand from his and covering her mouth. "What else did you find out?"

"That's the problem. There wasn't anything else. No one ever heard from Axel again. His family and friends knew nothing about the teen's disappearance. His body was never found."

Daisy felt herself go paler. Her voice was soft when she asked, "Are we going to connect the proverbial dots?"

"If we do, we might not like where they lead us. Axel Strow could be the murder victim that Trevor's caller was telling us about. On the other hand, we could be all wrong. It could just be a conspiracy theory."

"The Strows were from around here?"

"Oh, yes. They're from Willow Creek."

"We have dinner with my parents tomorrow night for the Fourth of July."

Though the line seemed to be a total non-sequitur, Jonas seemed to catch on. "Do you think they'll remember any history about this?"

"They might. You know my dad's memory is as good as it ever was. He could give us answers we might not find anywhere else."

"Then let's hold our questions until tomorrow night. In the meantime, I think I need some chocolate-chip cookies with more chocolate tea."

* * *

Daisy's parents' house had central air, which was a blessing on a hot, early-July day. Daisy, Jonas, Jazzi, and Iris had arrived early to help Rose prepare any last-minute food and to set the table.

Iris bustled around Daisy's mother, watching the boiled potatoes. "I'll be ready to mash these as soon as Vi and Foster arrive."

Stooping to the open oven door, Rose used a meat thermometer to test the internal temperature of the ham.

"We could have avoided a hot kitchen," Sean Gallagher proclaimed to everyone. "I offered to put burgers on the grill. Don't people usually have picnics for this holiday?"

Daisy, who had been setting the table with Jazzi, patted her dad on the shoulder. She murmured to him, "You know Mom likes to cook when we're all together. The kitchen will cool down as soon as we turn off the oven."

Jonas, who, on Rose's instruction, had pulled folding chairs from the closet and was setting them up, said to Sean, "Daisy, Rose, and Iris cook with love. That's why the food is so good."

"Young man, are you doubting the love in my burgers?" Sean joked.

Daisy studied her dad. His sandy-brown hair had turned mostly gray, but his blue eyes still sparkled with the life of a young heart.

"No, sir," Jonas returned with a grin. "But I have to admit, there is something special about a dinner with Rose's ham, mashed potatoes, and green beans in white sauce. Wouldn't you agree?"

Sean raised his hands in surrender. "I guess my burgers can't compete with that, right, Daisydoo?"

Jonas's eyebrow quirked up at Daisy's childhood nickname. Come to think of it, her dad hadn't called her that in quite a while.

When her dad saw her surprise, he shrugged. "With your upcoming wedding, I guess I'm reminiscing a lot. Your mom and I were going through photo albums yesterday." He leaned closer to Daisy. "She's feeling nostalgic, too."

Without thinking twice, Daisy gave her dad a hug. Big events brought up big emotions. Her wedding might do that for all of them.

Jazzi crossed to them. "Gramps, it's okay to cry at Mom's wedding, but promise me you won't cry when I leave for college."

He leaned away from Daisy to concentrate on his granddaughter. "I'll only promise that if you agree to text me at least once a week and send me selfies."

"Done," Jazzi agreed, with a special smile just for her gramps.

The front door of the Gallagher house suddenly flew open. Sammy toddled in with Foster reaching for him. Vi was saying, "It's okay, Foster. You know Gram has the house toddler-proofed."

"Still," Foster disagreed, "he's faster now than he's ever been. He can be in the midst of trouble before we can catch him."

Obviously taking offense, Vi argued, "Do you think I don't know that? You have to stop worrying about *everything*."

"*Somebody* has to," Foster shot back.

Jonas gave Daisy a concerned look, and she knew what it meant. It wasn't like Foster and Vi to be so contentious with each other.

As if understanding the unusual tension, too,

Jazzi flew into action and corralled Sammy as he ran to the sofa, where Felix was snoozing. Sammy and Felix were best buds.

Jazzi immediately sat on the floor with her nephew as Felix awakened and joined them.

Daisy assured the couple, "Jazzi will keep Sammy occupied until dinner."

Jazzi pointed to the stack of toys on the shelf of the coffee table, and Daisy nodded. She said to Foster, "There are plenty of puzzles there to keep him busy."

Foster was carrying a huge diaper bag with baby supplies as Vi toted the mixed-greens salad she'd prepared to the kitchen.

Daisy touched Jonas's hand and said in a low voice, "I want to talk to Foster." She and Jonas had discussed Vi's worry about her husband. Daisy had considered one way she might be able to help.

Foster's back was to her as he took Sammy's favorite toy this week—a stuffed panda—from the diaper bag. When her son-in-law turned toward her, she was surprised at the changes she saw in him. His russet-brown hair was mussed, which wasn't unusual. But even with his rimless glasses slipping down his nose, she could see the purplish smudges under his eyes and the fatigue in his stance. Like his dad, he was tall, and he didn't slump. But today there was a sag in his shoulders and tension in his jawline that she didn't usually see there. Foster's attitude throughout everything he and Vi had experienced had been fairly laid-back. He didn't look as if his attitude was laid-back now.

"Hey, Foster. How are you?"

He summoned up a smile that was a slipshod one. "I'm fine."

She could easily see that wasn't true. Ever since Gavin had mentioned the idea that he thought his son had taken on too much, Daisy had considered a few alternatives.

"Can I talk to you for a few minutes?" she asked, pointing to a quieter area near the stairs.

Although Foster looked wary, he nodded. "Sure." In the past, Foster had been agreeable but genuine. That genuine outlook was missing today. Simply a bad day? Or a week of bad days?

"I've been wanting to talk to you about my social media accounts."

Right away he jumped in. "I know I haven't been keeping up with the comments—"

She cut in. "It's not that. I think you know I hired April Jennings to take your place at the tea garden."

Less defensive now, Foster asked, "How's she working out?"

"She's doing very well, and I'm thinking about giving her more responsibility. She's going to manage the special tea for the covered bridge's one-hundredth-year celebration. I wasn't going to take it on at all when Amelia wanted me to do it, but April said she could handle it. Her ideas have been good. With wedding planning, it's really a relief to have her, though I *do* miss *you*."

"Good to know I'm missed," he said with some of his old humor.

"I know how busy you are with your new job and your website business. I could talk to April about taking over my social media postings, especially during the prep for the celebration."

"Daisy, you don't have to do that. Really. I can handle it."

"What about giving up the PR campaign for the homeless shelter opening, then? I'm sure the council can hire someone else."

"No," he said adamantly. "I want the payment from the town council to buy a play set for the yard for Sammy. I'm going to finally take responsibility for my family on my own."

"Your attitude is commendable, but you know we're all here to help."

Foster took a step back from her and the conversation. Stiff-lipped, he decided, "My family has done enough for us. Now *I'm* going to take over."

Daisy realized she couldn't suggest anything else. She could see why Vi was worried about her husband. Now Daisy was, too.

The aroma of smoked ham still filled the kitchen and dining area as Daisy cut slices of her mixed-berry pies to distribute around the table. Everyone seemed to enjoy dessert, including Sammy, who had berry stains on his shirt and around his mouth. Vi simply said, "Par for the course. But look at that smile. He's going to be a berry lover."

After coffee and tea and the remnants of crumbs on the pie plates were gone, Foster and Vi and Sammy left. Foster claimed he had work to do, and Vi's forehead was creased as she followed him out the door with Sammy.

Still sitting at the table, concern for Foster on all their faces, Jazzi was the one who said, "He's going to keep going until he can't, and then Vi's going to have to pick up the pieces." She sighed, then asked, "Can I be excused? I have some texting I want to do, and I'm sure Felix will help me."

After Daisy gave her a nod, Jazzi and Felix went to the living room and settled on the sofa together, Felix's head in her lap.

"More tea, anyone?" Rose asked, holding up the ceramic teapot with blue flowers coating its surface.

"I'm good," Daisy said.

Iris pointed to her teacup, and Rose poured some in.

After they were settled again, Daisy said, "Changing the subject a bit, Mom, I have a question for you, and maybe Dad, too."

"Go ahead and ask," her father directed.

"Can you tell me what you remember about Axel Strow's disappearance?"

Silence pervaded the room for a few moments.

"Wow, that's a name from the past," Sean said, rubbing his chin. "What was that . . . about twenty years ago? That was such a sad story, wasn't it?"

Iris gave a shrug. "I don't remember that much about it, truthfully. I didn't know the Strows. Did you?" she asked her sister.

"Oh, I remember them well," Rose recalled. "The family was the talk of the nursery. We'd gotten Gallagher's Garden Corner started, and business was slow. We were mostly selling trees and shrubs rather than flowering plants. It was spring when Axel disappeared."

"That was our busiest time," Sean remembered. "You know how gossip flies when anyone gathers anywhere, especially when it's about a family that's been around for a while."

"Tell us about that," Jonas invited, leaning forward with his elbows on the table.

"The Strows owned a farm that had been in the family for generations," Sean explained. "Axel and his dad did most of the work, but a couple of Axel's friends helped, too, and they got paid by enjoying the meals Susan Strow made."

"Susan Strow was Ernie's wife, right?" Jonas asked.

"Yes, she was," Sean said. "She had a baked goods stand at the farmers market and always sold out."

"Do you know anything more about Axel?" Daisy wanted to know.

Sean thought about it for a long moment, as if he were traveling back in time. "The word was that Axel and his friends were good kids. They got into mischief now and then, like letting a neighbor's bull out of his pen, annoying the goats that were clearing brush, drag-racing at midnight. Some of them had their licenses . . . some didn't."

"One thing always hung with me," Rose explained. "The day he disappeared, Axel had gone off with his friends. One of the boys' families had a pool. The Strows didn't sound an alarm until the next day because they thought he'd stayed over with friends."

Sean jumped in again. "The thing was . . . when the police asked the friends, they all said that Axel had left the pool mid-afternoon. They thought he'd gone home to do chores, but they never saw him again."

"Was there much follow-up?" Daisy asked.

"I don't know about that. I do know that both Ernie and Susan were heartbroken. Susan kind of folded into herself. She called the police every day, but she just seemed to fade away. She lost a lot of weight. Now they know she developed anorexia." Sean's face was sad. "She died in her forties from a heart condition that they thought the disease caused. After that, Ernie worked his farm."

"Why are you so interested in the Strow family?" Rose asked Daisy.

At one time Daisy becoming involved in a mystery would have upset her mom, but now they were on much better terms, and she hoped that wouldn't be the case. As concisely as she could, she explained about Trevor's podcast and what had come forth because of it.

Jonas explained further. "When we found out the Strow name, we decided to look into Ernie and his family. I don't know if that will lead anywhere, but it seems there are lots of questions about Axel's disappearance."

"He was never heard from again," Sean said. "A body was never found either, and that's why you're concerned, aren't you, Jonas?"

"I am," Jonas answered. "And there could be fifty reasons why they never heard from Axel again. Maybe he ran off. Maybe he was in an accident and never identified. There are so many maybes. On the other hand, maybe the police didn't investigate quite enough. Daisy and I would like to get more substantial information to give to the police so they might connect the two murders."

"You trust Rappaport and Willet to do that?" Sean asked.

"I do," Daisy responded. "They want answers, but they have limited resources."

"You go to it, Daisy girl," her father encouraged her. Then he shook his finger at her. "But be careful when you do."

The following evening after the tea garden had closed, Daisy walked into the Willow Creek Library.

She remembered her conversation with Jonas and Jazzi last night as they'd driven home from her mom and dad's, hearing the *pop* of fireworks in the distance.

Jazzi had asked, "Did what Gram and Gramps told you help you at all with this investigation, Mom?"

"I'm not sure. It's a lot to absorb, Jazzi." Daisy was still thinking about it all—about the farm that had been worked by generations . . . about a child who had gone missing . . . about a mother who had died from heartbreak.

Jonas had reached across to Daisy and placed his hand on her thigh. "I know you're thinking about the family, but I do know a few other things."

"What?" Jazzi had asked, practically bouncing on her seat. She'd gotten involved in this, and Daisy didn't know if she was happy about that.

Jonas had switched on his turn signal and veered toward the rural road that led to his and Daisy's home. "The Strow farm was sold a few years ago."

"Did you find that out from public records?" Daisy had asked.

"I did. The thing is, I couldn't find out where Ernie moved to. The year it was sold matches the date when the storage units were rented. If we could find out where Ernie moved, we might be able to find out more."

"Maybe Axel Strow and Henry Kohler went to school together," Jazzi had offered.

Taking it to the next step, Daisy had figured out what they had to discover next. Had Henry Kohler been a friend of Axel's? That was the clue Daisy was going to follow up on now at the library.

The scent of books and their physical presence was one that Daisy could wallow in. She loved libraries, and she wished she came to this one more often. She had run rampant in the children's section of the library on story-hour days during the summers when books were more important to her than the sports her sister, Cammie, pursued.

The library had a semi-musty scent along with an old-wood, leather, and paper aroma. The Willow Creek Library was small as libraries went. The computer area had taken over some of the book stacks. Her clogs tapped on the tile floor as she headed to the main desk. Daisy was glad to see Tabitha Seneft, the managing librarian, was there.

Tabitha was in her fifties and had a no-nonsense attitude. She ran the library with organizational skills she'd developed over the years in her career as a librarian. Her hair was black with a white streak over her temple. Cut short, it framed her face. She had a pointy chin, and her long, dangling silver earrings practically fell to her shoulders. Today she wore a navy-blue shirtwaist dress with huge silver buttons.

Tabitha had been studying her computer when Daisy approached. She looked up. "Hello, Daisy. I haven't seen you here for quite a while." Her tone was a bit disapproving but friendly.

"I know it's been a while," Daisy acknowledged. "But I'm here today, and I hope you can help me."

"Are you looking for recipes?" Tabitha asked. "We have the latest cookbooks."

"No, I'm looking for something specific, and I don't know if you have it."

"Give me the title," Tabitha said. "And the author's name."

"I'm looking for Willow Creek High School yearbooks from twenty years ago. What are the chances you have those?"

Tabitha thought about it, then turned to her computer. "Hold on a minute. I have notes on here about everything, as well as the logistics of what we have in storage."

Storage. Yes, Daisy supposed twenty-year-old yearbooks wouldn't be kept on the shelves since there was limited space.

Suddenly Tabitha raised her hand and beckoned to someone. A petite blonde about Jazzi's age came running over. "Yes, Mrs. Seneft. How can I help?"

"Delia here is one of our pages today," Tabitha said, introducing her to Daisy. Tabitha jotted something down on a piece of notepaper and handed it to Delia. "Mrs. Swanson is looking for the Willow Creek High School yearbooks for these three years. They're in the back section of the basement in the boxes labeled YEARBOOKS. There are ten years in each box, so they shouldn't be hard to find. If you need help pulling out the boxes, take Maria along with you. We're not busy now, and we won't need her up here."

Delia looked at Daisy. "We'll be back in a jiffy . . . promise."

"Delia and Maria are my two best pages. They'll find what you need. They'll pull yearbooks from nineteen, twenty, and twenty-one years ago. Do you have anything else you need help with?"

"No, I'll just wander over and look at the fiction titles."

While Daisy was doing that, she discovered she'd missed many titles from her favorite authors over the past few years. With Jazzi at college and Jonas possibly working in his new workshop, she'd have more time to read. Instead of focusing on the fiction titles, however, she found herself drawn toward the wedding planner shelf with a special display for the summer. Two of the books caught her attention. One was on floral displays for weddings . . . the other was about making your own table centerpieces. She'd taken both to a library table and sat down to go through them when Delia returned, three volumes of yearbooks in her arms.

"They were easy to find," she said to Daisy. "I hope they're what you're looking for."

"I do, too. Do you know if I'll be able to take these home?"

Delia leaned in conspiratorially. "Normally Mrs. Seneft doesn't let anybody take out items that have been in storage. But I bet you could convince her if you have a good reason."

Oh, Daisy had a good reason. "Thank you, Delia. Do you like being a page here?"

"I love books, Mrs. Swanson. My mom says my to-be-read pile is so high I'll never get through them all. She's wrong. I want to read fifty books this summer, and I will."

"That's a big order."

"I want to be a journalist, and the more I read, the better my vocabulary will be. By the way, I'm only a year behind Jazzi. I was on the committee to plan her graduation, so I run into her now and then." She looked over her shoulder and said to Daisy, "I have to go. I have a full cart to shelve from the book drop-off. It was nice meeting you."

"You, too, Delia."

Daisy pulled over the yearbook for the year she

was looking for. If she was right, Axel would have been a sophomore that year. She turned to the sophomore section and began going through the thumbnail photos. Since they were in alphabetical order, she came across Henry Kohler's photo first. Beth Ann had shown her a photo of Henry, and this was definitely his younger version. Back then, his hair had swooped over his brow and had been cut short above his ears.

Daisy was almost holding her breath as she ran her finger across the page and found Axel Strow's photo. Daisy felt her heart melt as she studied the young face, the slight gap in his two front teeth, a few freckles across his cheeks. He looked tanned as though he had spent a lot of time outdoors, and she supposed he had . . . on farm chores. His hair was parted to the side, but he had a cowlick that stood up right behind the part. He had a friendly smile, and she thought she caught a glimpse of teenage joy in his eyes. But maybe that was just her imagination.

For some reason, the story of this teenager who had disappeared squeezed her heart. She couldn't help but think—what if Jazzi disappeared? Would she die of heartbreak, too?

Her gaze drifted back to Henry's picture and then targeted Axel's once more. There had to be a way to figure this out. She saw one direction she could take. How could she find out who else ran in this crowd? How could she find out if Henry and Axel *were* friends?

CHAPTER ELEVEN

Gavin came around the house to the back patio, where Jonas and Daisy were sipping their mugs of coffee early the following morning. Daisy had made arrangements to go into work later. She and Jonas sat on the glider that Jonas had made for her, pushing slowly back and forth as they talked, watched Felix, and simply spent time in silence before they started their day. This meeting with Gavin had been planned. He was bringing over the plans for Jonas's workshop. At least, they were tentative plans.

"Let's go inside," Daisy said to Gavin. "It's already hot and humid out here, and it's only eight o'clock. Imagine what noon will be like. I have iced tea inside if you'd rather have that instead of hot tea or coffee."

"A glass of iced tea would be great. I've been making the rounds since six this morning." Gavin carried a cardboard tube that Daisy knew contained the paper-rolled plans.

Jonas whistled to Felix and the golden retriever

came running, glad to do his master's bidding. Once inside, Pepper wound around Daisy's ankles.

"Oh, no," she told the tuxedo cat. "You and your sister had breakfast with Felix. It's not treat time. This is grown-up time."

Pepper sat at her water dish and looked up at Daisy with her head tilted as if to say, *You're kidding, right?*

Jonas nudged Daisy's shoulder. "We're going to have a snack, aren't we? Didn't you make coffee cake for Gavin?"

"Gavin probably didn't have breakfast."

Gavin shrugged. "I hate to tell you, but I did— two doughnuts. Emily left for a babysitting gig this morning, and Ben was going over to his friend's. They're going to swim later. Emily sticks to her breakfast diet of yogurt, yogurt, and yogurt. Ben has his favorite cereal in the morning and nothing else. The doughnuts were left over from a job site yesterday, and I brought them home." Gavin pointed his finger at Daisy. "Don't you tell me I have to feed the kids healthier foods. There's fruit in the fridge for when they get home."

"I wouldn't deign to dictate your meals. Emily will probably do that for you."

"Yes, she does. '*Fish twice a week, Dad. We have to have fish twice a week for omega-3 oils*'."

Daisy laughed as Gavin laid the roll on the counter. By that time, Jonas had washed his hands and pulled the pitcher of iced tea from the refrigerator.

"This one is peach herbal," Daisy said. "Would you like sugar?"

"No, thanks. I just try to keep liquids going in all day on days like this." He hesitated before he took the lid off the cardboard roll. "Emily said you talked to her."

"I did." Daisy had stored the coffee cake in a container on the counter. Now she brought it over to the island and removed the lid. While Jonas pulled glasses from the cupboard, she found plates and set them on the island. "Did Emily talk to you about what we discussed?"

"Actually, she did. She approached me when Ben wasn't around. She said talking to you made her see life in my perspective. Those are her words, not mine. She said she doesn't want me to be lonely and she wants me to have fun, too. So, if I want to take somebody out to dinner, it's okay with her. We didn't go beyond that."

"You'll have to talk to her and Ben about each step and keep them informed. I haven't spoken to Ben yet. I thought I'd visit him tonight after work. You said he has a shift at the grocery store then."

"It sounds as if you had a pretty good talk with Emily. Don't expect that with Ben. He could go silent on you. His brother is doing the same thing with me now."

The idea that Foster wouldn't listen to Gavin either was troubling. "I tried to talk to Foster when we had dinner at my mom's. But he's not listening. I'm worried about him, Gavin." She summed up what Foster had said about the play set for Sammy.

"Jazzi was the one with the wisdom," Jonas told Gavin, coming over to the island. "She as much as said Foster will keep going like this until he can't. Then he won't have any choice but to give up some of the responsibilities."

"Your daughter is a smart cookie." Gavin took the glass of iced tea from Jonas and swallowed a few long gulps. When he did, Daisy said, "Emily would like to go to the paintball park in Lancaster soon. She might open up more to you there."

Gavin nodded at the suggestion.

Then they all sat at the island while Gavin unrolled the plans. Pointing to notes on the paper, he began, "The workshop would be built like a small barn, similar to the shape of your house. With the same siding and trim, it will look as if it belongs. Behind the garage, it won't interfere with your back lawn and garden. Felix will still have plenty of room to roam. These are just the sketch drawings, to give an idea of what you might want. For now, I have it sectioned off." Gavin dragged his finger across the sketch. "I've positioned your office in the front of the building and the workshop in the back. Have you both agreed you want to include a bathroom?"

"We did," Daisy answered. "It just seems practical." Gavin pointed to a note he'd made on the plans. There was a small box there. "I think you're going to want a sink in the workroom, too. One that's more industrial. And, of course, a superior ventilating system."

"I'll need plenty of electrical outlets, too. I'll have a planer in the workshop and a sander, a table saw, and a circular saw. The office doesn't have to be too large. I want most of the space just for working. It should be able to fit three people, maybe like Daisy's office at the tea garden."

"But you will need enough space for a computer, printer, and maybe a file cabinet?" Gavin asked.

"That's true," Jonas conceded.

"If you'd like to keep the area under the roof

for storage, too, we can easily do that. I can put an access point with stairs that pull down."

"Like an attic," Daisy said.

"The interior of the workroom itself can be barnlike," Jonas noted. "I don't want fancy finishes or anything like that—just a concrete floor."

"But you want your office modernized, don't you?" Daisy asked.

"Nothing fancy," Jonas repeated.

Daisy nudged Jonas's shoulder with hers. "Nothing fancy, but solid and maybe even cozy. You know what your window displays are like that draw people into Woods. I think your office should be like that. Maybe shiplap on the walls in a light color, furniture you yourself have made. We could hang a quilt piece or two on the walls . . . or a collage of the furniture you've created."

"Laminate flooring," Gavin suggested.

"That all sounds good. Maybe a double barn door at the back of the workshop so I can bring big furniture pieces in and out easily. One thing we haven't thought of . . ." Jonas looked at Daisy. "Should we extend the driveway back to the office and the workshop?"

"We'll have to, especially if you're unloading wood there and other supplies. It would make sense. I think we've given Gavin enough to start with. Gavin, can you put together an estimate for us?" Daisy inquired.

"That's why I'm here, to figure out what you want and how we can do it within your budget."

As Daisy served blueberry coffee cake, Gavin said, "Those blueberries make my mouth water."

"That's the idea," Daisy said with a smile.

"How's your search for the secret in the chest

going?" Gavin asked. "Gee, doesn't that sound like a Nancy Drew novel?"

Jonas shook his head. "I wish it was that tame. Tell Gavin what you found out."

"I went to the library yesterday and looked at old yearbooks. Hold on a minute and I'll get them. The librarian let me bring them home." Daisy went into the living room, found them on the end table, and brought them over to the kitchen island. Gavin was rolling up the plans for the workshop and stuffing them back in the cardboard tube.

She opened the yearbook that mattered the most and set it in front of Gavin. "Do you remember the names of the people involved?"

"Yes, I do. Henry Kohler and Axel Strow."

"Take a look at the thumbnails. The class picture with the kids on the bleachers, too."

Gavin ran his finger over the individual thumbnail photos just as she had. Then he looked up at her, his eyes narrowed. "They were both in the same class."

"They were," Jonas said. "I don't think that's a coincidence either."

"What are you going to do next?" Gavin asked curiously.

"I think I'll go to the farmers market and find out if any of the old-timers who still have stands there remember Susan Strow and what happened. She had a stand there and sold baked goods."

"You know, your friend Rachel Fisher might be able to help you with that," Gavin said.

Gavin had a very good idea, and Daisy was going to act on it.

* * *

Zeke Willet wasn't in the tea garden that afternoon but two minutes when Daisy saw the expression on his face. She was in for trouble. He was like a black cloud floating over to her. Well, not floating. Striding.

"Office, Daisy. I need to talk to you."

With her eyebrows raised, Daisy glanced at Cora Sue. Cora Sue said, "I'll cover. Go ahead."

In her office, Daisy sat at her desk, Zeke across from her. "Should I offer you something to eat and drink?"

"Not this morning. I'm upset with you."

"Tell me all about it," she said in a calm voice. If he was really upset, he would have called her into the station. "What did I do now?"

"You withheld information from me."

"What information is that?"

"Have you heard Lundquist's podcast this morning?"

She hadn't. She'd been too busy. "No, what did he say now?" She suspected she knew.

"You didn't tell me you had direct evidence that Henry Kohler's murder and Axel Strow's disappearance are connected."

"I don't have direct evidence. Not yet. The two men were in the same class in high school. I just discovered that yesterday. I went to the library and found the old yearbooks. When I went through them, I saw that they'd been classmates. Let me remind you that you said you didn't have time to look into Axel Strow, right?"

Sighing, Zeke admitted, "That was true then, but it's not true now. What exactly do you know?"

"I'm going to assume Beth Ann is in the clear, and you're looking for another suspect. That's why you're so upset . . . because you don't have one."

Zeke denied that conclusion immediately. "That's not true."

"Oh, that's right. You have the man who had a fight with Henry at the physical therapy center. How's that panning out?"

Running his hand up and down the back of his neck, Zeke said, "It isn't yet. We're still working on paperwork."

"Since Henry and Axel were classmates, other classmates might know something about Axel's disappearance," she pointed out.

"The police investigated back then," Zeke reminded her.

"How well did they investigate? It's not like now, when parents can go on social media, rile up the press, and put pressure on the police to look around."

"Daisy, you know we do our job."

"I know you and Morris do your jobs. I don't know what happened back then, and I don't even know if Chief Shultz would. But you might want to ask him."

Zeke's gaze sharpened as if that was a possible idea. "Don't you think he would have stepped forward if he knew something? He's gone over all the information we have."

"Including this new information . . . that the two men were classmates?"

"He was out of the office this morning."

After a few moments of silence while Zeke studied his hands, he looked up at Daisy, his gaze narrowed. "Let me ask you something. For an instant, let's say you're working on this case."

"I sort of am," she said with a bit of a smile.

His hand brushed that comment away. "What would you do next?"

"I think that's obvious, Zeke. I'd start talking to Axel's classmates who are still around. I'd ask Beth Ann if he was close to any of them now. I'm going to go to the farmers market and find out if any of the people at the stands there were around when Susan Strow was, too. If they were in Willow Creek when Axel went missing, they might remember something nobody else does. Oh, and sometime in the immediate future, I'm going to talk to Rachel because she knows them better than I do."

Zeke exhaled. "Let's have a cup of that chocolate tea while I think about whether I'm going to let you do that or whether *I* want to do all of it."

"If I can save you the groundwork, why should you do it?"

"Because it's my job," he practically growled.

"Your job is to keep Trevor under control, and follow up on anything I find, right?"

Zeke smiled. "As I've indicated before, does Jonas know what trouble he's getting into by marrying you?"

She wrinkled her nose. "Not if you don't tell him."

Quilts and Notions, Rachel and Levi Fisher's store, was kitty-corner across Market Street from the tea garden. Taking a short break mid-afternoon, Daisy crossed Willow Creek's busiest street,

feeling the heat of the asphalt up through her sandals. The plate-glass windows of Rachel's shop simply showed what was inside the store. There were
no decorating frills. The colorful fabrics and the
quilting corner were enough to draw tourists inside.

After Daisy opened the door and stepped in,
she could see the store was quiet for now. She was
tempted to daydream about a new quilt at the quilt
rack, but she could think about that later.

Hannah, Rachel's daughter, spotted Daisy. "*Wil-
kum,* Daisy. Can I help you?"

"Not today. I'm here to see your mom. Is she
busy?"

"Our customer line just fizzled. She went out
back to check on Brownie. She'll be giving him a
treat, I'm sure."

Rachel and her family were New Order Amish.
When at the store, her horse was hitched to a post
out back. Some days Levi dropped her and their
daughters off at the store, then came back to pick
them up at closing. Apparently not today. Daisy
went through the shop, down a hallway with a
storeroom and break-room cubbyhole, then out
the back door.

Rachel was murmuring something to Brownie
in Pennsylvania Dutch while she held her hand
open with carrot pieces. The leaves and branches
of the maples overhead swayed with the breeze
that kept the backyard shaded.

"Did Brownie need a treat, or did you need a
break?"

Rachel turned to her and smiled. "Probably a
little of both. Did you come for a visit?"

"Not exactly."

"Then it's true."

"What's true?"

"That you helped the police with Mrs. Kohler."

"My goodness. No one is supposed to know about that."

Brownie snuffled the last piece of carrot and crunched it.

"Oh, Daisy. Even before social media, we had chatting networks in Willow Creek. People saw you go to the station. They saw Beth Ann Kohler meet you at the tea garden. Do you not know that three and two have to add up to four if most people in this town say it does?"

Daisy rested her hand on Brownie's regal neck and stroked. "Morris called me in to help calm down Beth Ann. She'd just learned her husband had died and how. She was too upset to speak to them, and they needed to ask her questions. And we did meet at the tea garden. She had a question for me."

"And what's this about Trevor that has the town buzzing? What's he doing now? It's a far cry from those questions he asked me in March for his blog about English versus Amish values."

Ruffling her fingers through Brownie's mane, Daisy nodded. "I know. And I'm concerned he's getting himself in trouble. But because of him, the police have new leads."

"I don't listen to Trevor's podcast, but Luke does. That boy shares news like an over-pressured spigot."

Daisy smiled. Luke was in his *rumspringa*, his running-around years. He'd just begun courting a young Amish woman from his district. "Luke is full of enthusiasm."

"For sure he is," Rachel seconded.

"I'm trying to set facts straight for Zeke Willet. *I* know you don't gossip or believe in insubstantial rumors. So I've come to you."

Rachel stepped away from Brownie. "Just what could *I* have to tell you?"

"Do you remember when Axel Strow went missing?"

"Luke told me Trevor mentioned Axel Strow's name on that podcast. I'm certain sure I do remember. You talk about rumors. Those rumors developed into stories that many people believed."

"Did you?"

"After I gave it a lot of thought, I wasn't sure. Some people thought he took off for a different life. Farm work is hard work. No one knows that better than Levi. Others thought maybe he had a girlfriend that no one knew about and they left together."

Daisy pulled the yearbook she'd been carrying from under her arm. "Can you take a look at this?" She settled it on the hitching post, then opened it. "Axel was a sophomore when he disappeared."

Rachel studied the faces. "Going to Amish school kept me separated from everyone. You know that. I only knew the students in my school. Other than them, I saw you. Life was too hard and busy for much time for roaming."

Daisy knew that.

"Were these teenagers ahead of you or after you?" Rachel asked.

"They were a few years behind me. I was in college when Axel disappeared. I don't know if my parents tried to keep what happened to the Strows from me, or if I was just unaware because I was at Drexel."

After Daisy closed the yearbook, she asked Rachel, "What about Susan Strow, Axel's mother? Did you have any contact with her? With a stand at the farmers market, she would have been known to many people."

"I remember her stand, and my parents buying baked goods from her," Rachel recalled. "But then she stopped bringing baked goods and the stand was owned by someone else. The best thing you can do, maybe, is talk to some of the old-timers who are still there, who would remember her. I can tell you which ones. Toby Parker's stand has sold produce since I was a child. He is still there, though his daughter and son-in-law run it now. Another one to talk to is Bob Weaver. The Weavers have sold grass-fed beef there for as long as I can remember. Those would be two families to start with."

Daisy patted Brownie and gave her friend a smile. "Thank you. You've been a big help."

"I am hoping giving you a few families to talk to will not get you in trouble."

"It won't. I just want background. If I find out anything important, I'll turn it over to Zeke."

Rachel took her elbow. "Now let us forget about the awful that happened and talk about some good. I want to know all about your wedding dress."

Happily, Daisy described it to Rachel as they walked inside.

The grocery store at the east portion of town had been built within the last few years to service the growing population at that end. A medical park had also grown up, and more doctors were moving in. There would soon be other businesses extending Willow Creek to the east. The grocery store was an independent one. Mostly Ben helped the elderly folk who frequented the store by carrying their packages out to their cars or helping them to find what they needed in the store. It was a way for Ben to earn service hours for graduation and also learn the ropes so when he was old enough for a paying job, the store would possibly hire him.

Daisy parked in the lot at the front side of the store and watched men and women push their carts in and out. She was about to disembark from her car when she noticed Ben come out of the store and start collecting the carts in the parking lot that people had left at their cars. Maybe now was as good a time as any to pull him aside for a few minutes.

When he spotted her, he wheeled three carts over to her car. "Hi, Daisy. Did my dad send you to check up on me?"

He was grinning and joking, but he wasn't so far off the mark. "He told me you were working here, and I needed a few groceries for a meal tonight. I was hoping I'd see you."

Now Ben studied her a little differently. "Don't you usually shop at the other end of town?"

Ben was as smart as his sister and as quick as Jazzi in that teenage way they had of being perceptive.

"I usually do, but the truth is, I did want to talk to you for a few minutes. Can you take the time?"

"I'm not on a time clock," he mumbled. "So, if it doesn't take too long . . ."

There wasn't anyone around them and nobody to overhear. "I thought about asking you to stop in at the tea garden, but I didn't think you'd particularly enjoy a cup of tea."

He shuffled from one foot to the other, still holding on to the carts. "No, but I do like your chocolate-chip cookies."

Daisy's door was still open, and she reached to the passenger seat and brought out a bag. "I just happened to bring these along in case you need them for a break. Your dad said he wasn't picking you up until eight p.m."

"Is this a bribe?" Ben asked shrewdly.

She held out the bag, and he took it, still wary. Daisy leaned against the frame of the car and crossed one foot over the other, hoping to take a relaxed tone. "You and I are honest with each other, right?"

"We were about Foster."

"So, I'm going to be honest with you now. Your dad did ask me to come see you and feel you out about a certain subject."

Ben looked into the bag and took a whiff. He sighed. "What subject?"

"What would you think if your dad had coffee with someone?"

"Like you?" Ben asked.

"No, not exactly like me. Like, if he asked a woman to have coffee that he might want to take on a date."

Ben's expression was easy to read. The corners of his mouth turned down, and he was practically scowling. "I *don't* want to talk about it."

"Your dad knows you don't want to talk about it, and that's why he thought you might talk to me rather than him."

She stood at the other end of the grocery carts and dropped her arm to one of them. "Can you tell me why you don't want your dad to date anyone?"

Ben stammered, "He . . . he doesn't *have* to date. He has us. He has me and Emily, and Foster and Vi and Sammy, and you guys. Why would he have to date?"

After that little burst of venting, Daisy let the air settle a bit. "You know, don't you, that having us isn't the same as having a woman friend he can talk to, have fun with, so he isn't lonely."

"I don't want him to be lonely," Ben mumbled. Then he looked up at Daisy with big brown eyes that glistened. "But I don't want him to forget Mom either."

"Do you ever really think he could forget your mother? He has you and Emily and Foster to remind him every day. He has memories for all the years they were married. He has pictures of her and things that she held, and things that she loved. How could he *ever* forget?"

Ben looked away. "What if *I* forget? I'm younger than Emily. I wasn't around Mom as much. I don't remember as much. Sometimes I look at the photographs, and they don't seem real."

So *that* was a big part of this problem—he had only a shadow of his mom rather than a perfectly clear picture. "Maybe you and Emily and your dad can make a pact to share the memories you have of her on her birthday, on holidays, whenever you go someplace that she used to like to go. Would that help?"

"It might," Ben admitted. "I didn't think Dad liked to talk about Mom because it made him sad."

"Does it make *you* sad?"

"No. Emily and I talk about times we went to Dutch Wonderland or drove up to the Gettysburg Battlefield."

"Maybe you could share with your dad when you remember something that you want to try to keep more solid. It makes it more vivid in your memories. Looking through a photograph album together could be a start of that. I'm sure your dad would make the time."

"He often says he worked too much when we were little. On Sundays now we usually go for a hike or play board games in the wintertime or do something like that—family time."

"Ben, do you think you could talk to your dad about all this? He really wants to discuss any and all of this with you."

Ben's grip on the cart loosened, and he no longer appeared defensive. "I thought he just wanted to date somebody, and he didn't care about all the rest . . . you know, like our family time. Because if he was dating someone, then we wouldn't have family time anymore."

"You would still have family time. Maybe it would just be a little different."

"I don't know, Daisy. Maybe he should just wait until I'm out of high school and going to college. Then I won't care."

"Ben, I don't think that's true. I think you're always going to care. But it would help your dad if you could change the way you thought about it."

"I wouldn't care if he was dating *you*."

Taken aback at first, Daisy didn't know what to think. And then she laughed and showed Ben her ring. "I'm engaged, Ben. I'm going to be getting married to someone else. No chance of going out with your dad."

Ben gave her one of those teenage half shrugs. "I guess it would matter who he dates."

"Of course, it matters. Did you ever think that your dad might like to date a few different people before he actually finds somebody he really likes? It could take a while."

That thought brightened Ben's expression. "I can get onboard with that," he said.

Daisy almost laughed again. She didn't, though, because this was serious stuff.

A car drove into the parking lot and settled in the handicapped spot. "I'd better get back to work," Ben said.

"I understand." Daisy closed her car door, used the remote, and locked the vehicle. "Just think about everything we talked about, okay?"

"Okay," Ben said with resignation that Daisy hoped would open a door between him and his dad.

CHAPTER TWELVE

At the tea garden once more the next morning, Daisy was donning her apron and tying back her ponytail when Iris came to the office. "Tessa was telling me about the yearbooks you found. Can I take a look? After you were out of high school, I worked at the cafeteria there. I might be able to tell you if I recognize any boys from the pictures."

"Yes, take a look. I never thought about that. Do you remember Axel?"

"Not by name, but if I saw his picture, I might."

Crossing to the desk, Daisy opened the yearbook to the page where all the thumbnails were positioned. She didn't point anybody out. She just let Iris look.

At first, Iris swept her forefinger over the names. She studied each row and stopped at Axel's photo. "I remember him going through the cafeteria line. Like I said, I didn't remember his name."

"What about Henry Kohler?" Daisy asked.

Iris found his picture. "No, I don't remember him specifically. You know, when kids went through the line, they were talking to each other, ignoring us. And we only remember the ones who got in trouble . . . or who did say hello."

Then Iris's finger pointed to another picture. "I remember this boy."

Daisy looked over her shoulder. "Why do you remember him?"

"Dylan Meyer was a track star, and his dad was the coach. I remember his dad coming through with him now and then, telling him what he should eat for stamina. Henry's name didn't click when you first told me about him. But now, looking at their pictures . . . I seem to remember a group of them who came through together. Dylan and Axel. Maybe Henry, too."

Tessa peeked into the office and said to Iris, "Morris just came in. I don't know if you might want to serve him."

Iris blushed a little. "Sure, I'll serve him. I'll go right out. Take a look at Daisy's yearbook. Maybe you'll remember something."

"Trevor told me all about the yearbooks," Tessa said.

Daisy pointed to the one that was open. "This is the page with the individual thumbnails."

Tessa pulled it toward her. "I'm curious about the time period we're discussing. Yes, the boys were younger than we were, but that didn't mean we didn't see them around."

"I didn't remember any of them."

"You had your head in your studies, and I think you had a crush on Cade Bankert. So, no, you weren't looking around, but I was." She took a look at the photos. As she touched each photo,

Daisy watched her. Suddenly the tip of her finger stopped on a name no one else had mentioned—Brooks Landon.

"Are you sure you don't remember him?" Tessa asked Daisy.

"I don't."

"I remember him because he bragged about his dad all the time."

"Landon," Daisy repeated. "How do I know that name?"

"You know that name because he has the biggest tractor dealership in town. Residents from Lancaster, York, and all the small towns around here come to that dealership. Brooks has taken it over from his dad, from what I understand."

"Trevor doesn't realize what a source of information he has in you." Daisy grinned.

"I don't think he's figured out my worth yet," Tessa agreed. "But he will soon. I don't know if Brooks might have been friends with Axel, but there's the possibility their paths crossed."

"And there's the possibility that Henry Kohler might still have been friends with him . . . or at least acquainted with him. I think I should talk to Beth Ann again. If she doesn't know anything, Dylan Meyer or Brooks Landon might."

"Are you going to talk to them yourself?"

"I don't know. I'll see what Jonas thinks."

Tessa narrowed her eyes. "Are all your decisions going to become mutual ones after you're married?"

"I don't know about that. But I do know we'll ask for each other's advice. And you've got to admit, he's the former detective in the family."

"So, his opinion has more weight than Trevor's?" The lines around Tessa's eyes crinkled with amusement.

"For me, it does. I'm worried about what Trevor's doing, aren't you?"

Tessa gave a small shrug. "I'm keeping my eye on everything he's doing. If it gets too dangerous, maybe I can pull the plug . . . literally."

Daisy suspected pulling the plug on Trevor Lundquist would be a lot harder than Tessa imagined.

The farmers market was one of Daisy's favorite places to shop. It was open later on Fridays, and Daisy drove there after work. She always felt like she'd stepped into a fragrant world with so many excellent choices to eat healthy. Farmers and residents of Willow Creek had sold produce, baked goods, and other paraphernalia here for the past fifty years. At the beginning, the building had been fashioned of clapboard, almost like a barn. But then ten years ago, the town council had decided the farmers market needed to be preserved. Re-sided, it stood out. The siding was almost royal-blue and kept it from being just another shop on the road. The siding was unusual because it had been donated by a roofer who couldn't sell it. The roof had been re-shingled, too, in green shingles that didn't complement the blue. But none of that seemed to matter to residents of Willow Creek, who enjoyed going to the market three days a week—Tuesdays, Fridays, and Saturdays. Tuesdays, of course, weren't nearly as busy as the weekend days because then tourists stopped, too.

As soon as Daisy entered the market through the open wooden doors, she caught the scent of cinnamon buns. The baked goods stand sent delicious smells all through the market. There were also fresh potato chips from one of the many snack companies in the area. At the food service counter, grilled burgers and French fries sent those aromas into the air. The market was a wealth of sights, sounds, and good smells.

One of her favorite stands was Ruth Zook's. She carried varieties of apples and sweet potatoes. She also made wonderful jams, which Daisy bought for the tea garden. Next to Ruth, she found the larger stand that she was looking for. It was a refrigerated meat counter. Bob Weaver sold beef products like steaks, roasts, and fajita meat. He also had developed a section for pork and sausage, as well as a deli case, which showcased everything from pimento cheese to various salads. Bob was one of the sellers she'd come to see, and she hoped he was here and not just his family was running the stand.

A young woman at the refrigerated counter spotted Daisy and greeted her. "How can I help you?"

"I'm here to see Bob Weaver. Is he around?"

The woman glanced over her shoulder. "Hey, Bob. There's somebody here to see you. Do you have time?"

Wearing a white apron and a Phillies ball cap, the man came over to the end of the stand. Bob was probably seventy or more, and he had the creases on his face to prove it. His forehead wrinkled when he saw her. "Do I know you?" His mouth turned down in a puzzled expression, and his long jowls seemed to droop.

"I'm Daisy Swanson. I manage Daisy's Tea Garden with my aunt, Iris Albright." Maybe Bob would know her aunt.

He snapped his fingers and smiled. "You gals are the ones who serve tea and solve mysteries."

This wasn't exactly the way Daisy wanted to be thought of, but she was glad he recognized her . . . or at least her name.

"I'm gathering some information, and a friend of mine suggested you might know something about Axel Strow and what happened to him."

Bob frowned again. "I don't know *anything* about what happened to him."

"I worded that wrong," Daisy corrected herself. "I'm hoping maybe you remember some of the facts around the case. I wasn't living here then, so I don't know anything about it."

"Why do you need to know?"

Wasn't that a good question? "I'm assisting the police in gathering information."

"Yeah, I read some articles that you help them out now and then. So I guess you're legit."

"Did you know the Strows?" Daisy asked.

Bob motioned to her to come around the back of the stand. He stepped aside so she could walk behind the counter. Then he plucked out two chairs like you'd find at soccer games. "My knees don't hold me as long as they once did. Let's have a seat."

Daisy hoped that meant he had a lot to tell her.

After he settled in, he rubbed his knee. "I knew Ernie Strow."

She absorbed that. "I'm going to ask you something that might seem odd."

"The fact that Henry Kohler was murdered is odd. That reporter I listen to on my phone thinks

Henry Kohler's death and Strow's disappearance are connected."

"Do you think they are?"

"It seems too much like a coincidence. I don't believe in coincidences."

"If you listen to Trevor Lundquist's podcast, then you know this all started with a search for a few chests."

"Oh, those chests of Ernie's. He had a penchant for them. He and his wife and Axel each had one for personal belongings. Ernie also kept one in his living room that held books, and another in his barn to hold horse blankets. I think it was wicker."

That accounted for all five chests. "Do you know what happened to Ernie after his wife died?"

"Axel's disappearance and the death of his wife almost broke the man. He kept running the farm but eventually had to sell it for financial reasons. I heard he moved into a room with a family who took in boarders. Last year he tripped going down the stairs at the outside entrance and hit his head."

"Oh, no. Was he injured badly?"

"Very badly. He was in a nursing home for a few weeks, but then he had a stroke and died. That family had nothing but tragedy."

"And it started with Axel's disappearance," Daisy murmured.

"It sure did. Anyone who lived in Willow Creek during that time would have some peace if we all knew what happened to Axel. And now Axel's friend Henry dies suspiciously. I just can't figure out what's happening to the world . . . or to Willow Creek." After a pause, Bob asked, "Have you been talking to the police? Do they know who killed Henry?"

"They're following leads. That's mostly what they'll tell me. Did you know Henry?"

"Sure, I knew Henry. You don't get to be my age without needing physical therapy some time. I had arthroscopic surgery on this knee. I had known the Kohler family. I mean, after all, everyone in this town had connections with everybody else at some time or another, right?"

"I suppose that's true. I sure see a lot of it at the tea garden."

"I imagine you would. I had to go to physical therapy after the surgery, and that's when I met the adult Henry. He had gotten his master's in PT and come to work at the center. We talked while he taught me exercises. He was building a life for himself here."

"Do you know for sure if Henry and Axel were friends?"

"They ran around together, I know that. Them and some other guys."

Daisy's heart sped up. "Who are the other guys?"

"Perry Russo was one. Perry's an insurance broker now."

Daisy was going to add that name to her list.

"I saw Perry come into the PT center once when I was there, and he yammered with Henry for a while. I think they were going out for beers and to watch a game. That's about all I know. Are you really helping the police by looking into both murders?"

Daisy wondered if that was just a slip of the tongue on Bob's part. "Do you think Axel was murdered?"

"A boy like that don't just disappear. He was close to his family. He helped with chores. He loved that farm as much as his parents did. I can't see him just running off. But if he didn't run off, then something bad had to happen to him. I might have suspected an accident before Henry's murder, but now it sure makes you think twice, don't it?"

Yes, it certainly did make Daisy think twice.

Rushing from table to table was an occupational hazard on the weekends during the summer tourist season. Daisy was doing it this morning. Two buses had lined up in the public parking lot, and most of their riders had come to the tea garden. Chocolate tea was a big hit, even though it was a warm day. Cherry tarts, lemon tea cakes, and rice pudding were orders that she had carried back and forth at least twenty times already. She'd just served a table with two couples from Harrisburg when Trevor came rushing in. He had that expression on his face that she knew probably meant trouble, at least for her.

"I have to talk to you," he said with excitement in his voice as he approached her.

Daisy motioned to the busy tearoom, as well as the spillover area. "Not now, Trevor. I can't take a break."

"When can you?" he asked with his one-track mind.

She glanced around. "Meet me in fifteen minutes out back. I'll take a five-minute break."

By "out back," she meant outside the kitchen door, and he knew that. They would have some privacy there. She assumed he would need it.

Fifteen minutes later, she met him there. He was munching on a cinnamon scone. "These are good, you know that?"

"I do," she said with a nod. "How can I help you?"

"It's not how you can help *me*. *I* can help *you*."

"By telling me the police have solved this murder?"

"Not a chance. It's just getting more complicated, and that's what I came to tell you. I received another call on the tip line."

Oh, no, Daisy thought.

"Don't give me that look. This is good. The caller identified himself. It was Dylan Meyer."

She recognized the name immediately as one her aunt had mentioned.

"What did he have to say?"

"He was one of Henry and Axel's friends. He said a gang of them ran together. They even tried Wild Turkey that Ernie Strow kept hidden in the barn. So, we have lots of names to put together now—Axel, Brooks Landon, Henry, Perry Russo, and Dylan Meyer. But Dylan added a detail I didn't know about."

"Someone else who was close to this group?"

"Oh, yes. There was a girl who was younger who adored Axel and hung around with him. Her name is Stephanie Gallant. She's a librarian in York. I checked the library work schedule. The library's closed this weekend. But she'll be there on Monday. I think you should pay her a visit."

On Monday morning, with Jazzi and a part-time server covering for Daisy and Tessa at the tea garden, they stood outside the Martin Library in York. Daisy didn't let Trevor tell her what to do. However, when he'd explained his reasons for wanting her to meet with Stephanie Gallant, she'd agreed. Trevor knew he could be intimidating. He poked for answers in a much more aggressive way than Daisy did. Because of that, he thought Daisy would be the better interviewer.

After thinking about it, Daisy knew she didn't want to go alone, so she'd asked Tessa to accompany her. They'd gone on this type of jaunt before. No danger involved, simply questions.

The Martin Library was a colonial-style library. Located at the corner of Market and Queen Streets since 1935, it held the largest collection of books in York County. All age groups were encouraged to explore its services, from children to teens to adults. Stephanie Gallant helped with the children's services.

Not wanting to ambush Stephanie, Daisy had phoned the library that morning to speak with the librarian and explain what she wanted. Stephanie had seemed eager to meet with her and Tessa.

In her thirties, Stephanie was used to using technology. She'd texted Daisy a photo, and Daisy had texted her one back so they'd know each other when they met.

Tessa nudged Daisy's arm as they stepped into the library's lobby. "That's her, isn't it?"

The young woman was standing in the foyer. She was pretty . . . with a high forehead and a wide smile. Her golden-brown hair was parted on the right, and her bangs were brushed that way, too. She waved when she saw them. "Let's walk to a nearby café where we can talk."

They all agreed that was best.

Inside the café, Daisy requested a chai latte, Tessa green tea, and soon the three of them were sitting and sipping.

"I was surprised when you called," Stephanie said. She was wearing a cranberry pinstriped blouse with dolman sleeves. She was slim, and her tan skort came to her knees. Her beige espadrilles looked comfortable for any duty she might have to perform at the library. Her expression was wide and open, and her brown eyes glistened with memories.

"I have a photo to show you that was hidden in one of the chests," Daisy said, knowing this was her best lead-in.

Stephanie waited while Daisy pulled it from her purse. With a sad smile, the librarian studied the image of the woman in worn jeans and gray sweatshirt as she stood by a red barn, her arm around the boy beside her. "Susan was always affectionate with Axel, and he was embarrassed by it. She was so caring. Axel couldn't get away with anything with his dad, but his mom couldn't deny him much, even when he broke curfew or asked for a dozen cookies for his friends."

Daisy felt a kinship with a woman whose cooking and baking shared her love. She hurt with the idea that Axel's disappearance had broken his mother.

Stephanie pointed to the man in the photo, who was dressed in dusty jeans, a red flannel shirt, and a bucket hat. "Axel's dad was as hardworking as *my* dad."

After studying the photo along with Stephanie, Tessa crossed her arms on the table. "If Axel was sixteen, then you must have been thirteen or fourteen when you knew him?"

Stephanie nodded, took another sip of her coffee, and then set it down. "Yes, I was. I had a crush on him. He was the only boy who could make me blush. I thought he hung the moon, as my daddy would say."

"How did you know the Strows?" Daisy asked.

"We lived on the property beside them. We didn't have horses, and Axel's family did. So I often ran over there to visit the horses . . . and to visit him."

"Did he know you liked him?"

"He thought I was a bother, most of the time anyway. Most of Axel's friends didn't know it, but he liked to read as much as he liked to run track. The guy friends were more action-packed than Axel was. Do you know what I mean?"

"Not exactly," Tessa said. "Do you want to explain?"

"Axel and I talked books and computers. We particularly liked to talk about outer space. You know, taking a rocket to Mars and whether there were aliens or not."

Daisy remembered the article that had been secreted in the chest about a space mission to Mars. "Can you tell me about Axel's friends?"

"Sure, let me think. There was Henry Kohler, of course. Brooks Landon, Perry Russo, and Mick Ehrhart."

Mick Ehrhart's name was a new one, and Daisy mentally added it to her list. "Was he better friends with some than others?"

"I'd say Axel and Henry hung out the most together, but Axel had a lot of chores. Sometimes he joined his friends for adventures, and sometimes he didn't."

"What kind of adventures?"

"Let me think." She did so with her brows pulling together. "One time I was with Axel when Perry asked us to join him for a hike to the quarry. It was Axel, Brooks, Mick, Perry, and Henry. But, to my disappointment, Axel wouldn't let me go with them. He told me he didn't want me getting into trouble. I don't know what that was supposed to mean. Maybe they were going to indulge in beer and he didn't want me to know about that. He was protective of me, like a little sister, I guess."

"But you hoped for more than just being a little sister?" Tessa asked.

"There wasn't anything romantic between us." Stephanie looked deflated when she said it. "There couldn't be, not when I was just fourteen. But I'd hoped there would be in the future. I cried for weeks when Axel went missing."

Daisy waited a beat and let Stephanie take control of her emotions. She could see that even now, talking about Axel brought back bittersweet memories. "What do you think happened to Axel?"

"I don't know," Stephanie said. "But I do know two things."

Tessa and Daisy both leaned in to listen.

"I know Axel didn't run away. He cared too much for his family to even consider that. He loved his mom, and he respected his dad."

"Then what's the other thing?" Tessa asked.

"Something awful had to have happened to him. I know that for sure. He never would have wanted any of us who loved him to miss him and wonder what had happened. If he could have gotten back to us, he would have."

Daisy was beginning to believe that Stephanie was right.

CHAPTER THIRTEEN

Daisy was spending time alone. Jonas had been working on their wedding gazebo many evenings, and this was one of them. Last evening, Daisy had caught sight of a streak of white paint on his T-shirt before he changed clothes. She wondered if he was in the last stages of preparing the gazebo . . . painting rather than building. Working the evening shift at the Rainbow Flamingo, Jazzi had texted that she'd be home around nine thirty.

After Daisy returned home from the tea garden, she fed Marjoram and Pepper and immersed herself in her garden rather than Henry Kohler's murder investigation. It was hard to avoid thinking about all that Stephanie had revealed about Axel Strow. Could Trevor's podcast dig up more truth? Would his podcast affect the investigation? Would individuals he interviewed tell him truth or lies? Trevor wanted to interview Beth Ann on the air. Would she agree? What about Henry's co-workers and friends? Would they agree to let their ideas and views spread across Willow Creek and maybe much farther?

Stephanie Gallant's recognition of a young Axel in the photograph along with his parents kept swirling in Daisy's mind. Stephanie's expression had been so sad, tinged with her feelings for Axel and a crush that had stayed with her all these years.

Trying to focus on gardening, Daisy separated the green leaves of the zucchini vines and found two hidden squash. She hadn't eaten supper. Maybe after Jonas returned home, she'd fry bacon and sauté the zucchini and onions in the drippings. They could have BLTs with the sautéed zucchini.

After she pulled two more from the vines, she examined the tomato plants. By their wedding, they should have yellow cherry tomatoes along with a few red beefsteak tomatoes.

When she went inside, she placed the zucchini on the counter and washed up. She found Marjoram and Pepper curled together on the deacon's bench under the living-room window. They opened their eyes as she paused at the bench. Pepper directed her golden eyes directly at Daisy.

"I won't disturb you," she said.

Marjoram gave a small *meow*, as if to say, *You already have.*

Daisy had gone to her bedroom to change into raspberry-colored Capris and a white tank top when her doorbell rang. She checked her phone app and spotted Zeke at the door. Surprised, she pressed the talk live icon and told him, "I'll be there in a minute."

She tied her hair back in a ponytail and went barefoot to the door. After she opened it, she said, "This is a surprise. Jonas isn't home yet, if you want to talk to him."

Zeke shook his head. "I thought I'd take a look at the chests Lundquist is making famous."

"Are you thinking about taking them into your custody?"

"Not yet," was all Zeke responded when she motioned for him to come in.

"I would have called," he apologized as he headed for the corner of the room where the chests were located, "but I needed a break and took a chance you or Jonas would be home."

"He's working on the gazebo, and Jazzi's at work. How about iced tea and a cheese biscuit? I brought some home for supper."

"Let me take a look at the chests first, especially the one you found the photo inside of." Zeke shrugged out of his gray sports jacket and laid it over a chair. He looked tired but as handsome as always in a cream-colored T-shirt and blue jeans.

"The green one is Jazzi's. The other one is 'evidence,' if you want to call it that."

"She's going to take that to college?" Zeke asked.

"Yes, but we're going to paint and re-line it." Daisy opened it up and showed him the inside. "Nothing here to see." She closed it again.

Zeke opened the other chest and studied the compartments inside. "So, tell me what you've been up to."

She sank down onto the floor. Pepper jumped down from her napping spot on the bench and came to join her, crawling onto Daisy's lap.

"What makes you think I've been up to anything?" Daisy asked ingenuously.

He swerved his gaze from the chest to her. "I've discovered you don't back down when you go after something. What have you learned?"

"The manager at the storage units gave me the name of the person who had rented them. I might have used a little persuasion on him, something about his name being mentioned in Trevor's podcast."

Zeke groaned. "Don't tell me you're trading information for favors now, Daisy. I thought you were above that."

"Sometimes I am, sometimes I'm not. I've gotten better at delving into evidence."

Zeke shook his head and went back to studying the compartments in the chest. He removed the large, rectangular one. "So, tell me about the photograph you found."

"The family in the photo are the Strows—Ernie Strow, the dad and a farmer; Susan Strow, the mom and baker who had a stand at the farmers market; and Axel Strow, the sixteen-year-old who disappeared. Are you listening to Trevor's podcasts?"

"By the end of the day, the last thing I want to hear is Trevor Lundquist's voice," Zeke mumbled.

"Information is coming in to him, and you should be aware of it. I don't want to come running to you every time he or I learn something."

"Usually information doesn't come that fast," Zeke reminded her.

"I know, but this case is different. The podcast might make a difference."

"Daisy, it's not a case yet."

"Aren't you going to look into Axel Strow's disappearance?"

"Tell me more about what you've dug up." He took the second compartment from the chest.

"Someone called in to Trevor's show. His name

was Dylan Meyer. He knew the guys Axel ran around with, so we have some names."

Zeke thought about that and shook his head again. "I don't have the manpower to go after more interviews right now. We're bringing in the employees in Henry Kohler's practice. These interviews take time, Daisy. And then I go over the transcripts again for any hint of clues to follow up on."

"I have clues for Axel. Tessa and I talked with someone today."

"Who?" Zeke almost barked.

"No one dangerous, believe me. She was two years younger than Axel. She's a librarian now at Martin Library in York. Dylan Meyer, the man who had called in, knew about her. He said she was like a kid sister to Axel. So, Tessa and I went to the library to meet with her."

"Of course, you did." Zeke was kneeling now and looking at the fold-out compartment in the lid. "Did you find anything in here?"

"No. That would be an obvious place, wouldn't it? Apparently, Axel hid away what was important to him."

"What was this librarian's name?"

"Her name is Stephanie Gallant. She was very open and honest and guileless. She had a crush on Axel back then, and she admitted it. She was fourteen, and he was sixteen. Mostly she hung out with him because Axel's place had horses. She liked horses, and her family didn't have them. She said Axel was aiming to become an astronaut someday. He liked science and math. That article he kept about a rocket going to Mars proved that. The bottom line was, his dad didn't think he should be interested in math and science. Ernie Strow didn't want to hear about his son going to Mars or the moon. He wanted his boy to take over the farm someday."

"And Axel?"

"Axel loved his parents and respected them, and he would probably do what they said. But he had secret dreams, and that's what I showed you in that folder."

Zeke's head was practically in the chest now. The toolbox was still close by, and Daisy took out the chisel and the paint scraper. She showed Zeke how she'd used them to lift the teak bottom.

"Did Jonas teach you how to do this?"

"He did *not*. I figured it out on my own."

"I know," he sighed. "Women can do whatever men can do. Got it."

When he lifted the panel, he found the manila folder. "Why are you still keeping it in here?"

"I just felt that's where it belonged. I did make copies of everything that's in it, though. Do you want those?"

Zeke rubbed his hand across his forehead and ruffled his hair. It was short, and it stood up straight. "I'm going to say *yes*, but not because I think it's a case yet. The chief has to decide that."

"I understand. But you can convince him, can't you?"

"I need more to go on, Daisy. Tell me more about what this librarian knew."

"She knew that Axel liked to read as much as he liked to run track. She said that he often protected her. For instance, he wouldn't let her go along with him and his friends to the quarry. She suspected they drank there. I've also found out that Dylan Meyer, Brooks Landon, Perry Russo, and

Mick Ehrhart knew Henry and were classmates of Henry's and Axel's."

Daisy thought again about the Strow family and how brokenhearted they all had been after Axel went missing.

Zeke was looking at her now and asked, "What's wrong?"

"Axel's mom died of a broken heart. She developed anorexia. She died in her forties from a heart condition the disease caused. She'd lost her child, and that killed her."

Zeke was silent as awkwardness settled between them. He looked back into the chest, running his fingers over the bottom and then putting the teak panel back in place.

Daisy stroked Pepper's back, and the cat turned over in her lap, showing her white belly. Daisy ruffled it, giving affection and taking comfort. The cats were so good at that.

"Jonas looked into the public records," she finally said. "He found out that the Strow farm was sold just a few years ago. But he couldn't find out where Ernie had moved to. The year it was sold matches the date when the storage units were rented. Bob Weaver told me Ernie rented a room somewhere." Then she told Zeke about Ernie's fall and the stroke afterward.

Zeke seemed to think about all that. "I do have something to tell you, so don't say I never share," Zeke said.

"About the case?"

"About what you're working on. I contacted the storage unit manager, and I did get into the PO box. There were notices from the storage unit manager, as he said. I contacted the people at the address connected with the PO box, but they didn't know much because they didn't know Ernie before he rented a room, and he kept to himself. They told me about his fall."

"He sold the farm, put his belongings in storage, and moved into a one-room with a bath. It's sad, really," Daisy said.

"It surely is that a man's life boils down to that."

There was a noise in the kitchen. The sliding-glass doors had opened, and someone had come inside.

"You do have a code on those doors, don't you?" Zeke asked.

"I do."

Jonas called, "Daisy."

"In here," she called back. "Zeke's here. He came to look at the chests, and we're information sharing."

Jonas was wearing a smile when he came in and saw Zeke.

Zeke got to his feet, and Jonas clapped him on the back. "Information sharing, are we? That must mean you need our information, and you're willing to give a little to get it."

"Don't give up my strategy," Zeke complained. "Daisy has already learned to read me too well."

Jonas laughed. "She's a smart woman."

"I came over for a break, too. I just needed a half hour of downtime."

"I told him I'd supply iced tea and cheese biscuits, but better than that, we can make a quick supper. I have zucchini and bacon. How about it?"

"I shouldn't," Zeke drawled.

"But you're going to," Jonas supplied. "Come

on, I know how you don't eat when you're on a case. Daisy's zucchini will melt in your mouth, and we can cut open the cheese biscuits and put the bacon inside for sandwiches. What do you say?"

Zeke looked first to Daisy and then to Jonas. "I say yes."

Daisy was not a connoisseur of lawn mowers or tractors. However, Landon's Tractor Supply was impressive, even to her. Jonas had picked her up at the tea garden on her lunch break, and they'd driven there. The store was located at the south end of town. The facility might have started out small. But now it almost looked like a car dealership's showroom—a dealership that tantalized customers with the latest and best machines inside. The largest machines were located under a permanent awning outside. A service department sat at the rear.

Parking in the business's lot, Jonas made the comment, "They've added ATVs. That's a sure way to draw in a younger clientele."

As they disembarked from Jonas's SUV, Daisy looked around. There were both residential and commercial lawn tractors on display outside, as well as walk-behind mowers and riding models.

"Wait until you see the gear inside," Jonas said with some enthusiasm. "I might be able to come up with a Christmas list."

Daisy laughed at his enthusiasm, and when they entered the building, she could see what Jonas meant. There were blowers and edgers, hedge clippers, brush cutters, chain saws, pole pruners, and sprayers. She recognized most of the paraphernalia because of the models her parents used at their nursery.

"Which is the highest on your Christmas list?" she asked.

"Probably that pole cutter. I can see using that on some of the trees around the property. And I never needed a chain saw before. You never know where that could come in handy."

She swatted his arm. "You are kidding, right?"

"I'm not! What if a tree falls, and we have to saw it? It would be something good to have."

They were well inside the store, checking out the machines, when a man approached them. Daisy almost didn't recognize him from his high school headshot, but then she took another look. Brooks Landon had changed in several ways from his high school photo. Instead of his brown hair being brushed to the side, it was now brushed high on his already-high forehead. It curved back and looked as if it had seen hair product that day. His nose was well proportioned for his long face, but he must have decided he wanted to look more mature. His beard was short with thin, neatly trimmed sides, and his mustache connected to it on either side of his mouth. His face had filled out, too.

Brooks was wearing a LANDON TRACTOR SUPPLY dark-green T-shirt with white embroidery along with jeans. She imagined his sophisticated-looking Italian leather loafers wouldn't see tractor work. She suspected if Brooks turned around, she'd spot a designer label on the jeans. Did he want his clientele to notice or not to notice? That was the question.

His smile was just right, not too eager but friendly enough, as he held out his hand to Jonas first. "Brooks Landon. How can I help you? Are you interested in a lawn tractor?"

After he shook Jonas's hand, he addressed Daisy. "Not that I'm going to ignore the ladies. I have a model you might like, too."

Daisy did have a lawn tractor. Jazzi and Vi had taken turns using it when Vi was living there. Jazzi mowed after Vi had married, but Daisy helped. Since Jonas had moved in, he'd taken over the lawn care, and Daisy and Jazzi were appreciative of that. She had to admit she was appreciative of everything about Jonas.

She moved her thoughts back to where they belonged—on Brooks Landon. He was tall and lean, and she could see his forearm muscles and biceps under his shirtsleeves. Once an athlete, he still appeared to be built like one.

"Actually, I do have my eye on that pole cutter over there," Jonas told him. "But before I take a look at it, we have some other business we'd like to discuss with you."

Brooks tilted his head and studied Jonas. "And your name is?"

"I'm Jonas Groft. I'm the proprietor of Woods, a furniture store downtown. This is Daisy Swanson. She owns Daisy's Tea Garden with her aunt."

Brooks gave an acknowledging nod. "I've passed your businesses often. Is this community awareness you want to discuss?"

"This is community business in a way. Have you ever heard of Trevor Lundquist's podcast 'Hidden Spaces'?"

Brooks's mustache twitched. "I'm afraid I'm not

into podcasts. Much too busy around here. My dad has handed over the reins of the business since he's going to retire. I hardly have time to get a veggie wrap at lunch, let alone listen to podcasts."

How to explain the situation in the simplest way possible, standing here, in a business where customers could be coming in any minute, Daisy wondered. She dove in to the heart of the matter. "I'm helping the police look into Axel Strow's disappearance. I understand you were friends with Axel."

Brooks looked totally taken by surprise. If he had heard about Henry's murder, he obviously hadn't connected any of it yet.

"Axel went missing twenty years ago," he said. "I've never forgotten him, though. He was such a good guy." Brooks glanced toward the back of the showroom and gestured to them to follow him. "Come on. Let's go into the office. Then we can talk."

The office was about twelve-by-twelve with a massive desk and three chairs sitting in front of it. Daisy wondered if the elder Landon had meetings with his employees in here since it was large enough for that. A mission-style bench sat to the left of the door, which was the larger section of the wall. The polished concrete floor was covered by a rug under the desk that looked as if someone didn't like their feet on the cold cement. It was navy with a pile that looked plush. Brass and glass cases filled the back wall. Trophies lined the glass shelves along with car replicas and other knick-knacks. Her gaze lingered on those, then shifted back to the trophies. She commented, "Somebody has a lot to be proud of there."

"My dad does, I suppose. Some of them are his, and the others are mine." As if he was in no hurry, Brooks sat behind his desk and motioned to the chairs in front of it. "Have a seat," he said. "I don't know what I can tell you."

"We would just like some background information on Axel," Daisy suggested.

"Background about his life?" Brooks asked. "We were just teenagers doing the best we could . . . having fun whenever we could."

"Can you tell us what was going on the spring he disappeared?" Jonas asked.

Daisy knew that was the type of history that fed this kind of investigation.

Brooks rubbed the bridge of his nose. "I don't remember much about that spring. Twenty years ago. Do you remember what *you* were doing twenty years ago? We were all friends . . . just kicking around . . . glad we'd be out of school in a few weeks."

"Speaking of the track team," Jonas said, pointing to those trophies again, "Henry Kohler was on the track team, too, wasn't he?"

"Yes, he was. Many of my friends were."

"Was Axel on the team?"

"Yes, but it was difficult for him because he had so many farm chores to do. He was often late to training sessions or had to leave early."

The office's glass windows were open to the rest of the showroom on two sides. Daisy spied a man coming toward them, wearing the same type of shirt as Brooks. He looked to be about her dad's age.

She had the feeling this interview was going to come to an abrupt end. She wanted to get as much information as she could before it did. "Did you spend much time at Axel's farm?"

Brooks's smile and the sparkle in his eyes seemed reminiscent of his time spent there. "I did. We all did. Axel's mom was a sweet woman. She wanted to cook and bake for everybody. My own mom divorced my dad when I was fifteen because she found someone she liked better. Susan Strow was everything my mom hadn't been. Do you know what I mean?"

That was an honest remembrance, and Daisy had to give Brooks credit for sharing it. After all, they were strangers. However, it was something that must have affected Brooks deeply for him to talk about it with them. Losing a mom at any stage was tough. To lose a mom when he was a teenager, especially for that reason, had to have put a dent in his life that he'd remember always.

When the man who had approached the office stuck his head inside, Brooks said, "This is my dad, Gary Landon."

"Hi, there."

"This couple has some questions about Axel Strow and Henry Kohler," Brooks explained.

"It's a shame what happened to Henry," the elder Landon said. "But Axel . . . that was a long time ago. No use stirring all this up now. I sure as heck don't want to remember those years. Besides, we have a business to run, son. Come on. Let's get to it."

Brooks's dad backed out of the office and headed for another area of the showroom, where one of the salesmen was talking to a customer.

Brooks nodded toward his father. "He's still bitter about my mom leaving. I suppose I am, too.

She left and never looked back. I think she's in California somewhere."

"You didn't stay in touch?" Daisy asked, pushing a bit.

"My dad said there was no reason to. She betrayed us. After she left, we didn't hear from her again. At least *I* didn't. My dad had to sign the divorce papers. But like he said, that was a long time ago. We've moved on."

Life had gone on, Daisy supposed. But at what cost to a teenage boy and his dad?

Sarah Jane's Diner was a town landmark with its huge hex sign of birds on the front brick wall and a hex sign with hearts on the other side of the door. Daisy and Jonas had come to meet with Sarah Jane after the supper shift, when the restaurant was practically empty. Tonight, Sarah Jane, who was hostess as well as the managing chef, was standing at the sales counter. Strawberry-blond curls fell over her forehead and around her ears to her jaw. She was a little overweight, but she had the energy of someone much younger. Her blue gingham apron was a trademark look for her, as were her colorful sneakers, which today were red, white, and blue.

With a wide smile, she invited them, "Let's go to my office in the back. I have the catering menus printed out for you to look at."

Sarah Jane's office was tight. An L-shaped desk, a computer and printer setup, file cabinets, and pegboards hanging all over the walls above bookcases filled it. The bookcases were stuffed with cookbooks, some of them looking ancient. Corkboards with their colorful pushpins were covered with photos of her family, customers, and menus.

Sarah Jane pulled her rolling desk chair from around the back of the desk out to where two folding chairs were set up. She handed each of them a clipboard with a menu and a pen. "Without consulting each other, I want you to circle or checkmark your favorite foods. Not the foods you think should be served at your wedding reception, but your *favorites*. Then we'll go from there."

Daisy wondered if this was the process Sarah Jane went through with anyone who wanted her to cater their wedding reception. "It's going to be hot," Daisy began.

Sarah Jane swiped her hand across the room. "Don't think about that. Just think about your favorite foods. We'll talk about the heat after that."

Daisy circled *spaetzle* because she didn't make it often and she liked it. It was sort of a dumpling/noodle with nutmeg, eggs, flour, butter, and herbs. Her mom made it better than anyone she knew, but Sarah Jane's was good, too. Next, she checked egg-and-olive-salad sandwiches, as well as dandelion greens with warm bacon dressing. Some version of that was probably a possibility. She circled meatballs with pineapple glaze next. Sarah Jane's ham balls were the best. She also liked the idea of buttermilk biscuits with apple butter because Sarah Jane's chef made her own apple butter.

Try as she might to keep her mind on the menu, Daisy's head was spinning with other wedding plans. Not only that, but she was worried about the covered bridge tea that April was managing. Then there was their visit to Brooks Landon and possibly two murders twenty years apart. She could share in Beth Ann's grief even though she hadn't known Henry Kohler herself, but the picture of Axel, a hardworking, fun-loving young man tore at her heart. She truly wanted to find answers.

Sarah Jane peeked at what Daisy had circled. "You don't have a dessert circled yet."

Caught, distracted by her thoughts, Daisy looked up at Sarah Jane. "I . . . I had my mind on something else."

Jonas reached over and covered Daisy's hand with his. His was larger and stronger and all-encompassing. She loved it when he held her hand.

"Daisy and I have gotten involved in Henry Kohler's murder investigation. I think that's where her thoughts are. Not only on Henry Kohler, but on Axel Strow. Did you know the family?"

Daisy squeezed Jonas's hand, grateful he was the one to bring it up. She felt terrible because they were supposed to be discussing their wedding plans. But maybe both of them were thinking about Axel.

"I can remember when he disappeared. The police asked questions all over town, even into Paradise and Bird-In-Hand."

"Did you know the Strows?" Daisy asked Sarah Jane, giving up looking at the menu.

"No, not well. My family lived in town, and the Strows lived out on their farm. We passed by each other at the farmers market. Susan Strow had a reputation for being a good cook."

"That's what we've heard," Jonas confirmed. "Not only a good cook, but she liked to share her meals with anybody who was around."

"That's true. There was one thing I do remember about Axel."

"What?" Jonas and Daisy asked at the same time.

"He wore one of those red kerchiefs around his neck all the time. I asked him about it. He said he could pull it up and keep out the dust when he was working, especially when he was exercising the horses. It was his trademark, just like my apron," she said with a grin.

Daisy had set her purse on the floor. Now she picked it up and slid out the photo that she'd found in the chest. She showed it to Sarah Jane.

"Yep, that's the Strow family, all three of them."

Daisy stared at the photo along with Sarah Jane, who had been right about Axel. He was wearing the red kerchief. For some reason, Daisy felt that was important to know.

CHAPTER FOURTEEN

Customers at Pirated Treasures, the antiques shop where Vi worked, had to curb-park along the street. Daisy had driven there with April tonight. This store visit would be very different from her visit with Jonas yesterday to Landon's Tractor Supply.

As April opened the door to the antiques shop, a buzzer sounded.

Glancing around, April moved toward the first row of shelves. "I hope we can find what we need."

They were looking for china plates and cups, coasters, trivets, or anything else that might have a covered bridge design.

Otis Murdoch stepped from a side aisle. Seeing her, he said, "Daisy! What a treat. I haven't seen you since I stopped in for cherry tarts last month."

Otis was in his seventies. Daisy had met him when he'd been involved in a murder investigation. Otis's wispy white hair splayed over his ears. There were so many character lines on his face, she couldn't count them all. His chin, however, still had a determined point even though the skin on his neck sagged. His eyes were baby blue. Wearing a button-down white shirt with the collar open, he sported a tan cardigan sweater against the cool of the air-conditioning. He'd updated much about the shop when he'd taken on a partner. The air-conditioning was a huge improvement.

"What can we help you with today?" Otis asked.

April explained what they were looking for and why.

"Hmmm. I think my assistant can help you with that more thoroughly than I can. Vi, somebody you know is here."

Coming from the back, Vi smiled when she saw April and Daisy. "Did you just stop in for a visit?"

"No." April explained again why they were there. Then she said, "I'm printing pamphlets about the history of the covered bridge for the tea and to give out for the parade. Tessa drew the sketch of it for the cover."

Otis patted Vi's shoulder. "I'll be in the back if you need me."

"How's he doing?" Daisy asked once Otis had left the room.

"He's doing well. He's taking care of his house, and he's eating right. Keith helps with that."

Keith Rebert was Otis's partner.

Vi escorted April and Daisy to the rear of the store, where she pointed out a shelf. "I think there are coasters there and little vases. You could use them in the center of the tables."

"These are great," April said with enthusiasm as she ran her fingers over the picture of a covered bridge.

Vi asked Daisy, "Didn't Tessa do a series of paintings of the covered bridge at different times of the day? I remember the light hit it differently in the morning, at noon, and at night."

Daisy's gaze met April's. "Vi is right. Maybe Tessa would let us display those in the tea garden. What do you think?"

"That would be great. We could put one in the main room and two in the spillover tearoom," April said.

They sorted through small dishes and vases on the shelf and started picking out a few. Vi took them into her hands. "I'll put these on the counter. Keep looking. We're glad to supply anything you need."

"Who's babysitting Sammy tonight?" Daisy asked.

Vi's smile faded. "Brielle is babysitting him. Foster's working late again. He wants to show his boss his ambition and ingenuity, but he's hardly spent any time with Sammy or me in the past two weeks. I don't know what to do. And before you say *talk to him*, I already have. That doesn't seem to do any good. He has this attitude that he'll lose everything if he doesn't keep going every minute. It's unnerving for me and Sammy. Sammy watches him walk by, and Foster just gives him a pat on the head. Then he's out the door."

Wanting to restore Vi's equilibrium, Daisy commented, "Emily seems to be doing a good job with Sammy."

"She does. She plays with him the whole time she's there. What's not to like? He loves to see her come through the door. She said you stopped by to talk to her about her dad. What was that about?"

"Gavin wanted me to feel her out about something, and I did. I believe I got her thinking."

"You always do that," Vi said with a quirk of her

brow. "Maybe you're the one who should talk to Foster."

"I tried that. He wasn't any more open to me than he is to you."

"That says a lot in itself," Vi complained. "Jazzi told me Jonas suggested an intervention. Maybe that's what we need to do."

Since Daisy couldn't divert Vi's attention from what was worrying her most, she said, "Just let us know. We'll do anything you think is best."

April sidled up to Vi and pretended to whisper in her ear. "You can be grateful that she's your mom."

"Believe me, I am," Vi said. "I know you've lived on your own for a while. I admire that. Foster and I have accepted a lot of help, and I think that's what is driving him now."

That insight gave Daisy pause. Had they done too much for Vi and Foster? She wasn't sure, but she did know she'd always be there for Vi if she needed her.

Perry Russo's Insurance Agency was possibly the largest and busiest in Willow Creek. On her lunch break the next day, Daisy drew up to the office located between an accountant's practice and an exterminator's office. She had no intention of changing her auto insurance from the company she was presently with. Her agent worked by himself out of his house. Jonas had his policy with the same company. Nevertheless, Perry Russo didn't have to know anything about her intentions.

It was hard to tell how many cars were parked for the insurance company's attention because it was a public lot for all three businesses. She parked in the second line of spots, picked up her purse, and went inside.

The office was a modern space, all gray, chrome, and black, with a counter and then three cubicles over to the side. Perry Russo must have had two or three agents working under him. She knew what he looked like from his yearbook photo but also from a website photo, where he'd been front and center.

There was a young clerk behind the desk who greeted her as soon as she approached. After a glance over her shoulder, Daisy saw that two agents were in two different cubicles, giving their attention to customers.

"Hi, there," she said amiably. "I'd like to talk to Perry Russo if that's possible. I hope I don't need an appointment." From past experience, she knew face-to-face, impromptu meetings often produced the most information.

"You're in luck," the pixie-faced young woman said. "I just saw him go into his office. Let me see if he's free." Apparently, Perry had his own office away from the cubicles of the other agents.

Perry Russo was another thirty-something male with a beard. It must be the style for that age this year. He was smiling when he came from his office, and Daisy got a better look at him. He had a black anchor beard, which was pointed and traced his jawline. His black hair was curly but cropped short. His large glasses were navy with lighter-blue side pieces. Since he was wearing a pale-blue short-sleeved dress shirt with a navy striped tie and navy slacks, she guessed he was a man who took pride in his appearance.

He came to meet her in the walkway between the cubicles and the counter and extended his hand. "Hello. Shannon says you asked for me."

"My name is Daisy Swanson," she said. "I'd like to speak with you about car insurance. I'm looking for the best deal."

His grin was broad. "Let's see if I can give you the best deal. Come on into my office."

Daisy was in her work clothes—yellow Capris and a yellow-and-white polka-dotted shirt. He gave her a once-over, from her blond hair, which she'd arranged in a messy bun today, down to her white sandals.

He motioned her into his office, and she preceded him inside.

"How did you find me?" Perry asked with his most professional grin.

"Your name came up when I was speaking with friends."

"Word of mouth is the best way to engage clients," he commented. Then he took out a pen and moved a legal-sized tablet in front of him. "Now, tell me the make and model and year of your car."

"I have a Dodge Journey, 2018."

"That's a fine car," he said.

Daisy imagined he said that to everybody.

"Let me do some calculations. Do you have a few minutes?"

"Sure," Daisy responded.

In the next few minutes, Perry asked her the usual questions for a policy—whether she wanted comprehensive coverage and what deductible she was comfortable with. His fingers quickly moved over a desktop calculator. "I can plug these into the computer for a policy, but just to give you an idea of what we're talking about, I can do it faster this way." He came up with a number and told her what it was.

She frowned. "That's pretty much what I'm paying now."

"Ah, but do you get the service I could give you? My agents are on call twenty-four hours a day. If you have an accident or a claim, you don't have to dial an eight-hundred number or wait for a call back."

"Let me think about that," she told him. "But in the meantime, I wonder if I could talk to you about something else."

Behind Perry, a set of bookshelves displayed family photos, trophies, and other memorabilia. One photo was a picture of Perry and a woman around his age, along with a boy maybe ten years old.

She wasn't exactly sure how to begin with Perry, but again she thought honesty was the best way to go. "I understand you were friends with Henry Kohler and Axel Strow."

Perry's brown eyes behind the lenses of his glasses showed surprise, but his expression was stoic. "I was."

She'd been hoping he'd say more, but he didn't. So, she had to say, "I've become involved in looking into Axel's disappearance and Henry's death. Do you know Henry's wife, Beth Ann?"

As if he was resigned to the discussion since she'd brought Beth Ann into it, he nodded. "Yes, I know Beth Ann. Not well, but some of us have gotten together for barbecues and that type of thing."

"You and your group of friends from high school?"

"Sure. Sometimes we've had what you might call mini-reunions."

"Can you tell me who would come to these?" she asked.

He gave a shrug. "Brooks Landon, Mick Ehrhart, Dylan Meyer."

"So, you were all friends in high school?"

He grimaced. "As much as guys can be friends. Yeah, we tried to have each other's backs and cover for each other. Mick got into more trouble than the rest of us."

That was new information. "What kind of trouble?"

"In his late teens, he was arrested for shoplifting. I think the charges were dropped."

Teenage antics? A dare? "Did the rest of you get into any trouble?"

"Miss Swanson . . ."

"It's Mrs.," she said.

"Mrs. Swanson, I don't understand why you're involved in this."

"It's a long story, but I help the police from time to time and pick up information that they can't."

"Do you think they're going to interview me?" He didn't sound as if he liked that idea at all.

"It's possible. They've just started connecting Henry Kohler's death to Axel Strow's disappearance."

In spite of his beard covering a good part of his face, Daisy could see his frown deepen. "I don't understand how they could be doing that. Axel disappeared twenty years ago."

"New information has come to light. Can you tell me anything else about your friendship with Axel?"

"We were just guys . . . going to the same school . . . liking the same chicks. That's it." All of a sudden, Perry leaned forward in his chair and rubbed the middle of his back. "A back spasm," he said with a pained expression. "Sorry. It happens." He stood as if to soothe his muscles. "Is that all?"

She could see Perry was going to push her out. Could it have been a physical fight with Henry that caused that ache in his back? Or could the ache have come from dumping Henry's body into the creek?

"I own Daisy's Tea Garden with my aunt. I often strain my back from lifting trays." She didn't, but a little white lie wouldn't hurt.

"It's an old track injury. Then a few weeks ago, I made the mistake of skateboarding with my son. That didn't go so well. In fact, Henry was trying to convince me to go to PT. He said he had some strategies that would make it feel better. I really don't have time for lying around on a table or doing exercises. I'm just too busy."

Could it be true that Henry had tried to convince Perry to go to physical therapy? Maybe Beth Ann would know the answer to that one.

It was almost six when Daisy parked at the freestanding building on Market Street. Jonas was working on their gazebo on his friend's property. She'd stayed at the tea garden to catch up on paperwork till five forty-five, knowing that Beth Ann Kohler got off work at six. Daisy had texted her and asked if they could meet after work. She went inside the dental office, thinking she'd sit in the waiting room until Beth Ann was finished for the day.

All was quiet in the office until she saw Beth Ann walking toward her from the hallway, sweater over her arm, purse in hand. Beth Ann was dressed in what Daisy presumed was the dental office's uniform—navy slacks and a flowered scrub shirt. Though Beth Ann conjured up a wan smile, Daisy noticed how tired she looked. Grief could do that.

"How are you doing?" Daisy asked her.

"I came back to work hoping it would take my mind off everything, but it might be too soon. I'm off again tomorrow for a long weekend. I decided to have a memorial service for Henry next month when I bury his ashes. I couldn't handle it now. That will give me time to assemble photographs and ask his friends to give eulogies. How about if we walk to the frozen yogurt shop? I need to stretch my legs."

If Beth Ann needed time to pull herself together, a service in a month made sense.

The yogurt shop was about two blocks down Market Street. "Having yogurt for supper?" Daisy asked with a grin.

"That sounds good, don't you think? Maybe I can get a banana split with nuts and count them as protein."

Beth Ann was trying for levity, and Daisy went along with it, knowing their talk would turn serious soon enough.

As they began walking, Beth Ann took several deep breaths of the evening air.

After half a block in silence, Daisy decided to stay quiet and let Beth Ann vent or express free-form thoughts if she wanted to.

Beth Ann asked, "Do you have more questions for me about Henry?"

"Do you mind?" Daisy asked.

"Not if they get you some answers. When I signed my statement, the detective collected my DNA. I'm sure they'll call me back again. They as much as said they would."

Taking a spouse's DNA was standard procedure, as was locking in their story to see if it remained consistent. "I have a feeling they're busy with other interview subjects. I'd like to ask you about Henry's friends."

"Henry was friendly with everybody."

"I'm more interested in his friendship with the guys he went to school with."

"At college?"

"No. I mean high school. Did he have a present relationship with Brooks Landon?"

Beth Ann stopped walking as she thought about the question. "Henry bought a lawn tractor from Landon's Tractor Supply. I think Brooks was the one who sold it to him. But as far as much other contact, I don't think so."

"How about Perry Russo?"

Beth Ann shrugged and began walking again. "We have our auto insurance through Perry. I think Henry and Perry went to a few Orioles games to-gether. They were both baseball buffs. We went to a barbecue in the spring, and Perry and his wife and son were there. Come to think of it, Brooks Landon was, too, along with Dylan Meyer. Henry was better friends with Mick Ehrhart. They met now and then at Bases to watch games together and have a beer."

Bases was the town's go-to sports bar.

"Mick came over to the house now and then. Last fall he helped Henry split wood for winter."

"So, Perry's married, but Brooks and Mick aren't?"

"I don't know about Brooks but Mick has never married. Actually, he offered to help me with yard work if I need it since Henry's gone. Does any of this help?"

"I'm not sure. I do think I'd like to talk to Mick Ehrhart, though. Maybe Dylan, too. I want to get a feel for all the men in their group. That's hard to do with just a few questions."

They'd reached the yogurt shop. Daisy opened the door, and Beth Ann preceded her inside. No other customers stood at the counter.

"A banana split," Beth Ann told the clerk, as if just the idea of the treat could make her feel better.

Daisy hoped it could.

CHAPTER FIFTEEN

The following morning, Beth Ann's text was fortuitous because Daisy had taken the day off to run errands for the wedding—a stop at Sarah Jane's for up-front payment for the reception, an appointment at the flower shop to firm up colors for her wedding bouquet and the bridesmaids' bouquets, and a visit to the jewelers to pick up a wedding present for Jonas, a watch engraved with *Now and Always—Daisy*. The gazebo was his gift to her, and she wanted to give him something meaningful and lasting . . . besides a wedding ring.

When Daisy's phone beeped, Beth Ann's text read—*Mick Ehrhart is at my house now if you want to talk to him.*

Finishing up at the jewelers, Daisy texted back—*I'm on my way.*

Beth Ann had told Daisy she was taking off today to do some fix-up chores around the house. The ranch-style house was located in an older part of Willow Creek on Sycamore Avenue. Daisy pulled in to the short, concrete driveway and couldn't help but stare.

Mick Ehrhart, if that's who she was witnessing trimming Beth Ann's front-yard shrubs, was a fine specimen of manhood. Maybe not quite as fine as Jonas, she corrected herself swiftly, but fine nonetheless. He was shirtless as he worked using a gas-powered hedge cutter to trim boxwoods that were peeking up over what Daisy presumed was the living room's front picture window.

Leaving her purse in the car—this would probably be a short visit—she exited her Journey and headed for the front walk.

Beth Ann met her on the porch as Mick switched off the loud, buzzing machine.

Beth Ann was carrying what looked like a tall glass of lemonade, and she handed it to Mick, who set the hedge trimmer on the ground, swiped the sweat from his brow, and gladly took it. The look he gave Beth Ann was caring, and his quirk of a smile was . . . affectionate.

After he took a few swallows, he turned his attention to Daisy. "Hi, I'm Mick. Beth Ann said you'd like to talk to me about Henry."

"Would you like a glass of lemonade?" Beth Ann asked Daisy.

"No thanks, I'm good. Thanks for texting."

"I want answers, too," Beth Ann reminded her.

Beth Ann and Mick exchanged a look that told Daisy there was a connection between them. Merely friendship?

Daisy leaned against the porch railing, hoping to make this conversation casual. "I do want to talk to you about Henry and your friendship with him." She nodded to Beth Ann, who'd just gone inside. "Are you and Beth Ann friends?"

Mick ran his hand down his long, handsome

face and then raked it through his dark-brown
hair, which was swept to the side. Sweat glistened
on his biceps and the chest hair that swept down to
the middle of his six-pack. His brown eyes, almost
black, were clear and direct as he sighed. "We are.
I've been attracted to Beth Ann since I met her.
But it took me longer to grow up than Henry. He
dated her first, got engaged, and married her.
Henry always knew what he wanted. He went after
Beth Ann with single-minded purpose the same
way he went after his career. I've heard people say
he was the best physical therapist in Willow Creek."

"Which people are they?" Daisy asked, half serious and half joking.

"I'm a personal trainer. I have clients who
overdo it or hurt themselves, and they need PT to
get back to what they want to be."

"So, you recommended clients to Henry?"

"I did, but often I didn't need to because they'd
already heard he was great with sports medicine as
well as with elderly folks. Henry was a perfectionist. He did whatever he did with purpose and one
hundred percent accuracy."

"I'm not sure how that fits in with him getting
murdered," Daisy said, hoping to prompt Mick
into something more personal about Henry.

"I don't either," Mick admitted. "This whole
thing is crazy." He looked toward the house again.
"And don't think I'm going to go after Beth Ann
now. She needs time to grieve."

After a pause, Daisy asked, "So, you and Henry
were good friends in high school?"

"We were. We often rode our bikes up to the old
quarry to get away from adults and just be kids. We
even believed we could solve the world's problems

before it ended with Y2K. Then we laughed when it didn't."

"Tell me about Axel," Daisy invited.

"Beth Ann told me you're looking into his disappearance, too."

"I am, and so are the detectives. They think Axel's disappearance and Henry's murder might be connected. What do you think?"

"I don't know. It doesn't seem possible, but Henry was obviously involved in something that got him killed—if it *was* murder."

"It was," Daisy confirmed.

Mick shook his head and drank the rest of his lemonade. Then he set the glass on the porch floor. "You wanted to know about Axel. Everybody thought he was just a farm boy, but that wasn't true. Axel was smart. I mean, whip smart. He once set off one of those rocket ships in the barnyard, and his dad had a fit. He read whatever he could get his hands on. I think he even believed in life on other planets. You know Axel ran track, too."

"How did he manage that with all his farm chores?"

"He was motivated. There was this girl who lived on a nearby farm, the property adjacent to Axel's dad's."

"Stephanie Gallant?"

"Yeah, I think that was her name. She often did chores for him. His dad told him he could run the races if he could get his work done, too. He did somehow, even if he had to stay out there until midnight mucking stalls."

Daisy revealed, "I spoke with Stephanie. She said she was too young for Axel then, but she had a crush on him."

Mick picked up branches that had fallen from trimming the shrubs. "We all knew that. Stephanie hung around him as much as she could. He wasn't interested in dating anyone as far as I could tell. I had a different girlfriend every month. But Axel went home to study or do chores. I really think he wanted to become an astronaut."

Since Mick seemed to understand Henry and Axel well, and he was forthcoming, she asked, "How well did you know Perry and Brooks?"

"We all knew Brooks was being groomed to take over his dad's business someday. I don't know how happy he was with the idea he'd be tied down to the tractor store. I got the impression he wanted to travel. In fact, after high school he spent a year backpacking around Europe. But then he came back, took some business courses, and started working at the store."

"And Perry?"

"Perry never knew what he wanted to do. He was one of those kids who thought the world began and ended with athletics. But he got injured in college and somehow, he ended up in the insurance business. He's been a success, that's for sure. You should see his house. When he had the barbecue there, we were all impressed. Actually, I think that's why he invited us."

"To show off?"

"You could say so."

"What about Dylan Meyer?"

"Dylan always traveled the straight and narrow. He didn't pal around with us much. In some ways, the way we were as teenagers followed us through until now." Mick stopped gathering branches. "Tell

me something, Daisy. Are we all suspects because
we knew both Axel and Henry?"

"To be honest with you, Mick, anyone who knew
the victim . . . or victims . . . is a suspect until they
aren't."

Mick's eyes widened as if he'd never expected to
be considered a suspect. Was that mock-surprise?
Was he telling her all this so she wouldn't put him
on a suspect list?

With almost a scowl, he looked toward the interior of the house again. "Does befriending Beth
Ann now make me more of a target for the cops?"

"It could."

"Tough. I'm not going to quit when she
needs me."

What if Mick killed Henry so he could have his
wife? Daisy wondered. Rivals for love instead of
friends? Maybe Mick had decided his own happiness was as important as Henry's.

So, how did Axel fit into that?

Maybe he didn't.

"There's a reason we should talk to Callum
Abernathy," Jonas had decided when Daisy stopped
at Woods after her talk with Mick. "We'll need a
roofer for the workshop."

Daisy had discussed with Jonas everything she'd
learned from Mick Ehrhart . . . including how
he'd picked up the hedge trimmer once more to
indicate their conversation was over. Jonas had
suggested they talk to the roofer who'd had a beef
with Henry.

Together they headed for the roofer's office. It
was hardly an office, more like a warehouse with

roofing supplies. In a corner of it, there was a metal desk that was scarred and scraped. On the side door of the warehouse, an OPEN sign hung in the window.

Daisy and Jonas headed for that, not knowing how this interview would go. They could come away with a roofer . . . or with a suspect.

Jonas opened the door, and Daisy walked inside.

The smell of roofing supplies was strong in the air—rubber, vinyl, maybe even plastic. Some wood smells, too. Daisy was aware of all of them as the man at the scarred desk stood and faced them.

Beth Ann had described Callum Abernathy to Daisy, and he was easy to recognize—his wild, coarse blond hair, beard, and beefy arms. He seemed to be in his forties and was about five-eight, but he was broad and stocky with a bit of a beer belly. His tan T-shirt was patterned with black block letters stating ABERNATHY ROOFING.

"Can I help you?" he asked with a practiced smile that was hard to see in between his mustache and full beard. Jonas introduced himself and Daisy. To be clear, Jonas asked, "Are you Callum Abernathy?"

"The one and only," he said with a grimace. "What do you need? A roof? Vinyl siding?"

Jonas gave a look around the warehouse, seeing that it was well stocked.

"Daisy and I are building a workshop in back of our house." Jonas gave him the rough dimensions. "Have you ever worked with Gavin Cranshaw?"

"Sure, I know Gavin. From what I hear, he hardly has time to breathe. I think he added another crew. He's doing good."

"We're in-laws with Gavin, and he's going to be handling the construction on the workshop."

"So, why'd you come to me? These contractors usually have their own people they work with. Sure, I've worked with Gavin, but not regularly. And not since my business has been going downhill."

"Downhill?" Jonas asked, prompting a bit.

Callum backed up to his desk and leaned against it. "Yeah, downhill. I have a bum leg. I can't crawl up on the roof and supervise anymore, let alone work."

"What happened?" Daisy asked.

"I had a fall from a ladder. Surgery went okay, but the physical therapist botched my treatment. This work is my livelihood. Unless we're doing that workshop soon, I don't even know if I'll be in business in six months."

Jonas commiserated, telling Callum that he had his own shop, Woods, and that Daisy owned Daisy's Tea Garden.

"So, you two know how businesses work. When you can't be right there all the time, watching everybody who works for you, things can happen. Mistakes happen."

"Can I ask you who your physical therapist was?" she asked.

Callum's eyes darted here and there, and he was having trouble meeting hers. He obviously didn't want to answer her question. Finally he did. "Henry Kohler was my physical therapist."

"We really do need a roofer. But in addition, I'm trying to find out information on who wanted to kill Henry," she confided. "Do you have any ideas about that?"

He straightened from the desk and put his hand up as if he was pushing them away. "I knew the likes of you wouldn't come in here asking me to do your roof. Get out."

"We're just looking for the facts, Mr. Abernathy. We don't want to get anyone in trouble." Taking a last shot, Daisy asked, "Did you know the Strow family, particularly Axel Strow?"

Callum took a few steps toward them. "Out," he said, pointing to the door. "I don't have to talk to you, and I'm not going to. If you don't leave, I'll phone the police and tell them you're trespassing."

Jonas lightly touched Daisy's elbow, and she knew what that meant. Further talk with Callum Abernathy would only enrage him. If it was that easy for him to react out of anger, he was definitely another suspect for her list.

CHAPTER SIXTEEN

When Jonas appeared in front of the Victorian in a courting buggy, Daisy laughed. He'd said he had a surprise for her and was taking care of transportation to the covered bridge for today's parade and celebration.

She'd expected maybe a convertible borrowed from a friend.

She descended the steps from the tea garden, and he smiled at her with so much affection and love her heart tripled its rhythm.

Standing, still holding the reins, he waved dramatically at the buggy. "Your ride, ma'am."

The two-seater, open, horse-drawn buggy was usually given to a young Amish man when he was ready to court a girl in preparation for marriage—hence the name "courting buggy." It was fashioned with a bench seat for two occupants. Daisy recognized the horse pulling this buggy. It was Rachel's Standardbred, Brownie.

Jonas resumed his seat and offered his hand to Daisy as she stepped into the buggy. "What do you think?" Jonas's black hair blew in the breeze.

She brushed her own hair away from her face and said, "I think it's romantic."

They were both wearing jeans today and T-shirts that said in white print on red—*COVERED BRIDGE 100 YEARS.*

Teasing, he brushed his shoulder against hers and admitted, "We might have to buy a courting buggy if you think it's romantic. We could clomp the back roads, stargaze, neck."

"Sounds good," she said with a laugh. And it did. They should make every day of their marriage special if they could.

At the next intersection, Jonas joined up with other buggies, horses and riders, and vehicles decorated in red, white, and blue celebrating the covered bridge's anniversary.

"I think the whole town has come out for the celebration." Jonas nodded at the tourists and residents of Willow Creek standing along Market Street.

"All the seats for the tea are sold out. This is the first time I'm not going to be there when we have a special tea."

"I admire you, Daisy, for letting April plan the tea and trusting her to make sure it all runs smoothly. After all, Iris will be at the bridge, too."

Daisy lifted her phone. "I'm ready to answer anything April wants to ask me. Hopefully there won't be any problems. Or if there are, she'll be confident enough to handle them. Cora Sue and Tessa have her back."

Along their drive, Daisy and Jonas commented on the sights, pointed out people they knew, and simply enjoyed their buggy ride on this beautiful summer day. Although the sun was hot on their heads, Daisy couldn't think of a place she'd rather be.

"Did you see Luke Fisher and his girl in his courting buggy?" Jonas asked her.

"I missed them. Maybe we'll catch up at the covered bridge."

"I spoke to him for a while when I fetched Brownie. He'll be committing to his faith this fall. I doubt if wedding banns will be far behind."

"He's so young," Daisy commented. "But I was young, too. Still, I hope Jazzi waits until she finishes college to even think about marriage."

"Do you think she and Mark will last?"

"At separate schools, it's hard to tell."

"She might be a career woman," Jonas noted.

"She might, and that's okay, too."

Jonas reached over and took her hand in his.

Though a buggy was a slower means of transportation, the ride to the covered bridge seemed to be a short one. In no time at all, they were stepping out of the buggy and watching the spectacle unfold before them. Amelia and her husband had opened a field where everyone who brought their cars could park. They also had erected temporary hitching posts, where horses and buggies and single riders could hitch their horses. Daisy suspected the ceremony itself would last about a half hour until the mayor said remarks and presented the plaque that would be hammered onto the covered bridge. There were makeshift stands with canopies all around the area selling items for the day. The scene was quite a melée of people and merchandise.

Daisy and Jonas were standing by the buggy in

the field when she pointed to somebody. "There's Brooks Landon and his dad."

Suddenly Bob Weaver was standing beside Daisy. "Hi there," he said. "Hot day for this." He was wiping sweat off his brow.

"It is. But people love to come out for a celebration."

"I noticed you have your eyes on Brooks."

She introduced the two men, then said to Jonas, "I talked to Bob at the farmers market about Axel."

"You can't stop thinking about Axel, can you?" Bob eyed her with a wise man's eyes.

"You're right. I can't stop thinking about Axel."

Bob adjusted his cap and nodded to Brooks's dad. "He was hard on his son. He expected Brooks to win every track competition. But Axel, Brooks, Perry, and Dylan Meyer were competitive. That's what made their team of track runners great. There are lots of trophies for them in the case at the high school."

"I spotted trophies in Brooks's dad's office at the tractor supply and in Perry Russo's office."

Bob nodded as if he expected no less. "Those boys were proud of what they accomplished."

The mayor tested the microphone and spoke through the temporary sound system that had been set up. He welcomed everyone to the celebration, then motioned for Amelia Wiseman to come to the mike. "This woman is the one who set all this up. If it weren't for her, this covered bridge would be falling apart."

At the mike, Amelia spoke a few words and then showed the plaque that would be soon attached to the covered bridge.

Daisy leaned close to Jonas. "I see Bart over there. I'm going to talk to him for a few minutes." Bart Cosner was a patrol officer who was handling some of the crowd today.

"Do you think he'll tell you anything?"

"I can hope."

Bart had become her friend over the years. Once in a while he let something slip about an investigation the department was handling. She sidled up next to him. "Are you going to buy a T-shirt?"

He noticed hers and smiled. "Maybe . . . as a souvenir. My wife wants one."

"Are you just handling horse-and-buggy traffic, or are you keeping your eye on anyone in particular?"

"I'm keeping my eye on several people, many of whom Trevor Lundquist mentioned on his podcast."

"Where is the investigation headed? Are you still concentrating on Henry's murder?"

"Easy, Swanson, you know I can't tell you particulars."

"But you and the detectives want me to spill all the particulars that I find out about."

"That's true," he responded with no remorse. "I *will* tell you this. Zeke and Morris are more certain that Henry's murder and Axel's disappearance are connected. You were right about that. And one of Henry's friends has been cleared."

"Which one?" She hoped Bart would at least give her that much.

"Dylan Meyer. He was at a business meeting, and there's videotape with a time stamp."

Amelia was still speaking to the crowd. Perry Russo passed nearby with a can of beer in his hand, then stopped to talk to Brooks.

Daisy prompted Bart. "Have you spoken to them?"

"We've tried," Bart admitted. "Other than Meyer, none of them are happy about it, especially not Perry Russo."

"What do you mean?"

"He hired a lawyer, and he won't give us any useful information. Apparently, he's forgotten that he was ever friends with Henry and Axel. If that isn't suspicious, I don't know what is."

Was Bart right about that? Did Perry's actions put him in direct confrontation with the detectives? Bart was concentrating more thoroughly on him now. The question was—did Perry know something about Axel's disappearance and Henry's murder . . . or was he just protecting himself because he *could*?

Daisy had to admit she couldn't wait to see how the celebration tea was proceeding at the tea garden. Jonas dropped her off and took the courting buggy back to Rachel's farm.

Daisy walked in the front door instead of going through the back, simply to get a taste of the atmosphere. April was standing between two tables of six in the spillover tearoom, animatedly talking to their guests. Daisy always thought of them as "guests" rather than "customers." Cora Sue was overseeing service in the spillover tearoom along with April. Tamlyn and Ruth Zook's daughters, who often helped with service during Daisy's specialty teas, were busy in the main tearoom. She didn't see Ned but imagined he might be outside on the patio.

After she waved to Tamlyn, she went out there. Outside, she heard Ned's guitar. He was standing at the far side of the patio in a puffy-sleeved shirt and buckskin trousers strumming. It was nice background music along with birdsong. She brushed past the pots of herbs, and the scent of rosemary and thyme followed her. Stopping to say hello to regular customers, she waved to Ned.

Soon Jazzi came out from the side door to the tearoom with a tray of mini sandwiches and scones mounted on the tiered plate. She nodded at her mom as she went to a table for four, carefully setting out the glasses of iced tea and the tray of savory as well as sweet treats. Daisy was debating which table she'd approach first when Trevor came running out to the patio from around the side of the building. He looked upset, maybe even stricken.

Daisy didn't know what to expect, but she didn't want to disturb her clientele. She pointed Trevor to the path that led to the creek and met him there. "What's wrong?" she asked, because obviously something was.

"You need to have a talk with Zeke Willet." Trevor's face reddened with his words.

"Why would I do that?"

"Maybe Jonas should," he mumbled.

"Trevor, if you don't tell me what's wrong, I can't understand what the problem is."

"Zeke Willet accosted me at the newspaper office and practically threatened me."

Daisy doubted that. Zeke could be tough, but

she didn't think he'd threaten Trevor. "What did he threaten you with?"

"He told me they could hit me with an obstruction-of-justice charge."

"I've been threatened with that, too, not on this case, but on others. If they feel you're impeding the investigation, they have cause. You know they do."

"I'm not going to listen to him," Trevor said stubbornly. "Tessa thinks I should, but I'm not going to. I'm going to solve this case before they do. In fact, I'm releasing another podcast today. You won't believe how many comments I'm getting now. Sponsors are signing up. With the tourists this weekend, my podcasts should have even more listeners because word will get around among the celebration crowd."

"How do you think you're going to solve this case sooner than the police might?" Sometimes Trevor's tactics worried her.

"I get information first. I have callers who are telling me things."

"Exactly what things?" She could hardly believe they were standing here talking about murder with the scent of mown grass and a patio full of customers nearby. But this was Trevor. She had to deal with him, or he'd follow her wherever she went to say what was on his mind.

"I had a caller tell me that Axel's crowd used to hang around the abandoned quarry. When I told Zeke that, he looked as if I'd turned a switch on. I think he's going to go check it out. He stopped threatening me after that. I think he finally realizes the calls I'm getting are going to help him *and* me."

The abandoned quarry was now a lake with

fencing surrounding it and warnings posted. The kids these days, through a program at school, were warned not to go near it. The water was so cold that hypothermia was instantaneous if someone dove in . . . or fell in.

Was Zeke going to check it out because of the old crime or the new one? Maybe he'd simply given Trevor the impression he would check it out to redirect Trevor's attention. Knowing Trevor, however, Daisy suspected he wouldn't be easily redirected unless a new lead came in.

Did she hope it would . . . or hope it wouldn't?

CHAPTER SEVENTEEN

Standing by the vegetable garden that evening, Daisy and Jonas surveyed their backyard.

Jonas pointed to the area to the right of the vegetable garden. "I looked into canopies, and we could set up four back here easily or . . . would you rather have one huge tent?"

The summer day had cooled into evening. Swallows dove into the grass and soared above them over and over again. Right now, the yellow pompom marigolds bloomed along the edge of the garden while smaller rust and orange ones dotted the ground between tomato, zucchini, and pepper plants. The scent of grass, the sight of blue sky streaked with shadows of pink, the presence of Jonas beside her gave Daisy an emotional punch that almost brought tears to her eyes. Imagining their wedding and reception seemed like a dream.

When she didn't answer, Jonas immediately wrapped his arm around her shoulders as if he understood. Finally, she managed, "I think I'd like one big tent so our friends and family can mingle better."

"One big tent it is," Jonas agreed. "And white

wood chairs for the ceremony. After the ceremony, I have a couple of friends who will reposition them around the tables under the tent."

Daisy had turned toward the cement slab, picturing the gazebo that would be delivered there, when Mick Ehrhart came from the garage side of the property to the backyard.

Daisy spotted him first and said to Jonas, "That's Mick Ehrhart."

"Did you ask him to stop by?" Jonas asked her.

She shook her head, wondering why Mick had come. Had her talk with him at Beth Ann's raised questions for him? Was he trying to alleviate any of her thoughts that he could be involved in Henry Kohler's murder?

Mick was wearing a brown V-neck T-shirt with olive cargo shorts and black running shoes. He looked as if he'd just had a shower, and his wet hair was swiped to the side.

He gave them a slight unsure smile. "I don't mean to barge in, but I have something I'd like to show you." He'd addressed Daisy.

Daisy introduced Jonas to Mick. After she did, Jonas asked him, "Did you go to the front door first?"

Daisy suspected Jonas was trying to gauge Mick's forthrightness. Both of their phones would have sounded alerts if Mick had done that. They hadn't received any alerts.

"I didn't," Mick said. "I suspected you might be outside on a night like this."

"We have security back here, too," Jonas warned him, pointing to the eaves and the cameras over the patio.

"Noted," Mick said.

Apparently, Jonas was trying to determine if

Mick had been back here . . . or at the garage . . . the night Jonas had chased off an intruder.

After shifting back and forth on his sneakers, Mick took something out of one of his pockets. "I wanted to show you these."

They looked like photographs, and Daisy was eager to see them.

"I know Daisy is looking into Axel's disappearance as well as Henry's murder. I don't believe any of our gang had anything to do with either."

"That's easy to say." Jonas had his cop face on. "But that doesn't mean it's true."

Mick handed over the photos, two to Jonas and two to Daisy. "Henry had scanned these photos onto his computer a few months before he was murdered."

"How do you know that?" Daisy asked.

"Henry and I had gotten together at the sports bar Bases after work one night. After I showed him these, he took them along, told me he was going to scan them. He returned the photos to me a couple days later."

Had someone stolen Henry's computer because of these photographs? What about the originals that Mick held? Not important in *his* hands? If not, why not?

Daisy studied the two photos that she held carefully. The pictures depicted the boys on a farm, hamming it up for the camera.

Mick pointed to the two Jonas held. "Axel's mom took those."

"Where is this?" Jonas asked, pointing to the one in Daisy's hand.

"That's near the abandoned quarry before it was fenced."

Daisy made a comment about that particular photo. "Perry isn't in the picture."

"Perry took that one with Axel's mom's camera."

Daisy examined every detail of the four photos. Axel was wearing the red kerchief others had talked about. As she examined the photo more carefully, she noticed something hanging from Axel's belt.

"Do you know what this is?" she asked Mick.

"Sure. That was a compass given to Axel by his mother. He never went anywhere without it."

Daisy considered it, and the feeling of déjà vu came over her. Exploring every avenue, she asked, "Were you on the track team?"

"No, I wasn't. I had to work, not play sports. My mom and I had to scrimp for every penny to survive."

As a detective, Daisy assumed Jonas had never beaten around the bush. He didn't now. Staring at Mick, he said, "Tell me about the shoplifting charge."

"You did a background check?" Mick asked.

Jonas just shrugged, not revealing if he had done it or someone else had.

Mick's shoulders slumped a bit, and he didn't say anything for a few moments. Then he looked at Jonas and must have decided he might as well give it up. "The charge was dropped because my boss at the convenience store stood up for me. He said I could pay it back with the extra hours I was going to work."

"What I don't know is what you stole. What was it?" Jonas asked.

"It was a coat for my mom. She didn't have a winter coat, and she needed one."

"Needed one?" Daisy asked.

"She often went dumpster diving at night, even in the winter. She found things we could sell or use and food that was thrown out because no one had bought it."

Jonas gave Mick another once-over. "Is your mom still alive?"

"She is," Mick said, his shoulders going straighter. "And I buy her a new coat every winter."

After a bit more discussion about the photographs, Mick said, "You can hold on to those for a while if you need them. Show them to the cops. I don't care. I don't want to talk to the detectives any more than I have to."

"Understood," Jonas said. "I'll see that these get returned to you."

After Mick left and they heard his car rev up near the garage, Daisy asked Jonas, "What do you think?"

"I'm not sure. Either he's protesting too much or else he was a kid who turned his life around. We can hope it was the latter."

Dinner at Daisy's parents' house on Sunday was a monthly occurrence. She and Jonas walked up the path to her childhood home with Felix trotting beside them.

Hot-pink wave petunias bloomed along the walk. Rocket snapdragons in shades of purple and yellow circled bushlike bee balm blooming with pink blossoms. The scents of roses—rich red Chrysler Imperial, dark-pink McCartney, and yellow tipped with peach Peace conveyed the care Daisy's mom took pruning the bushes. Yellow and red knockout roses formed a border of sorts between the Gallaghers' property and their neighbors. The riot of color visibly spelled summer for Daisy, both in her childhood and in the present.

"Your mom probably has more wedding plans for us. She might want to go over the menu again."

"That's her way of showing us she cares."

Jonas touched Daisy's elbow to halt their progress. "Your mom doesn't feel as if she's doing enough."

"I don't know how to convince her I forgive her for everything that happened when I was little. It's not as if I didn't have plenty of support from Dad and Aunt Iris."

Jonas's expression conveyed his understanding. Aware of what had happened between Daisy and her mother, he had seen their story play out and the healing begin.

When Daisy thought about her childhood with her mom and her sister, Camellia, those years still produced a measure of sadness. Circumstances of the causes and emotional distance from her mother and sister hadn't come to light until Violet had given birth to Sammy and experienced postpartum depression. Rose had revealed to Daisy that she'd experienced postpartum issues, too, for a year after Daisy had been born. She hadn't experienced it after Camellia had been delivered, and the doctors back then hadn't been in tune with a new mother's issues, emotions, and hormones.

For that first year of Daisy's life, Rose hadn't bonded with her second-born. Daisy's dad and her aunt had taken up the slack, but that lack of bonding had led to an insurmountable distance between Daisy and her mom. Rose had favored Cammie and had a strong bond with her. But for years, Daisy and her mom had seemed at odds. In college,

Daisy had been eager to leave Willow Creek permanently for a life with her new husband in Florida.

When Violet had experienced such a rough time after Sammy was born, Rose had come forward to share her experiences, in part because she'd wanted Vi to have a bonded, loving relationship with her son . . . and because Rose had wanted to mend her relationship with Daisy and start over.

They had . . . slowly. Now they were in such a better place.

"I'm so glad you and Mom have a good relationship now," Daisy said to Jonas.

At first, Rose hadn't approved of Daisy dating Jonas. She'd believed he'd lacked ambition. But her opinion of him had slowly changed. She'd come to realize Jonas was a man who would love and protect Daisy until his dying breath.

"I had to grow on her—like one of her plants."

His tone was so wry, Daisy laughed.

As they climbed the steps to the front door, she said, "Jazzi texted me that she'll be here later. A shipment of cruise wear came in, and she had to sort it."

Jonas nodded as if that made perfect sense.

Rose had opened the inside door before Daisy could open the storm door. Daisy noticed immediately her mom's ash-brown-blond hair had seen a recent cut. She was wearing her favorite shade of pink lipstick. Her blue-and-yellow-flowered short-sleeved chiffon blouse seemed a little dressy for a family dinner, but it looked cool. Her slacks were powder blue.

Rose gave Daisy a giant hug. "Come in. Get out of the heat."

The day had been a hot one, hitting ninety degrees. Daisy had worn mint-green shorts and a

mint-and-yellow floral blouse. She'd fastened her
hair in a topknot with jade hoops on her ears that
Jonas had given her for Christmas. Cognac-colored
gladiator-style leather sandals graced her feet.

As her mother propelled her into the living room
and Felix dashed in beside her, Daisy suddenly regis-
tered the number of women there. She'd hardly
taken a breath before they all yelled, "Surprise!"

All the women whom Daisy loved and admired
were gathered in her childhood home. There was
something heart-tugging and extraordinary about
that. Her gaze traveled around the room from her
aunt Iris to Tessa to Vi, Jazzi, and Emily. She took
in the presence of Rachel, April, Tamlyn, Cora Sue,
Eva, and even Sarah Jane. Glorie Beck propped on
her cane and her granddaughter, Brielle, beamed
at Daisy. Brielle's mother, Nola, stood beside her.
Her mother had even thought to invite Adele,
Felix's original mom, as well as Amelia Wiseman.
Overwhelmed by the show of friendship, Daisy
gasped when her sister, Cammie, appeared from
the kitchen, calling her own "Surprise!"

Daisy went around the room hugging them all,
brushing tears away. "I didn't expect this," she said
to her mom as she came back to her.

"That's exactly why we wanted to do it for you.
Come sit at the table, and we'll bring out your cupcake cake."

Just then, Iris carried a huge white wicker tray
from the kitchen. A layer of cupcakes was iced to
resemble one huge sheet cake. *CONGRATULATIONS*
was written in script across the top in blue icing.
Beneath that, each cupcake was decorated like a
daisy with yellow centers and white petals on a
background of blue.

"It's gorgeous," Daisy said, her voice thick with emotion.

"And easy to serve, too," Cammie offered.

"Sarah Jane made it," Iris revealed. "And there are other snacks in the kitchen. Come on, everyone, let's eat and chat, then Daisy can open her presents."

A card table had been positioned next to the sofa. Presents wrapped in blue, white, and silver were stacked high.

Jonas touched Daisy's elbow. "Felix and I are going to drive to Four Paws and visit. We'll be back for you later."

Whenever he could, Jonas volunteered at Four Paws Animal Shelter. He'd adopted Felix from there.

"I can catch a ride home with Tessa," Daisy said.

"You might want to stay after everybody leaves, to talk with Cammie."

He was right about that. She wouldn't see her sister again until the wedding, and then they might not find time to talk.

Jonas leaned in and kissed Daisy. She felt a little dizzy as he stepped away.

"Save me a cupcake," he quipped, then left the bevy of women.

In the midst of sampling triangles of chicken-salad sandwiches, cucumber sandwiches, mini–asparagus quiches with pancetta, and chocolate truffles, Emily took a seat beside Daisy. "Are you nervous?"

Daisy laughed. "I think I'm too excited to be nervous. Why?"

"Foster told me once he was shaking in his shoes during his wedding."

Daisy laughed. "I hope I won't be. I hope we all just have a really enjoyable night."

Daisy migrated around the room again for a while, talking with everyone even if in a short conversation. She was grateful they had all taken the time to come, including Rachel, who mostly just attended her district's gatherings.

Adele said to her, "I'm so glad you invited me. It's nice to get out to a party and see somebody other than folks in my retirement community."

"I hope you'll enjoy the wedding, too. And you can come visit me whenever you want. Jonas or I can pick you up and bring you over."

"Or I can," Iris offered, overhearing.

After Daisy spent a few minutes with Glorie, Brielle, and Nola, Nola took her aside. "I listen to Trevor Lundquist's podcasts. Interesting stuff there. I understand the detectives are questioning a lot of people."

"Anyone who was involved with Henry Kohler and all of Axel Strow's old friends."

Nola seemed to debate with herself for a moment. And then she made a decision. "Our law firm is representing two of them." After Nola's divorce, she had joined another area law firm. She and her husband had been partners, and the breakup had been difficult. But now she was settled again.

"Two of them?" Daisy asked.

"They aren't my clients. I don't handle criminal law. They've been quite vocal in their complaints about the detectives. It's public knowledge they're being represented by our firm."

"Let me guess," Daisy said. "Brooks Landon is one of them."

"You guessed right. Perry Russo is the other."

"The detectives are just doing their jobs," Daisy said.

"I figured as much," Nola agreed. "But both men have egos to protect. They're both prominent in the community."

"I've spoken to both of them," Daisy said. "They were fairly open with me, but I didn't press too hard, and I'm sure the detectives did and will."

"You be careful," Nola warned her.

"I will. I'm not going to do anything to jeopardize getting married in less than two weeks."

For the next hour or so, Daisy sat on the sofa and opened presents. The women in her life had decided on a theme—flowers. All her gifts somehow revolved around them. She received aromatherapy essential oils in rose and lavender, pillowcases embroidered with bluebells, daisy-embossed potholders, a trivet in the shape of a hydrangea, and pressed-flower coasters. The next surprise was Tessa's present, which she carried in from the den—a set of TV tables each painted with assorted flowers—irises, daisies, camellias, violets, and jasmine.

"Beautiful!" Daisy exclaimed. "I can't believe you took all that time to paint these for me."

"It's helped me get back into painting again," Tessa said. "I've missed it. There's nothing better than painting a gift for someone you love."

Daisy hugged her best friend, so thankful they'd stayed friends all these years.

Jazzi and Vi together presented their mom with a vase engraved with the wedding date. Jazzi said, "And we want you to use it, not just let it sit around looking pretty."

"You know I will. I like to bring in fresh flowers."

Camellia was next. She handed Daisy a bottle of expensive wine for her wedding night. "It's rosé, so I kept with the flower theme," she said with a chuckle.

"It's just right. I know Jonas and I will enjoy it. We'll have the whole night to ourselves before we leave for the Grand Canyon the next day."

"Are you flying to Phoenix?" Cammie asked.

"Yes, and then driving up through Sedona to Flagstaff. There's a B and B there Amelia said we should try."

"It will be great for you to get away. My trip to Florida really helped me think about what I want to do next."

"What do you want to do next?" Daisy asked her sister.

"I think I want to quit my job. I have some feelers out with nonprofit foundations and organizations. I think that will be more fulfilling work."

After everyone left, Daisy wanted to explore that conversation more with Cammie. For now, she gave her a tight hug.

Daisy had brought home the rest of the lemon-blueberry cupcakes that had made up her bridal shower cake. After the guests had departed, she'd sat and had a productive conversation with Cammie and Jazzi. Cammie had reiterated again her desire to change jobs and move wherever that job would take her. She would even consider going abroad for a clean water foundation. Daisy couldn't quite see her sister, who liked glam, roughing it in a small village in Africa. But she'd been wrong about Cammie before. She could be wrong again, and this time for the right reasons.

It was almost 1 a.m. when Jonas put on the pot for tea and they ate more cupcakes and the left-over cucumber sandwiches at the kitchen island.

"I'm just going to consider this breakfast," Jazzi said. "I'm glad I don't have the first shift tomorrow at the dress shop."

"Iris told me to stay home tomorrow morning," Daisy admitted. "But I'll go in mid-morning."

Motioning to the boxes and gift bags they'd carried into the living room, Jazzi teased, "You have all that to put away."

"Maybe I'll use that chest we found Axel Strow's secrets in." To Jonas, Daisy said, "Do you think the chest will fit at the bottom of the bed?"

"It will if you want it there. I could line the inside with cedar, and you can use it for storage for whatever you want."

Daisy put a cupcake on a plate for him. "You have the best ideas. Maybe you can have *two* cupcakes."

Jonas laughed. "I think I've had so many cupcakes that icing is going to start spurting from my ears. I'll warm a couple of those quiches in the microwave. They'll be good with the tea."

"That's what I should be eating," Jazzi moaned. She took her finger through the icing on the top of the cupcake. "But I do so love sugar."

Felix had sidled up next to Jazzi as she broke a cupcake in two, hoping crumbs would fall his way. "How about a peanut butter biscuit, boy. I think that's more your speed," she told him.

Marjoram and Pepper were asleep on the dea-con's bench, and they hadn't stirred.

"I bet cats get a high score on deep sleep when they nap," Jazzi observed. "Look at them. It's like they don't even know we're here."

Jonas protested, "I saw one golden eye open when we came in. They know we're here. They just don't care."

They were all sipping chocolate tea when Daisy's phone played. "I wonder if Cammie forgot to tell me something," Daisy mused as she went to the counter to pick up the phone that was charging. Instead, however, she said to Jonas and Jazzi, "It's Trevor!"

She answered the call. "It's late, Trevor. I hope this is important."

She put Trevor on speaker so Jonas could hear him, too. The thing was . . . she only heard mumbling.

"Trevor? I can't understand you. What's wrong?"

"I need help." Trevor's voice sounded weak.

"What happened?"

"I can't think straight, Daisy. Can you come get me at the convenience store at the west end?"

"The convenience store."

"Yes . . . by the dumpsters. Please."

"Are you hurt?"

"Daisy, just come and pick me up. Don't do anything else until you get here, okay?"

"Should I call Tessa?"

"No, don't call Tessa. Just come, please."

"We'll be there. Stay on the phone with me."

Felix didn't go along this time but stayed with Jazzi and the cats as Daisy and Jonas hurried to Jonas's SUV in the garage and hopped in. On the road, Jonas drove in silence while Daisy kept in contact with Trevor.

When they arrived at the convenience store, there were a couple of cars in the parking lot. Daisy recognized Trevor's sedan as they parked beside it.

Over the phone, Trevor reminded her weakly, "By the dumpster."

Jonas ran that way and found Trevor first. "His head's bleeding."

Trevor was sitting with his back against the dumpster. His knees were propped up, his elbows were on his knees, and his head was in his hands.

Daisy dropped down beside him. "I'm going to call an ambulance."

"No ambulance."

"Then we're taking you to the emergency department at the Lancaster hospital. Come on, Jonas. Help me get him up."

"I'll bring the SUV over," Jonas said. "Trevor, do you think you can stand until I do that?"

"Yes, I can stand. My head's throbbing and things are spinning a little, but I'll manage it."

Daisy kept her arm around Trevor's waist. Sweating and breathing heavily, he sagged against her. She wanted to swipe the blood from the side of his head but didn't know if that was the best thing to do right now. He might need stitches, and it was better to let the professionals look at the wound.

She and Jonas managed to help Trevor into the front passenger seat. Daisy sat in the back, keeping her eye on him as they drove.

"I called Morris to meet us there," Jonas said. "Tell me what happened."

"Stupidity happened." Trevor sounded disgusted with himself.

"Your stupidity or someone else's?" Jonas asked.

"Mine. Someone called my hotline. His voice was disguised. At least I think it was a guy. The caller told me that Axel Strow knew Mick Ehrhart stole. The informer also said Axel threatened to turn Mick in. When I poked for more, the guy said if I wanted to know the whole story, I needed to come to the back of this parking lot at midnight. I did. When I reached the dumpster, someone came around from the back and conked me. How stupid was that? I think I passed out for a few minutes. Everything was spinning. I had lights in front of my eyes. I waited until I felt more stable before I called you."

Apparently already sifting through the information Trevor had given him, Jonas wanted to know, "Do you think the story about Axel is true?"

"I don't know. It could be, or it could be a hoax. I know one thing for sure. Whoever hit me meant it as a warning. I'm getting close to figuring out what happened, and they know it. If this was meant to dissuade me, whoever the person was that conked me, got it all wrong. I'm going to figure out who killed Henry Kohler and why Axel Strow disappeared."

CHAPTER EIGHTEEN

Although Trevor hadn't wanted Daisy to call Tessa, she had. The doctors had decided that Trevor needed to have a CAT scan since he'd passed out. Reluctantly he'd agreed. After a long night of tests and observation, the doctor had discharged Trevor, and Tessa had insisted he come home with her. This morning Daisy and Jonas sat with Tessa and Trevor in her living room above the tea garden, waiting for Morris, who'd wanted to question Trevor further than he had when he'd recorded the basics last night at the hospital.

Tessa's boho sense in fashion was evident in her apartment. The colors of pillows along the back of her kidney-shaped sofa varied from red, to blue, to orange, and wine. The fabric pattern on the sofa included diamonds and chevrons in the same colors as the throw pillows. A low coffee table in front of the sofa held a scarf runner in bright colors, too.

Jonas sat in a platform rocker with wooden arms and a burnt-orange fabric while Daisy, Trevor, and Tessa sat on the sofa. Soft valances in burnt orange, red, and yellow draped over the rods in the front windows above bookshelves.

Tessa asked if anyone wanted tea or coffee ... or soda. When they all passed, she said, "The doctor told Trevor to stay hydrated. He thinks he can do that with orange soda."

Trevor held a can of orange soda and took a few sips before he explained what he wanted to do next on the podcast. "I'd like to explain who exactly Henry Kohler was by sharing interviews with his friends and his wife. I asked Beth Ann to do an interview. She said she will if it will catch his killer."

"Trevor," Tessa began, but he brushed her worry away with his hand.

"I want to do the same kind of podcast about Axel. I put in a call to Stephanie Gallant, and she, too, is willing to talk to me and let it go on record—how she knew Axel and what she knew about his family."

"Are you going for the sensational aspect?" Jonas asked. "Or do you simply want to turn up more facts?"

"Both," Trevor said honestly. "I didn't get this conk on the head for nothing. I'm thinking of finding a producer, someone who could put the taped interviews together expertly with music in the background. That way I can concentrate on the script."

Script, Daisy thought. A script conveyed a pre-fashioned story. How would all that impact the investigation? Could interviews on the podcast corrupt witnesses for the police investigation?

A doorbell buzzed. Tessa rose to her feet and went down the stairs to the door to the apartment.

Daisy could hear Morris's voice as he spoke with Tessa while they ascended the stairs.

Once in the living room, Morris crossed his arms over his chest and studied Trevor. "I didn't want to come down on you last night. You had an awful headache, and I get that. But don't you see now that what you're doing is dangerous?"

"If you've come to lecture me, Detective, you can just leave again. If you've come to pick my brain, to find out what can help your investigation, then have a seat."

Jonas rose and waved to his chair. "I'll get one of the kitchen chairs. Go ahead and sit, Morris."

The detective looked tired . . . more than tired. He looked frustrated. "Tell me again what the caller told you, word for word."

"He told me that Axel knew Mick Ehrhart stole. Axel threatened to turn Mick in. If he did, that's motive."

"*You* think it's motive. *I* think it could be hogwash. Someone merely wanted to coax you to that convenience store. Someone wanted to make sure you'd stop these podcasts."

"If that's the case," Trevor said belligerently, "then I'm doing something right."

Morris targeted Tessa. "Can't you reason with him?"

"You can see how easy that is," she jibed.

Morris's shirt was rumpled, and his jacket was creased. He was without a tie this morning, and Daisy thought she saw the stain of something on his shirt lapel. Coffee, maybe?

"I've spoken to Mick Ehrhart twice now," Morris said. "The second time was this morning. He told me what happened when he stole a coat for his mother. But that's all he ever stole, and that was out of necessity."

Trevor pretended to be playing a violin. "Does that tug on your heartstrings?"

"Lundquist, I've interviewed enough witnesses to know when they're telling me a lie and when they're telling me the truth. Ehrhart was never arrested for anything else. He told me the convenience store manager let him take day-old doughnuts home as well as cans that were damaged. He helped him and his mom. Because of that, Ehrhart was determined to build a life that didn't include handouts."

"I'm planning to devote an episode on my podcast to Axel. Maybe we'll turn up something in his past that shows you Mick Ehrhart is lying," Trevor countered.

"Mick seemed forthcoming to me," Daisy agreed, "though I've been wrong before. He showed me and Jonas some photos of his gang of guys. Though he does seem to be interested in Beth Ann Kohler."

"How do you know that?" Morris barked.

"Beth Ann knew I wanted to talk to Mick, and he was at her house trimming bushes one day. I went over to talk to him. He as much as told me he'd thought about dating Beth Ann, but Henry got to her first."

"He gave you a motive for murder," Morris grumbled.

"Maybe, or maybe he was just telling me something I could see with my own eyes when he was around Beth Ann. Why deny it when it's right there?"

"This case has so many moving parts it's making my head spin."

"It's a double case," Jonas pointed out. "Whether you want to or not, you have two investigations going at once. Are you and Zeke trying to work them both, or are you each taking one of them?"

"Trying to work them both. The chief has given the go-ahead on that. Did you know he was a patrol officer when Axel disappeared?" Morris asked.

"I had no idea," Jonas said.

His guard down some because of his fatigue, Morris said, "Chief Schultz pulled out the old files. They were buried in the basement, not on the computer."

"What did he think of the investigation back then?" Trevor asked.

"He was involved in the search party that went looking for Axel. He'd organized volunteers from the town who wanted to help. Strow's farm was home base. Susan Strow made sandwiches and coffee for everyone."

"She needed something to do to keep herself busy," Daisy murmured.

Morris glanced at her. "That's probably so. The chief said they searched long and hard for a week from one end of the town to the other, but they had all become convinced that Axel had run off. The underlying conviction was that he wanted more than farm life. He was a smart kid, and his dad didn't want to hear about him going to college. He wanted him to stay on the farm."

Suddenly Morris stood. "I've got to get going. Lundquist, I wish you could give me something about who attacked you."

"I wish I could, too. I don't even know what I was hit with."

"Whatever it was, your guy or girl took it with them. It could be anything from a bat to a two-by-four from what the doc said who stitched you up. You were lucky, but don't count on that luck to hold. I'm interviewing Dylan Meyer again this afternoon, shaking all the trees to see what falls out. But his alibi seems solid." Morris headed for the stairs.

Daisy caught up with him there.

"After your next interview, why don't you stop by the tea garden and let Aunt Iris get you an iced tea and a snack. It's on us."

Morris gave her a twitch of a smile. "Thanks, Daisy, but you know if I had any chance with your aunt, this case has probably messed that up. I hardly have time to breathe, let alone think about romance. Take care of yourself and stay away from Lundquist."

The detective jogged down the stairs. What Morris had just revealed meant he was thinking about Aunt Iris a lot. That counted.

That evening, after Jonas parked his SUV about a quarter mile from the quarry on a gravel road used for utility vehicles, he and Daisy hiked to the quarry. The temperature had dropped as the sun met the horizon with orange and purple streaking the sky.

"Can you tell me again why you wanted to come out here?" Jonas asked as they walked up the hilly terrain.

They both wore T-shirts, jeans, and sturdy trainers. "I know it doesn't make sense, but Axel and his friends spent time here. I just want to take a look around."

"It's different now than it was twenty years ago," Jonas reminded her.

"It might be. But I can imagine it as it was back then. Really, the only thing that's changed is the fencing and the DANGER and KEEP OUT signs. I called Bob Weaver to ask him about the quarry and that's what he told me. He said the fear of God is drummed into kids nowadays to stay away from here."

Even though the heat of the day had diminished, Daisy felt sweat beading on her back as they walked.

"Some kids would take that as a dare," Jonas concluded.

"Maybe." Daisy wasn't convinced of that. She caught a glimpse of the fence as they climbed higher. Finally it was in full view.

"Do you know who paid for the fencing?" she asked.

"The township and the landowner went together on this for the safety of Willow Creek residents. But I don't know if anyone ever comes out here to check on it."

"Can we walk the perimeter?"

"I don't think we'll have time before darkness falls. And I don't believe you'll want to be out here after dark."

"You don't think it would be romantic?" she teased.

"I think I'd prefer your backyard for romance,"

he said, leaning close and nudging her shoulder. "There could be critters out here. I've heard about coyotes in the area."

"Now you tell me," she joked, but she scanned the area.

"We can't walk the entire perimeter, but we can walk some of it," Jonas said.

They began trekking along the chain-link fence.

"Trevor's new podcast goes live tonight." Daisy removed her phone from her pocket. "I could stream it as we walk. I have a good signal."

Jonas nodded. "Go ahead."

Daisy stopped walking for a few moments to access Trevor's website and the link for streaming.

His voice played in the silence. "*This is Trevor Lundquist with my true crime podcast, 'Hidden Spaces'.*"

"He's upped his game," Jonas said, "by putting his podcast into the true crime category."

"*You should know what happened to me this week. Someone wants me to stop these podcasts. I could have been killed.*"

Daisy and Jonas exchanged a look.

With anger and frustration in his tone, Trevor explained, "*Someone called my tip line in a disguised voice with the accusation that Axel Strow had known one of his friends was a thief. That friend supposedly had a motive to silence Axel. And, yes, the caller named names. He said he'd give me more information if I met him at the convenience store. I did and ended up in the hospital with a concussion. Did this person kill Axel Strow?*"

Trevor went on. "*The mysterious disappearance of Axel Strow continues to plague this Willow Creek, Pennsylvania, community. I have more and more questions about Axel, who was sixteen when he went missing. I've spoken to old-timers who remember Willow Creek twenty years ago. Let's listen to what Bob Weaver has to say about Willow Creek and Axel Strow."*

"Trevor must have taped this interview last week," Daisy said, talking fast so she didn't interrupt listening.

Next, they heard Bob Weaver's voice. *"Willow Creek was different then . . . smaller. We were more of a farming community. Still, kids wanted to leave. In many cases, they didn't want the lives their parents had made. A couple of my children were like that. They couldn't wait to see life in the big city . . . couldn't wait to get away from the stink of manure. Folks thought Axel was like that, that he'd just run off to find another life."*

After a moment's pause, Trevor's voice sounded again. *"That's what some people thought, but I spoke with one of Axel's teachers, Mrs. Caruso, who taught him mathematics."*

A high woman's voice rang clear. *"Axel was so smart . . . beyond his years. I was a young teacher when I taught him. I'd only been in the classroom for three years, but I realized how talented he was. One doesn't usually associate talent with mathematics, but Axel had a gift of computing, analyzing, and calculating. He was at least two years ahead of his peers in math. He did calculations on his own just for the fun of it."*

Trevor's voice again. *"Would he have run away?"*

"I don't think so," she said. *"I was determined to find him scholarships if he wanted to go to college. If he ran off, he couldn't continue his education. I believe something happened to him, but I don't want to imagine what."*

"None of us want to imagine what happened," Trevor said. *"But we have to in order to solve this mystery. One of Axel's friends agreed to talk to me about Axel,"* Trevor went on. *"Here's Dylan Meyer."*

*"Axel was a good kid. I didn't know him as well as
some of his other friends did. Sometimes he blew off practice because his dad needed him on the farm. I can't believe he'd help anyone steal anything."*

"I asked Dylan if he thought Axel ran off," Trevor
continued. *"And here's what he thought."*

*"I don't believe so. He cared about his parents and
what they wanted. He was really torn about whether he
should go to college. I just don't see him running away.
And if he was in an accident, wouldn't he have had some
kind of ID on him?"*

"Isn't that a good question?" Trevor asked dramatically.

Suddenly Jonas clamped his hand on Daisy's
arm. "Look there."

She'd had her mind on Trevor and his interviews and hadn't been paying attention to anything else. But now she looked where Jonas pointed.
"Kids?" she asked.

"Probably."

The fence had been cut and pushed aside. There
was enough room to walk through and enter the
area around the quarry.

"Let's take a look," she said in a soft voice.

No longer focused on Trevor's podcast, Daisy
swiped off his website and pushed her phone back
into her pocket.

Jonas took her hand. "Are you sure you want to
explore?"

"Yes. I'm not sure if I'm fascinated by the quarry
or by the idea of Axel and his friends coming
here."

Once inside the fenced area, they didn't have to
go to the edge of the quarry to see down inside.
The sides of the quarry were striated with colors of

limestone—layers of gray were dabbled with tan, cream, and yellow, all made to look otherworldly by the rays of the descending sun. Cedar bushes grew along portions of the edge. Daisy thought she'd glimpsed more layers down farther. Some kind of ground cover, too. Maybe moss and lichen?

"Limestone and dolomite," Jonas murmured. "Willow Creek is smack-dab in the middle of a limestone valley."

"The water is reflecting the sun and the vertical walls. It's fascinating. I can see why kids would come here. But the depth of the water and the cold temperatures make it so dangerous."

Daisy noticed Jonas staring at the circle-like hole of limestone and the surrounding edge. "What are you thinking?"

"I'm thinking if Axel died here, no evidence would ever be found."

Daisy was afraid Jonas was right. The only way they'd know what had happened to Axel was if someone confessed.

On Tuesday, a pile of receipts sat next to Daisy's keyboard on her office desk. She'd stayed at the tea garden after everyone else had left for the day. Her bookkeeping program was open on the screen, and her playlist sounded from a small Bluetooth speaker on the credenza. Jazzi, with the help of Ned Pachenko, was putting together a playlist for the wedding reception. Both Jazzi and Ned had asked Daisy and Jonas for a list of favorites, and they'd obliged.

Daisy was concentrating on the monitor screen and her keyboard when her phone stopped playing music and erupted with the tuba sound. Quickly glancing at her phone, she saw that Jazzi was calling.

She picked up the phone and answered. "Hi, honey, what's up?"

"Hi, Mom. I just wanted to let you know I won't be home for supper. I'm going over to Mark's. His mom is making lasagna for us. Hers is the best. She's making all of Mark's favorite meals before he leaves. He says he's already gained five pounds. I think that's an exaggeration."

Daisy understood that in each meal Mark's mom made, she was telling him how much she'd miss him.

"Maybe you should stop at the chocolate shop on your way to show your appreciation," Daisy suggested.

"Good idea. Truffles go with everything."

"I'll be getting home late tonight anyway. I'm catching up on bookwork. I don't want to fall behind before the wedding."

"Portia told me she'd received your email invitation. I'm surprised Gram didn't talk you into sending out engraved invitations." There was amusement and fondness for her grandmother in Jazzi's voice.

"She knows we want to keep the wedding somewhat casual."

"And elegant, too," Jazzi pointed out. "I know you. Your wedding gown will set the tone."

Jazzi had accompanied Daisy to the seamstress yesterday for a final fitting. Details were all coming together. "Jonas is putting the finishing touches on the gazebo tonight. It's going to be delivered tomorrow." Daisy couldn't wait to see it.

"Are you getting wedding jitters?"

"No, not exactly, but excitement is building. I keep telling myself it's just a ceremony. Then I think about all the ways marrying Jonas will change my life. All good ways."

"I've seen the way you look at him and he looks at you. I hope to have that kind of love someday."

"I hope that for you, too." Tears came to Daisy's eyes and seemed to jam her throat.

"You're not crying, are you?" Jazzi asked teasingly, hearing Daisy's emotion.

"Yes, I am," Daisy acknowledged. "It's an emotional time."

"As long as you're happy."

"I am," Daisy assured her daughter. Even though she'd be sad Jazzi was leaving for college, Daisy was happy for her, too.

"I've got to go, Mom, if I'm going to stop for chocolates. Do you want me to bring a box home, too?"

"I'll never turn down chocolate candy."

They both laughed. Jazzi ended the call with, "I'll see you later, Mom."

After the call, Daisy didn't tap the icon on her phone for her playlist once more. She pushed the stack of receipts back into the accordion folder and settled it all in her desk drawer. It was time to go home. Maybe she'd stop at the grocery store on the way and pick up chicken tenders for a stir fry. After Jonas got home, that would be quick to make.

Taking one last check around the tea garden, she made sure all the lights were off. With her purse under her arm, she pushed her phone into her pocket, set the alarm, and left through the kitchen's back door.

She'd no sooner locked the door when a nearby male voice said, "I'd like to talk with you, Mrs. Swanson."

Swinging around, she saw Gary Landon, Brooks's father, standing there.

A silver truck was parked next to her Journey. He must have known what her car looked like from when she and Jonas had visited the tractor supply store and assumed she was inside. She didn't like the feel of this encounter . . . at all.

Still, she told herself she was just being paranoid.

"Hello, Mr. Landon. I'm on my way home." She reached for her phone in her pocket and lifted it. "I just texted my fiancé that I was on my way."

He studied the phone in her hand. It was obvious she was taking a precaution. She could always press 9-1-1.

Gary Landon was dressed in his obvious business uniform—khakis and his LANDON'S TRACTOR SUPPLY T-shirt. His face went from a frown to a more settled non-threatening expression. "I merely want to have a word with you about what you're doing."

"What am I doing?"

"You're digging up old pain and memories for no good reason. You have friends looking at each other with suspicion."

"Henry Kohler's friends? Or Axel Strow's friends?" The questions had shot out before she could filter her thoughts.

His mouth twisted with disgust. "Axel Strow's history couldn't have anything to do with Henry's death. Axel could be in South America right now or drinking a mai tai on a beach. I think you should stop messing around where you don't belong."

"How about the detectives, Mr. Landon? Do you think they're messing around, too?"

Landon shifted and gave a sigh. "The detectives are doing their job. They'll find Henry's killer. But poking around in twenty-year-old history is just causing pain. Brooks and I—" He stopped. After he cleared his throat, he continued, "Brooks's mother left that winter. Those days are hard for both of us to remember. It's taken us years to move on. I especially don't want to see that progress stopped for Brooks. He's dating someone, and I don't want the past to interfere with his present."

"I understand, Mr. Landon. Really, I do. The police are handling the investigation, and I'm going to concentrate on my wedding next week."

"Really? You're getting married? Are you a widow?"

"I am. I know about memories and moving on. I wish you and your son nothing but the best with that."

As if he believed her and was reassured by her words, Gary Landon nodded and took a step back. "I hope you have a wonderful wedding day."

"I intend to," she said with an almost-genuine smile.

The owner of Landon's Tractor Supply gave a wave of his hand and walked fast back to his truck and climbed in. Daisy watched him start it, back up, and drive out of the parking lot.

Was Gary Landon being a protective dad? Or was his little visit meant to be a warning?

CHAPTER NINETEEN

In spite of her best intentions to forget about Trevor and what he might do next, Daisy found herself in her living room in the corner of the sofa with her laptop. Jonas had suggested she stay inside while he oversaw the assembly of their gazebo. She'd put chili in the slow cooker, did laundry, and baked chocolate-espresso cookies. But she'd known another podcast had been posted, and she told herself she was simply going to listen to it so she knew what was going on in Trevor's head. However, that was an impossibility. Still inside with the two cats, she'd have quiet to concentrate on the stream.

As soon as she was settled, Pepper and Marjoram came over to see what she was doing. Pepper jumped up onto the back of the sofa and looked down over her shoulder. Marjoram, on the other hand, stayed on the coffee table, her golden eyes on Daisy.

"I feel like you two are guarding me. It's either that or you want to find out what Trevor has to say as much as I do."

Pepper's tail swished along the side of Daisy's head. Marjoram made herself more comfortable in a bread-loaf position, the better to see what Daisy was doing.

Trevor's video opening came up. He was dressed in a cranberry collarless shirt, his hair slicked back, his smile wide as he explained about another episode of "Hidden Spaces." His intro was a little different tonight.

He said, "*This podcast has become a true crime one. 'Hidden Spaces' is doing a deep dive into the recent death of Henry Kohler and the disappearance of Axel Strow twenty years ago. Secrets can't stay buried, and it seems as if there are a lot of them in Willow Creek. If you've been following along, you know that Daisy Swanson found the clues in the chest she bought at the Small Town Storage auction. A photograph of Axel and his parents started her on her search to find out what happened to Axel. The Willow Creek Police Department understands that there's a link between Axel Strow's disappearance and the murder of Henry Kohler because Axel and Henry were friends. They were on the same track team in high school. There were others in their orbit. Twenty years ago, on a spring night when Axel disappeared, someone had to know something. Maybe that person had been Henry Kohler. We're going to find out more about that today from his wife, Beth Ann Kohler. Here is the interview I taped with her yesterday.*"

Trevor was moving fast, putting all his energy and effort into "Hidden Spaces." Was he doing it to solve the crime, or because it might find him a new career? Was he doing it for the people who remembered Axel . . . or for Beth Ann and anyone who had loved Henry? It was so hard to say. The interview started out with Beth Ann and Trevor talking about her job, her life, and how heartbroken she was now that Henry was gone. Then Trevor pushed with the hard questions.

"*Most people are familiar with crime shows,*" he said. "*I'm sure you are, too. The closest person to the victim is always the best suspect. Do you feel that you are a suspect?*"

Beth Ann responded, "*I loved Henry with all my heart. The idea that the police think I could have hurt him, well, it just . . . it just devastates me.*"

"*Have they been hard on you?*" Travis asked.

"*I've had several talks with the detectives,*" she admitted. "*The truth is . . . at first I couldn't answer their questions. I was completely lost. Hysterical, I guess, after I found out that Henry had been murdered. The police brought in Daisy Swanson to calm me down and ask me a few questions. She made the transition easier. I could talk to her.*"

"*Were the detectives in the room when you spoke to her?*"

"*Not at first,*" Beth Ann answered. "*She kind of led me into talking about everything. It made it so much easier. She had brought tea, and that bolstered me.*"

"*What happened next?*" Trevor pressed.

"*Then I spoke to Detective Morris Rappaport. He was a bit gruff, but he was kind enough and went slowly.*"

"*What type of questions did Mrs. Swanson ask?*" Trevor pushed.

"*She wanted to know about my life with Henry . . . about him. She wanted to know if anything unusual had happened.*"

"*Had it?*"

"*His laptop had been stolen from his car a few weeks ago,*" Beth Ann revealed. "*We talked about what he might have kept on his laptop.*"

"Anything else that was significant?"

Trevor knew the answers to some of these questions before he asked. But the point was to put emphasis on them.

"I thought about some other things, so I met with Daisy at the tea garden to talk about them," Beth Ann related. *"I told her about Henry's nightmares, and about the fact that he never seemed to be able to sleep well. He was secretive about his dreams. He wouldn't talk to me about them."*

Trevor followed with, *"And that upset you?"*

Daisy could hear Beth Ann's hesitancy, but she finally went on. *"It did. But we all have private things, things maybe we're scared of or ashamed of or embarrassed about. I wasn't going to force it. I thought when the time was right, he would tell me. But the time never became right."*

Trevor wasn't going to let his questions stop there. *"Did anything else come up in this talk you had with Mrs. Swanson?"*

"Well . . . yes. I told her about a patient that Henry had who was very upset with him."

"And what did Daisy tell you to do?"

"She told me that when I signed my statement, I should talk to the detectives about all of it. They would figure out whether it was important or not."

"Did you do that?"

"I did. But to tell you the truth, Mr. Lundquist, I don't think they're getting anywhere."

Trevor pounced. *"Why do you say that?"*

"I had another interview a few days ago. They've spent hours talking to me."

"Do you have an alibi?"

"No. I was home alone waiting for Henry. I'd made

supper, and it got cold and I started to worry. No, I didn't have an alibi like some others did."

Again, Trevor was quick to jump on Beth Ann's comment. *"Others?"*

"I hear they're talking to many of Henry's friends, too. They did let it slip that one of them has a solid alibi, Dylan Meyer. He's the one who called in to you."

Even though Trevor had known about Dylan's alibi, he pushed Beth Ann. *"Yes, he did. What was his alibi?"*

"He was at a business meeting, and his colleagues could verify it. There was also a video confirming he was there."

"What about Henry's other friends? Have the detectives mentioned them?"

"I don't know about the others," Beth Ann maintained. *"I do know Daisy talked to more of Henry's friends, though. She grilled Mick Ehrhart quite thoroughly when he was over at my house."*

"You made the meeting possible?"

"I did. I'm willing to do anything that helps. I want to catch whoever did this to Henry. I think Daisy will have more luck with that than the police. She gets people to open up. They talk to her."

Trevor's voice was knowing as he responded to Beth Ann's statement. *"That's exactly how she's been able to help solve nine other murder cases. I'm not sure the police could have done it without her."*

Daisy really hated this conversation. She didn't like the way it was going at all. Her name had been mentioned too many times. Not only that, but she suspected Henry's friends wouldn't be happy that their names had been brought up. Did Trevor really understand the dangerous pot he was stirring?

Sensing Daisy's discomfort, Pepper used her shoulder to step down from the top of the sofa and then hop to the sofa cushion. She sank in close to Daisy's lap and purred. Daisy listened as Trevor asked a few more incidental questions and Beth Ann answered them. Her interview came to a close.

Daisy was about to exit Trevor's website when he said, *"Whether the police department is actually making headway on solving this case or not, we're going to proceed with another interview. The man's name is Callum Abernathy. Some of the people in this community heard the quarrel between him and Henry Kohler at the physical therapy center. It was heated, if not physical. We'll decide whether it had anything to do or not with Henry's death after you hear Callum Abernathy speak."*

Daisy wondered if it was possible that Trevor could be sued for this podcast. Seriously, the way he put it, he didn't actually say Abernathy was a suspect, but the subtext sure was there.

"Mr. Abernathy, thank you for talking to me."

"No problem," the man said in a strong voice.

"Many people from the physical therapy center have told me about the argument you had with Henry Kohler a few days before he died."

"So what?" the man asked belligerently. *"People argue all the time. Why is it so important that I argued with Henry?"*

"It's important, Mr. Abernathy, because Henry's dead. You were upset with him. Can you tell our listeners what that was about?"

"It wasn't no secret. Henry told me when I started physical therapy that if I worked hard, I could get back to a normal life."

"Did you work hard?"

"I certainly did. Session after session, I was in pain. I iced, I used the medication the doctor gave me, I exercised, but I didn't get better. Oh sure, the pain let up maybe ten percent, possibly twenty, but my leg will never be what it was. I can't do my job. I'm a roofer. If I can't climb on roofs, what am I supposed to do?"

"You almost came to blows with Henry Kohler."

"He started getting pretty hot, too, saying he never promised that I'd be where I was before my accident. He sort of did. That's what 'normal' meant to me."

"Have the police questioned you?"

"Yes. I told them I had nothing to do with what happened to Henry, and I didn't. I just wish everybody would let me alone. I even had a woman and a man come into my office to question me about this. She said she worked with the police. I didn't care, I told her to leave."

"Was the woman Mrs. Swanson?"

"Yes, it was. She had no right to question me about anything. It was probably her fault the police called me in."

"I doubt that that's so, Mr. Abernathy. The police bring in anyone and everyone who they suspect might have had something to do with Henry Kohler. One person could give one little bit of information that could lead to them finding out if another person has more information. That's the way it works. Daisy facilitates that process."

Daisy groaned. She wished to heck Trevor wouldn't keep mentioning her name. She could imagine her customers at the tea garden questioning what she did and how she did it. They were curious, and she didn't blame them. She had a streak of curiosity, too. Right now, though, all she wanted to do was concentrate on her wedding next week. The thing was . . . Trevor's podcast had her totally entranced. She was concentrating on it so hard that she didn't even hear Jazzi come in the sliding-glass doors.

Suddenly, however, she heard three voices from the kitchen—Jazzi's, her mom's, and Aunt Iris's.

"Come on, Mom, you've got to see this," Jazzi called to her. "Gram, Aunt Iris, and I are going to help you get ready for a wedding."

Daisy hadn't expected her aunt Iris and her mother to drive over tonight. Just what were they planning?

The delivery of the gazebo *was* a momentous occasion. Jonas had spent the last couple months getting it ready for them. It was his wedding present to her. Daisy watched as finishing installations were completed on the white gazebo, absolutely perfect for a wedding as well as a future together. Elijah Beiler, a local craftsman and sometimes store clerk at Woods, had helped move the gazebo from his property to theirs that afternoon.

As soon as the men stepped away from the completed structure, seemingly satisfied, Daisy ran to Jonas and flung her arms around him.

She hugged him hard, tears burning in her eyes. "It's perfect," she murmured. "Thank you."

He kissed her soundly and held her close.

Jazzi joined them. "Okay, there will be enough time for that after the wedding. Iris, Gram, and I have work to do."

Daisy and Jonas stepped away from each other, laughing.

"What work?" Jonas asked as his friends waved and started for their truck, ready to leave. Jonas waved back with a shouted, "Thank you," then he turned back to Jazzi to listen to her answer.

"It's a very pretty gazebo, but it's going to be even prettier with tons of fairy lights." She pointed to Iris and her gram on the patio.

Iris gave a wave and lifted the string of fairy lights she was unraveling.

"They're solar," Jazzi said.

Daisy studied the twelve-foot octagonal gazebo that had been built by the man who loved her. Fairy lights would easily wrap around the spindles and handrails. As Iris brought a ladder and a string of lights toward Jazzi, Daisy realized Jazzi would be wrapping them around the decorative roof brackets, too.

When Jazzi positioned the ladder, Daisy tapped her shoulder. "You're making this so special for us."

"You're the one who told me once that you didn't believe in fairy tales anymore. If you believe you and Jonas will be happy, then I can believe in happily-ever-after."

Daisy gazed at her daughter, so proud of the woman she was becoming.

"Don't cry, Mom," Jazzi warned. "We want to trim the gazebo with the lights before the sun sets."

As Jonas circled Daisy's waist with his arm to lead her toward the patio, her phone played its tuba sound. She plucked it from her shorts pocket and murmured, "I hope it's not Trevor."

Jonas chuckled. "That knock on the head should have taught him something."

Before she could say anything to Jonas about Trevor's latest podcast and her thoughts about it, she checked her screen. The caller wasn't Trevor; it was Vi.

"Hi, honey. What's up?"

"I'm at the hospital. Can you come?"

Daisy pressed the icon for the speakerphone so Jonas could hear, too. Her heart was beating in triple rhythm, and her breath stuck in her chest. She finally managed, "Is it Sammy?"

"Sammy is with Brielle at our house. It's Foster. He couldn't breathe. He scared me out of my mind. They did an EKG and are monitoring him. Can you come?"

Daisy's gaze met Jonas's. She could see his worry, too. "Did you call Gavin?" she asked her daughter.

"Foster doesn't want me to call him, but I did. His phone went to voicemail. I'll try again."

"We'll be there as soon as we can."

Fifteen minutes later, Daisy and Jonas arrived at the hospital for the second time that week. Vi was waiting. As soon as she saw Daisy, her face crumpled. "I was so scared, Mom. He wouldn't let me call an ambulance, so I rushed him here. Thank goodness Brielle was home to watch Sammy."

After a long hug, Vi took a deep breath. "They think it was a panic attack. Only one person can go back with me."

Jonas said, "I'll wait here for Gavin."

Daisy and Vi passed the desk, and Vi nodded to the woman there. Vi led Daisy down the hall. They stopped at the second cubicle.

On the gurney, Foster appeared completely dejected in a hospital gown with his glasses on the side table. He looked like a kid who had lost his way.

"Hi, Daisy," Foster said, looking embarrassed.

She knew chastising him at this point wasn't

going to make anything better. With a gentle smile and trying to react to all this calmly, Daisy sat beside his bed. "How are you feeling?"

"Better. When I first got here, they put oxygen on me, and I realized I just had to take deep breaths and relax to feel better."

"Foster, I don't know what to say to you. I don't want to act like a mother-in-law right now."

He gave her a weak smile. "But that's what you are."

Vi said, "I'm going to step out so the two of you can talk."

After his wife left, Foster said, "Vi read me the riot act."

"I expected she would. You scared her to death."

"I scared myself, too. She wants me to go to this yoga group she attends sometimes. Daisy, yoga?"

"It would do you good. You're going to have to find a way to relax so this doesn't happen again."

"I know that, but yoga?"

"You can always do a spa day every couple of weeks and get a massage."

He crinkled his nose at her. "You can't be serious."

"But I *am* serious, Foster. That's the point. This is serious. You have to find something to do that lets you shed the weight of your world."

"What if I take Sammy to the park on weekends? Like, every Saturday morning, he and I do something together?"

"That would be a start. That will work if you don't have something else to do for your job. Can you carve it out? Can you say, 'that's what I'm doing, no matter what'?"

"I'm not supposed to be in the office on Saturdays. I was just trying to prove I was a great employee."

Daisy just listened.

"It's more important that I'm a good husband and a good father, isn't it?"

"*You* have to answer that question for yourself. But you also have to realize that before you can be a good father and husband, you have to take care of yourself."

"Lying here and having other people taking care of me, I thought a lot about this."

"What have you decided?"

"First of all, the doctor wants me to see my family physician and have a stress test."

"That makes sense."

"The doctor also suggested I cut caffeine out of my diet."

"Can you exist without it?" she joked.

"I'm going to have to. It makes my heart speed up, and that doesn't help with anxiety."

"And?" Daisy prompted, expecting that there was more.

"And I'm going to tell the town council they'll have to find someone else to do their PR campaign."

"That's sensible," Daisy agreed.

"If you think she's able, let me talk to April about taking over your social media commentary and your website. The way I have it set up, she can make changes easily, and I can talk her through the process."

"All the changes you're suggesting are good ones. Does Vi agree with them?"

"She does, and she suggested that once your

wedding's over, maybe Jonas could help me build a play set for Sammy. Maybe I could find a way to relax doing that."

Daisy covered Foster's hand with hers. "You're a good man, Foster. You're a good husband and father."

He started shaking his head. "Not for the last couple of months."

"We all get off track sometimes."

"And just how do I keep on track, Daisy? What if this happens again?"

"You can't be afraid that it will, or it will. You just have to make the changes that you think will make everything better. I trust your judgment, Foster."

He grimaced. "I think I need a personal Yoda."

Daisy laughed. "I don't know about that. But I do know you have to consider your family as your compass to keep you on the right track. They're your North Star. If you listen to them, I think you'll know what's too much and what's just enough."

"A compass," Foster said thoughtfully. "Maybe Vi can get me one for Christmas. Then I'll have something tangible to hold in my hand or keep in my pocket so that I remember."

A compass, Daisy thought. And then a picture came into her mind—a compass on a chain . . . a compass on a chain on a belt . . . Axel's belt.

Vi returned to the room. "The doctor has your discharge papers. We can get you out of here." She looked at her mother. "What's wrong, Mom?"

Daisy felt a little light-headed at what she'd recalled. "Nothing, Vi. Maybe I'm just remembering the last time I was here. I'm going to get some air. I'll tell Gavin he can come back if he's out there."

"He is," Vi said. She glanced at her husband. "You can expect a lecture from him, too."

Daisy went out to the waiting room. When she saw Gavin, she said, "You can go back now. He's ready for you. But don't be too rough on him. He's rough enough on himself."

Gavin shook his head. "He's a chip off the old block," he said, then he headed toward Foster's room.

Daisy pulled Jonas aside. "Let's go outside. I have some calls I have to make."

He followed her out the sliding-glass doors. "Who are you calling?"

"Mick Ehrhart. I need him to verify something."

Jonas didn't ask what. He waited for her to complete her conversation with Henry and Axel's friend.

After that call, she turned to Jonas. "It's time to call Zeke. I think I know who killed Axel, and maybe Henry, too."

A few minutes later, Daisy was speaking to Zeke with Jonas listening in. Daisy had slipped the photos Mick had given her out of her purse. She showed Jonas exactly what she was talking about as she explained to Zeke, "Mick Ehrhart had pictures of the gang of friends when they were teenagers. In one of the photos of Axel, I could see a compass hanging on a chain from his belt. Mick said he always wore it. His mother had given it to him. I just spoke with Mick again. He told me Susan Strow told Axel his home was his compass. He could always come back there, no matter what. The compass was engraved with *YOUR NORTH STAR—MOM.*"

"What does that have to do with his disappearance?" Zeke asked.

"I saw that compass. I'm almost sure it was the exact same compass."

The detective sounded doubtful. "Where did you see it?"

Quickly, she told him about her visits to Brooks Landon's and Perry Russo's offices. She couldn't remember exactly on which shelf she'd seen the compass, but she was sure it had been displayed on one of them.

"Your thoughts about this don't give me probable cause for a warrant, Daisy. But I'll nose around. You need to be very careful. Remember what happened to Lundquist."

"My wedding is next week. Of course, I'm going to be careful."

After she ended the call with Zeke, Jonas took her into his arms. "Of course, you're going to be careful," he repeated.

Famous last words.

CHAPTER TWENTY

Nerves plagued Daisy the next day as she tried to stay busy . . . busier than usual. She'd come into the tea garden at 6 a.m. to help Tessa and Iris get ready for opening. Usually, she didn't arrive until 8 a.m. That had been her schedule since the business had opened.

There was a pre-opening list of everything they had to accomplish. Iris, Tessa, and Eva readied the morning baked goods and salads. Tamlyn and April arrived before the shop opened at 7 a.m. to serve their first customers. When Daisy arrived, she started the soups. Today, however, she went from item to item on the list before Iris, Tessa, or Eva could get to it. Her mind was racing from Foster and his physical and mental condition to what she'd revealed to Zeke.

Zeke was always meticulous when he went by the book the same way Morris did. Would the detectives be talking to Brooks and Perry today? Would they be able to secure warrants to search the shelves in both men's offices? If they did, would they find the compass? Would it be the one that had belonged to Axel? She'd texted the photos she'd scanned to Zeke.

Last night she and Jonas had talked about why either man could be the killer. Either could easily say Axel had given the compass to them. But was that feasible, since Mick's photo had the date the photo was taken . . . a date only a few days before Axel went missing?

Jonas had said something that had chilled her. *"That compass could also be a killer's trophy."*

Finally, Tessa, who was mixing dough for chocolate whoopie pies, stepped in front of Daisy to prevent her from opening the walk-in refrigerator. "What's going on?"

Tessa knew Daisy so well. The first thing Daisy told her was, "Vi took Foster to the emergency department last night for a panic attack."

Overhearing, her aunt told Tessa, "He was overwhelmed by everything he's been trying to accomplish. I think he's too much of a perfectionist."

Daisy had called both her mother and her aunt last night to tell them what had happened.

Daisy's phone played, interrupting their conversation. Yanking it from her apron pocket, she saw the caller was Vi.

She told the others, "It's Vi. I have to take this."

They all nodded with understanding. Iris squeezed Daisy's arm, showing her support.

Without a greeting, Vi said, "Our doctor had a cancellation and gave Foster the appointment. We're on our way now."

"And Sammy?"

"Emily is free. She came over as soon as I called Gavin."

There had been a time when Vi wouldn't have

called her father-in-law for help, but rather, would have let Foster do it. Daisy was happy to see Vi and Gavin were growing closer.

"Call me and let me know what the doc says," Daisy said.

"I will. Today she'll probably just order tests. Don't worry, Mom. We'll handle this."

Don't worry. Now that Vi was a parent, she should know worry about her child would never end.

Daisy had wandered into her office to take her call with Vi. Now Tessa poked her head in. "Is everything okay?"

Daisy sank into her desk chair. A headache was beginning to throb between her temples.

Tessa came farther into the office and pulled the door partway shut. "Is there something else besides Foster?"

Not knowing exactly what to say because Tessa was dating Trevor, Daisy hesitated.

"Is this about Trevor?" Tessa sank down on the corner of the desk. "Honestly, you'd think getting clobbered by a killer might put some fear into him. But it hasn't. If anything, he's even more motivated to find answers."

Daisy was hoping Zeke and Morris would be finding answers today. But what if she was all wrong? She didn't know how much to say to Tessa.

She finally settled on, "It's about the investigation."

"Has something happened?"

Again, Daisy didn't speak right away.

"Daisy, we've been friends a long time. Your friendship means so much to me. I'd never jeopardize it."

"You *cannot* tell Trevor, at least not for the next couple of days, until the detectives can wrap this up."

"I understand."

Daisy could see her best friend *did* understand.

After a deep breath, Daisy leaned down to her desk drawer, opened it, and took the photos Mick had given her from her purse. "These are the photos Mick Ehrhart gave me."

"The boys looked so carefree," Tessa commented as she studied each photo.

Daisy knew photos could be deceiving. Although Daisy didn't know exactly what had happened among the boys, there must have been some kind of tension there.

Tessa's orange and purple smock swept across the desk as she turned toward Daisy. "What has you troubled?"

Standing, Daisy came around her desk where she could look at the photos with her friend. She pointed to the picture where she could easily see the compass dangling from Axel's belt.

Tessa studied the photo. "Is that a pocket watch?"

"It's a compass on a chain. Axel's mom gave it to him."

"So, he could always find his way home," Tessa guessed.

"Exactly. Mick said Axel wore it all the time, unless he was training or running."

"I get the feeling the compass is important somehow?" Tessa handed the photos to Daisy.

"I think I saw it." The more Daisy thought about it, the more she was sure.

Tessa's eyes grew wide. "Where? You mean, not in the photo?"

"Not in the photo. When I went to visit Perry Russo, there was a set of shelves in his office behind his desk. When Jonas and I went to Landon's Tractor Supply, there was a case of trophies in the back of the room behind Brooks's desk. I remember a compass on a chain lying on a shelf, but I can't remember whose set of shelves. I can't recall if it was in the midst of trophies or just knickknacks, like antique replicas of cars. Isn't that awful? I can't make myself remember."

"You're trying too hard," Tessa suggested. "You have to *let* yourself remember."

"I called Mick to verify the details of the compass, and then I called Zeke. He insists that's not enough info for a warrant, but he is going to bring in Brooks and Perry to the station for questioning again."

"Today? No wonder you're nervous. The thing is—how are they going to know the compass belonged to Axel?"

"There was an engraving on the back. *Your North Star—Mom.* Mick Ehrhart says Susan Strow gave it to Axel on his thirteenth birthday."

"When he became a teen," Tessa noted.

"Probably when he wanted to become more independent."

Daisy crossed to her office door. "More than that. According to Mick, that's when Axel began talking about becoming an astronaut."

That fact floated in the air between Daisy and Tessa.

Tessa laid her hand over her heart. "Not a word to Trevor or anyone else. I promise."

* * *

Two busloads of tourists flowed into the tea garden around noon. Storms were predicted for the afternoon, so tourists walked from store to store, apparently sure the rain wouldn't start for a while.

Distracted, Daisy helped serve customers, going from table to table to pour more tea or take further orders. Was she so distracted by wedding plans and Jazzi's departure that her memory wouldn't focus on what she needed it to? *Where* had she seen that compass?

As Tessa had advised, if she relaxed, maybe her memory would target what she needed to know.

Around 2 p.m. Tessa came to her and pointed out, "You didn't take your lunch break."

Her friend was right, she hadn't. As the sky had grown darker, her servers had gone on their breaks, and Daisy had covered them. That's what they all did on busy summer days . . . covered for each other.

Glancing around the tearoom, she could see traffic had slowed inside as well as outside along the street. The tourist buses must have loaded up and left for other Lancaster County travels or for home.

"I'll take my break, stop at Rachel's to see if the material to line Jazzi's chest came in, and then walk down to the frozen yogurt shop."

"That's lunch?" Tessa asked knowingly.

"A banana split with walnuts will be." Beth Ann's logic made sense.

"Go for it," Tessa said. "Maybe Jonas will go with you."

"I'll text him when I finish at Rachel's and see if he's free."

In her office, Daisy shed her apron and grabbed her shoulder bag from her desk drawer.

Her aunt poked her head into the office. "You'd better grab your umbrella. We could have a downpour any minute."

Daisy could hear the rumblings of thunder, though they still sounded far away. A spare umbrella patterned with cats who smiled at her when it was open hung on her coat tree. She grabbed it, told her aunt, "I won't melt," and waved to her staff as she left the tea garden.

On the curb, waiting for a sorrel horse and a gray-bonneted buggy to pass, a loud *boom* of thunder startled Daisy, and she jumped.

"Get a grip," she muttered to herself, then jogged across the street.

After she pulled open the door to Quilts and Notions and went inside, she spotted Rachel's daughter Hannah at the counter. After peering around the store, she noticed Rachel was nowhere in sight.

Crossing to the sales counter, she greeted Hannah. "Hi, Hannah. How are you today?"

"Just fine, Daisy."

Today Hannah was dressed in a mint-green cape dress with her black apron. Her brown hair straggled from under her *kapp*.

"*Maam* isn't here. *Dat* picked her up so they could prepare at home for the storm. *Dat* says it could be heavy rain."

Looking outside, Daisy realized everything seemed grayer than when she'd walked in. "How about *you*? How will you get home?"

"A friend with a car will drive me home."

Transitioning to business, Daisy asked, "Did the fabric Jazzi ordered come in yet?"

"I think it did," Hannah said, the strings of her heart-shaped white *kapp* floating forward as she stooped to a shelf under the counter. She brought up a roll of fabric. She gave Daisy a peek at the confetti-colored, polka-dot fabric on a blush background.

"Jazzi decided on something different than an animal print," Daisy said.

"She did. Jazzi said that this was cheerier and will complement the robin's-egg blue of the outside of the chest."

"It will. We hope to paint it this weekend," Daisy confirmed.

After Hannah bagged the fabric, Daisy bid her good-bye and left the shop. She stood on the sidewalk for a minute, assessing the sky, the humidity in the air, and possibility of a downpour before she and Jonas could reach the yogurt shop. She poked the fabric parcel under her arm and slid her phone from her purse.

She had texted Jonas, *Are you free for a frozen treat?* when the dark-green SUV pulled up beside her along the sidewalk. A drumroll of thunder sounded above. It took Daisy's attention for a few seconds, but in those few seconds, the driver of the SUV had jumped out, come around to Daisy, and smiled at her as if they were old friends.

They weren't.

It was Brooks Landon. Her phone vibrated in her hand. She'd turned it on silent but vibrate before she'd left the tea garden. Before she could check if Jonas had sent a text, before she could even back up or make a sound, Brooks had opened the passenger-side door.

"Get in," he ordered. He snatched her phone from her hand, holding a revolver in his.

When she took a horrified step back, he said again, "Get in. I have Jazzi. She's tied up but unharmed. For now. If you don't follow my orders, I can't guarantee her safety."

A light rain began dripping from the stormy clouds. Daisy's head spun as panic overtook her. Her baby. Brooks had Jazzi. She wanted to run.

But if his threats held even a possibility of truth . . .

He poked her in the ribs with the nose of his gun, a wide smile still on his face, just in case anyone was watching.

"If you scream, you'll be dead . . . just like Henry . . . just like Axel. Think about what I could do to your daughter."

Suddenly Daisy's phone vibrated again in Brooks's hand. He tossed it into the back seat without watching where it fell.

She was getting married to Jonas next week. At least she hoped she was. Jazzi was going to be her bridesmaid. If she tried to escape now, Brooks would kill her . . . and her daughter.

The rain transformed from drips to a steady beat on the hood of Brooks's SUV.

She knew kidnap victims shouldn't go with their captors. She knew it. But what choice did she have?

"You're too smart, Daisy. Get in so we can have a little chat. I won't say it again."

In his car, he'd have to keep his gun on her

while he was driving. Maybe she'd be able to distract him . . . find out where he was keeping Jazzi . . . grab the wheel.

As she slid onto the bucket seat, her umbrella wristlet fell off her wrist, and the umbrella fell to the ground along with her package.

"Leave them," he demanded and slammed shut her door.

He was inside the SUV with her with the door locked before she could even fight tears and catch her breath. She was scared beyond thought as he drove down Market Street and turned onto a side street. She knew she had to gather her wits about her.

Rain streamed down the windshield, and Brooks turned his wipers on higher. Puddles were already gathering along the curbs.

"Why me? Why now?" she managed.

"Why *you*? Because your friend Zeke Willet called. He wants me to come in to the station again."

She bit her lip and tasted blood. "He's calling in many of Henry's friends for more interviews."

"Let me tell you, Willet smells something. I could see that when he questioned me before. Henry pretended to be a friend, but ever since we were teens, he'd been keeping a secret. And he was about to reveal it. I saw that as soon as I heard that idiot's podcast about the chests. I realized Henry could have been the only one to call Lundquist. If it wasn't for Lundquist and you digging around and asking questions, I'd be free and clear. Now, shut up until we get where we're going."

She heard the quiet vibration of her phone in the back seat. Daisy couldn't keep the fear and hope from her voice when she asked, "To Jazzi?"

He said grimly, "We'll see."

Daisy began to shiver. Her thoughts jumbled together. How was she going to escape Brooks and free Jazzi? Could she save her daughter?

Brooks's gun lay on his lap. He wasn't paying attention to her phone, which was vibrating again on the leather seat.

For a few minutes, Daisy could only be aware of sounds rather than her fear and thoughts—the *thrum* of the tires hummed, the *splash* of rising water flew against the doors, the windshield wipers *tick-tock*ed as they swiped on high speed. The vibration of her phone was a sound she was used to that was almost comforting as her nerves jangled and her skin prickled. Wind brushed against her door, buffeting it with more force. Daisy was so afraid that she felt almost claustrophobic. Now she knew how Foster must have felt. Taking the advice the doctor had given him, she inhaled deep breaths.

Brooks was driving faster than the weather conditions warranted. She had to keep her eyes open and her senses clear. The SUV sloshed through a puddle and veered to the left over the center line. If she did try to snatch the wheel or hit him with her purse, she could end up dead that way, too. And Jazzi?

"Where are we going?" Daisy asked, trying to keep her voice from shaking.

"I told you to be quiet."

"I have a right to know," she shot back.

"You have no rights with me." He gave her a laser-like sideways glare and put his attention back on the road, one hand on his gun, one hand on the steering wheel. That gun was turned toward her. His finger was on the trigger. Why had she gotten into his car?

Because of Jazzi.

"You underestimate me, Daisy Swanson," he suddenly said. His voice had a gravelly harsh edge.

Maybe she had. Maybe she'd thought Zeke could take care of this investigation. Maybe she'd been too involved.

They bumped off the paved road onto the two-lane track that she and Jonas had taken to the quarry. Her heart hadn't sunk to her toes before. It did now.

"Lundquist broadcast the fact that *you* were the one calling the shots. You questioned Beth Ann Kohler for the detectives. You spoke with Callum Abernathy. Who else did you question?"

She remained silent as the SUV tossed her back and forth. The tires sunk into potholes . . . climbed back up on the road . . . kept going forward.

"Perry Russo, I'm sure," Brooks went on. "And Mick Ehrhart. Lundquist swallowed my tale about Axel knowing that Mick stole."

"All of it was a lie," Daisy said in a small voice.

"Oh, I'm good at lying," Brooks agreed with a chuckle. "I've lied to my dad about sales figures. I've lied to him about profits. I've lied about how I can't wait to take over the business. I can't wait to sell it," Brooks almost spit out the words.

"I have friends and staff who will miss me and look for me."

"They'll never find you." He seemed completely sure about that.

"How do you expect to get away with killing me?"

"This isn't my car. I borrowed it from Perry. As soon as I get rid of you, I'm driving to Harrisburg and catching a plane out of here. I have a flight booked to South America. Maybe after I leave, my father will realize his retirement isn't going to be as secure as he thought it would be."

"You stole from him."

"You bet I did."

Daisy's insides felt as if they'd been shaken up and rolled around. The SUV rocked her against the seat belt and the door. They climbed up the hill to the fencing around the quarry. She could hardly see the fencing in the pouring rain, but she knew it was there. Where could he be holding Jazzi? Was he going to tell her? Would he let someone else know so they could go get her? Was this going to be the end of her life as she knew it?

Not if she had anything to say about it. She had a daughter to save. She had vows to recite. She had a family to love.

Brooks seemed to be in his own headspace when he said, "We thought this quarry was a magical place—all that limestone, all those levels, fifty feet high, fifty feet wide . . . and then another level, deep and wide. Abandoned, it was like a playground. No fence back then. We came up here to smoke and drink, at least Perry and I did. Axel and Mick . . . I'm not so sure why they came, maybe just because they wanted to be part of the gang. I guess Axel came because he was fascinated by anything that had to do with science. He wondered whether there were quarries on the moon. Can you imagine?"

Actually, she could. She wanted to imagine that more than she wanted to imagine what was going to happen next.

Brooks jerked the SUV to a stop. Gun in hand,

he said, "Stay put. I can shoot you through the window."

The sarcastic little voice in her head asked, *What does it matter if he shoots me now or later?* But she had to take every chance she could. She unhooked her seat belt and opened her door. Brooks was already there. Daisy's clogs sank into the muddy grass. The smell of rain and dank earth was heavy.

The nose of Brooks's gun against her yellow T-shirt seemed cold as the fabric grew wetter from the rain and stuck to her skin.

"Move it," Brooks ordered, poking her harder.

He gave her a push forward, and she almost fell. The rain let up to a drizzle. Her heart pounded in her ears.

She had to distract him so she could swing around to hit the gun out of his hand. "Tell me about Axel. How did you get his compass?"

As they went through the fence opening, Brooks gave her another shove. "I used bolt cutters on this, thinking I'd bring Henry up here."

"But you didn't." She wanted to hear this . . . all of it. She looked over her shoulder at Brooks. Were those headlights down the two-lane track they'd driven on? Could someone have followed them?

She blinked, and the lights were gone. Had that merely been her hopeful imagination playing tricks on her?

Brooks glanced behind him where Daisy had looked. Nothing was there. With the gun still trained on her, he ordered, "Move closer to the quarry, and I'll tell you about Axel."

Brooks's clothes were getting wet, too. His tan sports shirt and khaki cargo pants had dark spots from the rain. He didn't seem to mind. He brushed damp hair from his forehead.

She took about ten steps, losing a clog in the gravelly, soaked soil as she did. Stopping, she was determined not to get any closer to the edge.

Brooks took a quick look down at the water, where pools formed and shimmered with the plopping of the rain. Daisy swiped her hand over her wet face, tensed her shoulders, and readied herself to make a move.

With a shrug, as if what Daisy learned now was of no consequence, Brooks said, "Axel and I were on the track team. He was never serious about it. But I was. My dad was constantly on me about it. He cut off my privileges when I didn't place or win. Axel missed practices, and he didn't care. But he was fast, fit, and good. I needed college scholarships. I needed college recruiters to see me as a top runner. I pleaded with Axel to throw an important race. I needed to have the best time, to be the star."

From what she already knew of Axel, she suspected where the story was headed. "Axel wouldn't throw the race," she said as a statement, not as a question.

"No, he wouldn't. We fought up here. His compass caught on my belt and pulled off of his. He fell over the edge into the water and hit the side on the way down. No way was I jumping into that cold water to save him. I'd get hypothermia in no time. With those slick walls, there'd be no way for me to climb out."

So, Brooks had just let his friend drown. Daisy was shivering, whether from cold or Brooks's hard-hearted attitude, she didn't know.

Brooks's hand still held the gun steady. She had to shake him up somehow. Something she said, or he said, had to affect his emotions. "How did Henry get involved?" She fought to keep her teeth from chattering.

"When Axel went over the edge, I heard a shout. Henry had followed us up here. He saw Axel go over. He was afraid to dive in, too. So, we made a pact. We'd both keep our mouths shut."

Daisy kept her focus on Brooks's revolver, and then she watched his expression for any hint of his humanity rather than the coldness that characterized his words.

Brooks let out a frustrated sigh. "Henry and Beth Ann started thinking about having kids. After all these years, Henry grew a conscience. After he called in to Lundquist, we met up. He intended to go to the authorities. I couldn't let that happen."

"You said you were going to bring him up here, but you didn't. Why not?"

Holding the gun pointed at her heart, he revealed, "Henry wouldn't come with me, not even for friendship's sake. Maybe he suspected what I was going to do. He started to get into his car. I grabbed him. He was parked in the last row of cars, where employees parked. I knew the security camera didn't reach back there."

Her voice was low and quavering when she said, "And you strangled him."

"I did, but I won't strangle you. A gunshot will be quicker. You won't even feel the cold water. And by the way, I don't have Jazzi. I told you I was a good liar. I had to convince you to come with me somehow, didn't I?"

The wind blew, and she swayed with the sound

of it whistling around the limestone circle. Mist seemed to hang over the quarry. Daisy felt as if she'd dropped into a surreal universe, where fear sang through her and her pulse spiked to an unbelievable pace.

Jazzi was safe. He didn't have her daughter. But what if that was just another lie?

Another rumble of thunder echoed across the quarry, filling all space between the wet grass and the sky as rain seemed to spurt from the gray heights again. Daisy spied a figure behind Brooks.

She was unsure who it was until Trevor Lundquist tossed something at Brooks's right shoulder and shouted to Daisy, "Duck!"

She not only ducked as Brooks's gun skittered to the edge of the quarry, but she found a rock and threw it directly at his midsection so she couldn't miss.

Brooks cried, "Oomph" and fell to his knees.

As sirens wailed a quarter mile down the two-track road, Daisy saw Trevor jump on Brooks's back and hold him down. She also saw what Trevor had hit him with—a can of orange soda.

Daisy slipped and slid on one shoe toward the gun. Once it was in her hand, she pointed it at Brooks. "Where's Jazzi? So help me, if you don't tell me the truth, I'll shoot."

Brooks raised his head just as red, blue, and white bar lights played over them. Brooks must have seen the wild, raw determination in her eyes. "I don't know where she is," he said. "I never had her."

They were all soaking wet as Zeke, Morris, and Bart took over handcuffing Brooks.

Free from his responsibility of capturing Brooks,

Trevor put his arm around Daisy's shoulders. "Why are you asking him about Jazzi?"

"Because I have to make sure—"

Before she could finish the thought, Jonas was wrapping his arms around her. When she fell against him, he explained, "When you didn't answer my text, I used that app we all put on our phones to keep track of each other. But then Trevor called me and said Brooks had taken you. He saw him pull up. He kept track of the license numbers for Henry's friends' vehicles."

Daisy held on to Jonas and with a sob asked, "Where's Jazzi?"

Puzzled, Jonas said, "Let's get you out of the rain."

"I'm not in shock," she practically shouted at him. "Brooks said he had her. That's how he convinced me to come with him."

Jonas took hold of Daisy's shoulders. In spite of the rain pouring down on them, he looked directly into her eyes. "Jazzi is at the tea garden. She was trying to get ahold of you because her car wouldn't start. She came to the tea garden to catch a ride home with you. She's safe, Daisy. She's safe, my love. And so are you." He swept Daisy's soaked hair behind her ear, kissed her forehead, and then held her tight.

He held her so tight, Daisy knew he'd never let her go.

EPILOGUE

Daisy felt an almost-ethereal happiness as dusk fell over the white gazebo. Fairy lights blinked around the upper brackets, circled the waist-high rails and spindles, and were interspersed in the front arch of flowers, made up of blue delphiniums, daisies, blue and pink hydrangeas, and white roses. Those flowers also trimmed the sides of the gazebo.

Daisy's eyes glistened with love for Jonas as she promised, "I vow to keep hold of your hand no matter what forces try to separate us . . . to love you with a heart full of gratitude for each and every day . . . to respect your opinion even if it differs from mine . . . to provide you solace as well as seek it from you. I love you, Jonas Groft."

She saw his eyes were wet, too, as he vowed, "I will make you my home . . . cherish your family as you do . . . and walk beside you through sunny days as well as stormy ones. I will hold you in my heart, remembering our path is united until this life passes into the next. I love you, Daisy Swanson."

After Reverend Kemp blessed their union, they turned to face their family and friends to applause that filled Daisy with so much joy that she felt her heart would explode.

A slight breeze ruffled the folds of her creamy lace-and-chiffon gown and blew a strand of her hair along her cheek. She'd worn it down with a circle of baby's breath and gardenias in her hair. As she turned toward her new husband, she thought he'd never looked sexier or more hand-some in his relaxed-fit white guayabera shirt with its vertical pin tucks and embroidery. Her father, Gavin, Foster, Zeke, and even little Sammy were also wearing that style of shirt. Jonas had said he'd surprise her, and he had. Felix was the male wear-ing a bow tie collar. She'd laughed when she'd seen him sitting at the entrance of the gazebo like a butler.

When Jonas kissed Daisy, the applause from the white wooden chairs increased until Ned Pachenko began strumming a recessional. Daisy and Jonas walked down the grassy aisle between their guests and tiki torches, ready to eat, drink, dance, and be merry in celebration of their marriage.

The night seemed to whirl by Daisy, but not so fast that she didn't appreciate her mother's, sister's, Tessa's, and Rachel's hugs, her father's heartfelt congratulations, her aunt Iris's beaming presence as she sat beside Morris Rappaport enjoying fried chicken and sweet-and-sour meatballs. Morris had been her aunt's choice for a hopefully serious rela-tionship. Portia, Jazzi's birth mom, and her hus-band, Colton, expressed sincere good wishes, as did Jonas's Philadelphia friends.

After Jazzi sliced the lemon wedding cake topped

with swirls of creamy and edible pearls, Vi helped serve. Foster sat with Sammy on the patio, letting his little boy sleep on his shoulder as Felix sat on guard beside them.

Fireflies sparkled in and out of the gardens and high into the velvet sky as Zeke pulled up a chair beside Daisy and Jonas. "Do you want to talk about the case, or leave it until after you return from your honeymoon?"

Daisy exchanged a knowing look with her new husband. "We've been so busy preparing for the wedding, I tried to put Brooks out of my mind. But I think we both want to know where the case against him stands."

"What my wife said," Jonas agreed, with a tender look for her.

Zeke faced them, his cop face on now. "First off, let me just say we've got him sewn up. We were in the midst of warranted searches when Brooks Landon kidnapped you and drove you to the quarry."

"I think he'd gone a little crazy," Daisy said.

"I don't know about crazy, but I think he's got a sociopath's soul," Zeke admitted. "We found Axel's compass on him wherever he was headed to spend the money he stole from his father. I guess he couldn't bear to leave his token behind. On top of that—" Zeke hesitated, as if he was debating with himself how much they wanted to hear.

"Go ahead, Zeke," Daisy said. "I can take it. After all, I survived the quarry."

"Thanks in part to Trevor's can of orange soda," Jonas said, nodding to cans of soda on the beverage stand, where they'd included the orange flavor.

"It was Lundquist's fault you were in that mess," Zeke said. "I'm glad he got you out of it. I wish I could arrest him for something, but I can't. At times, his podcast aided our investigation. And . . . he did save your life."

"So, what else did you find?" Jonas asked.

Zeke ran his finger around the collar of his white shirt even though it wasn't tight, even though it matched Jonas's for a night under the stars.

"We found a tin box under Brooks's bed in his town house. It held newspaper clippings about Axel's disappearance, but it held one other thing, too—Axel's red kerchief. Brooks confessed it had slipped off Axel when they were fighting. He let slip that he'd rolled Axel from the edge of the quarry. It wasn't the accident he claimed to *you* it was."

"Voluntary manslaughter for Axel, first-degree murder for Henry, aggravated assault for Trevor, and a kidnapping charge for Daisy?" Jonas asked.

"Yes," Zeke responded. "Brooks had also left Henry's laptop behind on his desk at his town house. He was going to be drinking margaritas in Brazil and didn't need it. I guess it didn't matter what we found once he'd flown away. There was a file Brooks had tried to delete on the laptop, not only with old photos, but with a letter from Henry in case anything ever happened to him. It plainly stated that he'd witnessed Brooks's fight with Axel, and he saw Brooks push Axel over the edge into the quarry."

Jonas was shaking his head when Zeke added, "And one more thing that nailed the case for the district attorney. Brooks answered a phone call from his father around the time he was dumping

Henry's body in the creek. There was a ping on a nearby cell tower. With GPS in his phone, smart watch, and vehicle, we can trace his movements from the physical therapy center to the creek and back to his town house."

"Do you think Brooks's dad was aware of what his son was doing when he called him?"

"No, we don't. Brooks could lie without losing a beat, and I'm sure he lied to his father," Zeke said. Then he stood and capped Jonas's shoulder. "The case is tied up. Now it's time for the two of you to take your first dance together as a married couple."

Ned was waving at them from the patio, which had been ringed with multicolored party lights. He'd put together a playlist with Jonas's and Daisy's help. Jonas had chosen the song for their wedding dance, "Perfect" by Ed Sheeran.

As Jonas guided Daisy to the patio's dance floor, Daisy thought the song was the most romantic sentiment she'd ever heard. Into her ear, Jonas whispered, "When we get home from our honeymoon, we'll come out here and dance, just the two of us with no audience."

Suddenly there was a commotion near the side of their house facing the garage. Their dance complete, Daisy looked up at Jonas with questions in her eyes.

He merely smiled and said, "Our transportation has arrived." Threading her arm through his, he walked her to the side of the house, where a courting buggy stood waiting for them, a beautiful gray horse standing at attention.

"What's this?" she asked, amazed.

"It's our transportation to the bed-and-breakfast,

and it's ours—for good. We'll be keeping it at Rachel and Levi's."

"The horse, too?" she asked, laughing.

"The horse, too. His name is Silver Star."

In no time at all, Daisy and Jonas's family and friends lined up to see them off. After Jonas helped Daisy into the buggy, he climbed into the other side and took the reins from Rachel's son, Luke, who had driven the buggy there.

When Jonas flicked the reins and clucked to the horse, they were off down the driveway. Daisy leaned close to her husband, ready for new adventures, ready for a life with him.

ORIGINAL RECIPES

Ham and Cabbage Soup

Ingredients
   2 cups ham broth (I bake the ham for a dinner and use the broth in the soup)
   1 can chicken broth (14 ounces)
   1 cup water
   8 cups cabbage, cut into small chunks
   3 cups potatoes, cut into small cubes
   1 cup sliced carrots
   1 cup sliced celery
   2 cups chunked baked ham
   ¼ teaspoon black pepper
   ¼ teaspoon garlic powder
   ¼ to ½ teaspoon salt (to taste)

Pour liquid ingredients into a soup pot. Add cabbage, potatoes, carrots, celery, ham, and spices. Stir and bring to a boil. Reduce heat to simmer and cook until cabbage and potatoes are tender—about 45 minutes.

Serves 10–12.

Egg and Olive Salad

Ingredients
  5 jumbo-sized hardboiled eggs
  2 tablespoons mayonnaise (I use Hellmann's
     Olive Oil Mayonnaise Dressing)
  1 teaspoon mustard (I use French's)
  ⅛ teaspoon salt
  Pinch of pepper
  5 chopped green olives without pimento
     (add more to taste)

Shell, chop, and put eggs into a medium-sized bowl. Add the remaining ingredients and mix thoroughly.

This recipe makes 4 to 5 scoops of salad to serve on a bed of lettuce . . . or it will fill 4 to 5 sandwich rolls.

Rhubarb Muffins

Topping

I mix the topping first so it is ready when I spoon the batter into baking cups. I use paper liners to make cleanup easier.

Ingredients
- ¼ cup grated butter
- ¼ cup light brown sugar
- ¼ cup flour
- ¼ cup cooking oats
- 1 teaspoon cinnamon
- ¾ cup chopped pecans

Grate the butter while it is cold. Set it aside. Mix sugar, flour, oats, and cinnamon, then fork in the butter until mixture is crumbled. Stir in pecans until they are roughly mixed in.

Muffins

Ingredients

  1½ cups light brown sugar
  ½ cup vegetable oil
  2 eggs
  ½ cup plain yogurt
  1 teaspoon baking powder
  1 teaspoon baking soda
  1 teaspoon salt
  2 teaspoons vanilla extract
  2 cups chopped rhubarb
  2½ cups flour

Mix light brown sugar and vegetable oil with electric mixer until well blended. Add eggs and beat until smooth. Mix in yogurt. Add baking powder, baking soda, salt, and vanilla extract. Mix in chopped rhubarb. Add flour ½ cup at a time until batter is well blended and smooth.

Put 18 paper baking cups in muffin tins. Evenly distribute batter into baking cups. Fill them ¾ full. Top with a spoonful of topping.

Bake at 350 degrees for 25 minutes for muffins. You can also pour the batter into an 8½"-by-4" loaf pan and bake for 55 minutes until a toothpick inserted in the center comes out clean.